HERALD'S DOOM . . .

Surrounded before she could even think of calling out for aid, Talia fought with every trick she'd learned from the weapons master, but it was hopeless. Struggling, she was half-carried, half-dragged to the river bank, and tossed up into the air, landing in the icy waters of the river with a shock that drove what little breath she had from her lungs.

Unable to breathe, or to cry out for help, her mind shrieked in incoherent fear.

Then, like a gift from the gods, a trumpeting neigh split the air and something huge plunged in beside her. Strong teeth seized her collar, pulling her within reach of a broad, white back that rose beside her like magic.

"Rolan!" she gasped, trying to make her fingers work enough to grab mane or tail. For a moment it almost seemed as if it would work. Then Talia's fingers loosed their grip and she began sliding away, dragged by the strong pull of the current. And as the water closed over her head, darkness closed over her mind. . . .

ARROWS
OF THE
QUEEN

Mercedes Lackey

DAW BOOKS, INC.
DONALD A. WOLLHEIM, PUBLISHER

375 Hudson Street, New York, NY 10014

DAW Book Collectors No. 702.

Dedicated
to Marion Zimmer Bradley
and Lisa Waters
who kept *telling* me I
could do this . . .

First Printing, March 1987

5   6   7   8   9   10   11   12

PRINTED IN THE UNITED STATES OF AMERICA

One

A gentle breeze rustled the leaves of the tree, but the young girl seated beneath it did not seem to notice. An adolescent of thirteen or thereabouts, she was, by her plain costume, a member of one of the solemn and straight-laced Hold families that lived in this Borderland of Valdemar—come there to settle a bare two generations ago. She was dressed (as any young Holdgirl would be) in plain brown breeches and a long, sleeved tunic. Her unruly brown curls had been cut short in an unsuccessful attempt to tame them to conform to Hold standards. She would have presented a strange sight to anyone familiar with Holderfolk; for while she sat and carded the undyed wool she had earlier cleaned, she was reading. Few Hold girls could read, and none did so for pleasure. That was a privilege normally reserved, by long-standing tradition, for the men and boys of the Holdings. A female's place was not to be learned; a girl reading—even if she *was* doing a womanly task at the same time—was as out of place as a scarlet jay among crows.

If anyone could have seen her thoughts at that moment, they would have known her to be even more of a misfit than her reading implied.

*   *   *

Vanyel was a dim shape in the darkness beside her; there was no moon, and only the dim light of the stars penetrated the boughs of the hemlock bushes they hid beneath. She only knew he was there by the faint sound of his breathing, though they lay so closely together that had she moved her hand a fraction of an inch, she'd have touched him. Training and discipline held her quiet, though under other circumstances she'd have been shivering so hard her teeth would have rattled. The starlight reflected on the snow beneath them was enough to see by—enough to see the deadly danger to Valdemar that moved below them.

Beneath their ledge, in the narrow pass between Dellcrag and Mount Thurlos, the army of the Dark Servants was passing. They were nearly as silent as the two who watched them; only a creak of snow, the occasional crack of a broken branch, or the faint jingling of armor or harness betrayed them. She marveled at the discipline their silent passage revealed; marveled, and feared. How could the tiny outpost of the Border Guard that lay to the south of them ever hope to make a stand against these warriors who were also magicians? Bad enough that they were outnumbered a hundred to one—these were no simple barbarians coming against the forces of Valdemar this time, who could be defeated by their own refusal to acknowledge any one of their own as overall leader. No, these fighters bowed to an iron-willed leader the equal of any in Valdemar, and their ranks held only the trained and seasoned.

She started as Vanyel's hand lightly touched the back of her neck, and came out of her half-trance. He tugged slightly at her sleeve; she backed carefully out of the thicket, obedient to his signal.

"Now what?" she whispered, when they were safely

around the ledge with the bulk of a stone outcropping between them and the Dark Servants.

"One of us has to alert the King, while the other holds them off at the other end of the pass—"

"With what army?" she asked, fear making her voice sharp with sarcasm.

"You forget, little sister—I need no army—" the sudden flare of light from Vanyel's outstretched hand illuminated his ironic smile, and bathed his white uniform in an eerie blue wash for one moment. She shuddered; his saturnine features had always looked faintly sinister to her, and in the blue light his face had looked demonic. Vanyel held a morbid fascination for her—dangerous, the man was; not like his gentle lifemate, Bard Stefen. Possibly the last—and some said the best—of the Herald-mages. The Servants of Darkness had destroyed the others, one by one. Only Vanyel had been strong enough to withstand their united powers. She who had little magic in her soul could almost feel the strength of his even when he wasn't exerting it.

"Between us, my Companion and I are a match for any thousand of their witch-masters," he continued arrogantly. "Besides—at the far end of the pass there isn't room for more than three to walk side by side. We can hold them there easily. And I want Stefen well out of this; Yfandes couldn't carry us double, but you're light enough that Evalie could easily manage both of you."

She bowed her head, yielding to his reasoning. "I can't like it—"

"I know, little sister—but you have precious little magic, while Evalie does have speed. The sooner you go, the sooner you'll have help here for me."

"Vanyel—" she touched his gloved hand with one fur mitten. "Be—be safe—" She suddenly feared more for him than for herself. He had looked so fey when the

King had placed this mission in their hands—like a man who has seen his own death.

"As safe as may be, little sister. I swear to you, I will risk nothing I am not forced to."

A heartbeat later she was firmly in the saddle, Evalie galloping beneath her like a blizzard wind in horse-shape. Behind her she could feel Bard Stefen clinging to her waist, and was conscious of a moment of pity for him—to him, Evalie was strange, he could not move with her, only cling awkwardly; while she felt almost as one with the Companion, touched with a magic only another Herald could share.

Their speed was reckless; breakneck. Skeletal tree-limbs reached hungrily for them, trying to seize them as they passed and pull them from Evalie's back. Always the Companion avoided them, writhing away from the claw-like branches like a ferret.

"The Dark Servants—" Stefen shouted in her ear "—they must know someone's gone for help. They're animating the trees against us!"

She realized, as Evalie escaped yet another trap set for them, that Stefen was right—the trees were indeed moving with a will of their own, and not just random waving in the wind. They reached out, hungrily, angrily; she felt the hot breath of dark magic on the back of her neck, like the noisome breath of a carrion-eater. Evalie's eyes were wide with more than fear; she knew the Companion felt the dark power, too.

She urged Evalie on; the Companion responded with new speed, sweat breaking out on her neck and flanks to freeze almost immediately. The trees seemed to thrash with anger and frustration as they eluded the last of them and broke out on the bank above the road.

The road to the capital lay straight and open before them now, and Evalie leaped over a fallen forest giant to gain the surface of it with a neigh of triumph. . . .

*   *   *

Talia blinked, emerging abruptly from the spell her book had laid on her. She had been lost in the daydream her tale had conjured for her, but the dream was now lost beyond recall. Someone was calling her name in the distance. She looked up quickly, with a toss of her head that threw her unmanageable hair out of her eyes. Near the door of the family house she could make out the angular figure of Keldar Firstwife, dark-clad and rigid, like a stiff fire iron propped against the building. Keldar's fists were on her hips; her stern carriage suggested that she was waiting Talia's response with very little patience.

Talia sighed regretfully, put up her wool and the wire brushes, and closed the worn little cloth-bound volume, laying aside the rocks she'd used to hold down the pages as she'd worked. Though she'd carefully marked the place, she knew that even without the precious scrap of ribbon she used to mark it she'd have no trouble finding it again. Keldar couldn't have picked a worse time; Herald Vanyel was alone, surrounded by the Servants of Darkness, and no one knew his peril but his Companion and Bard Stefen. Knowing Keldar, it would be hours before she could return to the tale—perhaps not even until tomorrow. Keldar was adept at finding ways to keep Talia from even the little reading she was grudgingly allowed.

Nevertheless, Keldar was Firstwife; her voice ruled the Steading, to be obeyed in all things, or suffer punishment for disobedience. Talia responded to the summons as dutifully as she could. She put the little book carefully away in the covered basket that held carded and uncarded wool and her spindle. The peddler who had given it to her last week had assured her many times that it was worthless to *him*, but it was still precious to her as one of the three books she owned and (more importantly) the only one she'd never read before. For an hour this afternoon she'd been transported to the outside world of Heralds and Companions, of high adventure and magic. Returning to the ordinary world of chores and Keldar's sour face was a distinct letdown. She schooled her expression with care, hoping none of her discontent showed, and trudged dully up the path that led to the Steading, carrying her basket in one hand.

But she had the sinking feeling as she watched the Firstwife's hardening expression that her best efforts were not enough to mislead Keldar.

Keldar noted the signs of rebellion Talia displayed despite her obvious effort to hide them. The signs were plain enough for anyone with the Firstwife's experience in dealing with littles; the slightly dragging feet, the sullen eyes. Her mouth tightened imperceptibly. Thirteen years old, and *still* fighting the yoke the gods had decreed for her shoulders! Well, that would change—and soon. Soon enough there would be no more time for foolish tales and wasted time.

"Stop scowling, child!" Keldar snapped, her thin lips taut with scorn, "You're not being summoned for a beating!"

Not that she hadn't warranted a beating to correct her attitude in the past. Those beatings had done precious little good, and had drawn the feeble protests of her Husband's Mother—but it was the will of the gods that children *obey,* and if it took beating to drive them into obedience, then one would beat them with as heavy a hand as required, and pray that *this* time the lesson was learned.

It was possible that she, Keldar, had not possessed a hand heavy enough. Well, if that were indeed the case, *that* situation would be corrected soon as well.

She watched the child trudge unwillingly up the path, her feet kicking up little puffs of dust. Keldar was well aware that her attitude where Talia was concerned was of a harshness that bordered on the unfair. Still, the child drove her out of all patience. Who would ever have imagined that so placid and bovine a creature as Bessa could have produced a little scrap of mischief like this? The child was like a wild thing sometimes, intractable, and untamable—how *could* Bessa have dared to birth such a misfit? And who would have thought that she'd have had the poor taste to die of the birthing and leave the rearing of her little to the rest of the Wives?

Talia was so unlike her birth-mother that Keldar was perforce reminded of the stories of changelings. And the child *had* been born on Midsummer's Eve, a time long noted for arcane connections—she as little resembled the strong, tall, blond man who was her father as her plump, fair, deceased mother—

But no. That was superstition, and superstition had no place in the lives of Holderkin. It was only that she had double the usual share of stubbornness. Even the most stubborn of saplings could be bent. Or broken.

And if Keldar lacked the necessary tools to accomplish the breaking and bending, there were others among the Holderkin who suffered no such lack.

"Get *along,* child!" she added, when Talia didn't respond immediately, "Or do you think I need hurry your steps with a switch?"

"Yes ma'am. I mean, no ma'am!" Talia replied in as neutral a voice as she could manage. She tried to smooth her expression into one more pleasing to her elder, even as she smoothed the front of her tunic with a sweaty, nervous palm.

What am I being summoned for? she wondered apprehensively. In her experience summonings had rarely meant anything good.

"Well, go in, go in! Don't keep me standing here in the doorway all afternoon!" Keldar's cold face gave no clue as to what was in store. Everything about Keldar, from her tightly wrapped and braided hair to the exact set of her apron, gave an impression of one in total control. She was everything a Firstwife should be—and frequently pointed this out. Talia was always intimidated by her presence, and always felt she looked hoydenish and disheveled, no matter how carefully she'd prepared herself for confrontations.

In her haste to edge past the authoritative figure of the Firstwife in the doorway, Talia stumbled a little on the lintel. Keldar made a derogatory noise in the back of her throat, and Talia felt herself flush. Somehow there was that about Keldar that never failed to put her at her faultiest and clumsiest. She regathered what little composure she had and slipped inside and into the hall. The windowless entryway was very dark; she would have paused to let her eyes adjust except for the forbidding presence of Keldar hard on her heels.

She felt her way down the worn, wooden floor hoping not to trip again. Then, as she entered the commonroom and she could see again in the light that came from its three windows, her mouth suddenly dried with fear; for *all* of her Father's Wives were waiting there, assembled around the rough-hewn wooden table that served them all at meals. And all of them were staring at her. Eight pairs of blue and brown eyes held her transfixed like a bird surrounded by hungry cats. Eight flat, expressionless faces had turned to point in her direction.

She thought at once of all her failings of the last month or so, from her failure to remember her kitchen duties yesterday to the disaster with the little she was supposed to have been watching who'd gotten into the goat pen. There were half a hundred things they might call her to account for, but none of them were bad enough to call for an assemblage of *all* the Wives; at least, she didn't *think* they were!

Unless—she started guiltily at the thought—unless they'd somehow found out she'd been sneaking into Father's library to read when there was a full moon—light enough to read without a betraying candle. Father's books were mostly religious, but she'd found an old history or two that proved to be almost as good as her tales, and the temptation had been too much to resist. If they'd found that out—

It might mean a beating every day for a week and a month of "exile"—being locked in a closet at night, and isolated by day, with no one allowed to speak to her or acknowledge her presence in any way, except Keldar, who would assign her chores.

That had happened twice already this year. Talia began to tremble. She wasn't sure she could bear a third time.

Keldar took her place at the head of the table, and her next words drove all thought of that out of Talia's head. "Well, child," she said, scowling, "You're thirteen today."

Talia felt almost giddy with relief. Just her Birthing Day? Was *that* all it was? She took an easier breath, and stood before the assemblage of nine Wives, much calmer mow. She kept her hands clasped properly before her, eyes cast down. She studied the basket at her sturdily-shod feet, prepared to listen with all due respect to the lecture about her growing responsibilities that they'd delivered to her every Birthing Day she could remember. After they were sure that she'd absorbed all their collective wisdom on the subject, they'd let her get back to her wool (and not so incidentally, her tale).

But what Keldar had to say next scattered every speck of calm she'd regained to the four winds.

"Yes, thirteen," Keldar repeated significantly, "And that is time to think of Marriage."

Talia blanched, feeling as if her heart had stopped. Marriage? Oh, sweet Goddess *no!*

Keldar seemingly paid no heed to Talia's reaction; a flicker of eyes betrayed that she'd seen it, but she went callously on with her planned speech. "You're not ready for it, of course, but no girl is. Your courses have been regular for more than a year now, you're healthy amd strong. There's no reason why you couldn't be a mother before the year is out. It's more than time you were in a Household as a Wife. Your Honored Father is dowering you with *three whole fields,* so your portion is quite respectable."

Keldar's faintly sour expression seemed to indicate that she felt Talia's dower to be excessive. The hands clasping the edge of the table before her tightened as the other Wives murmured appreciation of their Husband's generosity.

"Several Elders have already bespoken your Father about you, either as a Firstwife for one of their sons or as an Underwife for themselves. In spite of your unwomanly habits of reading and writing, we've trained you well. You can cook and clean, sew, weave and spin, and you're trustworthy with the littlest littles. You're not up to managing a Household yet, but you won't be called to do that for several years. Even if you go to a young man as his Firstwife, you'll be living in your Husband's Father's Household. So you're prepared enough to do your duty."

Keldar seemed to feel that she'd said all she needed to, and sat down, hands folded beneath her apron, back ramrod straight. Underwife Isrel waited for her nod of delegation, then took up the thread of the lecture on a daughter's options.

Isrel was easily dominated by Keldar, and Talia had always considered her to be more than a little silly. The Underwife looked to Keldar with calf-like brown eyes for approval of everything she said—nor did she fail to do so now. She glanced at Keldar after every other word she spoke.

"There's advantages to both, you know; being a Firstwife and being an Underwife, I mean. If you're Firstwife, eventually your Husband will start his own Steading and Household, and you'll be First in it. But if you're an Underwife, you won't have to ever make any decisions. And you'll be in an established Household and Steading—you won't have to scrimp and scant, there won't be any hardships. You won't have to worry about anything except the tasks you're set and bearing your littles. We don't want you to be *unhappy*, Talia. We want to give you the choice of the life you think you're best suited for. Not the *man* of course," she giggled nervously, "That would be unseemly, and besides you probably don't know any of them anyway."

"Isrel!" Keldar snapped, and Isrel shrank into herself a little. "That last remark was unseemly, and not suited to a girl's ears! Now, child, which shall it be?"

Goddess! Talia wanted to die, to turn into a bird, to sink into the floor—anything but this! Trapped; she was trapped. They'd Marry her off and she'd end up like Nada, beaten every night so that she had to wear high-necked tunics to hide the bruises. Or she'd die like her own mother, worn out with too many babies too quickly. Or even if the impossible happened, and her Husband was kind or too stupid to be a danger, her *real* life, the tales that were all that made living worthwhile, would all but disappear, for there would be no time for them in the never-ending round of pregnancy and a Wife's duties—

Before she could stop herself, Talia blurted out, "I don't want to be Married at all!"

The little rustlings and stirrings of a group of bored women suddenly ceased, and they became as still as a row of fenceposts, all with disbelief on their faces. Nine identical expressions of shock and dismay stared at Talia from the sides of the table. The silence closed down around her like the hand of doom.

"Talia, dear," a soft voice spoke behind her, breaking the terrible silence, and Talia turned with relief to face Father's Mother, who had been sitting unnoticed in the corner. She was one of the few people in Talia's life who never seemed to think that everything she did was wrong. Her kind, faded blue eyes were the only ones in the room not full of accusation. The old woman smoothed one braid of cloud-white hair with age-spotted hands in unconscious habit, as she continued. "May the Mother forgive us, but we never thought to ask you. Have you a vocation? Has the Goddess Called you to her service?"

Talia had been hoping for a reprieve, but that, if anything, was worse. Talia thought with horror of the one glimpse she'd had of the Temple Cloisters, of the women there who spent their lives in prayer for the souls of the Holderkin. The utterly silent women, who went muffled from head to toe, forbidden to leave, forbidden to speak, forbidden—life!—had horrified her. It was a worse trap than Marriage; the very memory of the Cloisters made her feel as if she was being smothered.

She shook her head frantically, unable to talk around the lump in her throat.

Keldar rose from her place with the scrape of a stool on the rough wooden floor and advanced on the terrified child, who was as unable to move as a mouse between the paws of a cat. Keldar took her shoulders with a grip that bruised as it made escape impossible and shook her till her teeth rattled. "What's *wrong* with you, girl?" she said angrily, "You don't want an Honorable Marriage, you don't want the Peace of the Goddess, what *do* you want?"

All I want is to be left alone, Talia thought with quiet desperation, *I don't want anything to change—* but her traitorous mouth opened again and let the dream spill.

"I want to be a Herald," she heard herself say.

Keldar released her shoulders quickly, with a look of near-horror as if she'd discovered she'd been holding something vile, something that had crawled out of the midden.

"You—you—" For once, the controlled Keldar was at a loss for words. Then— "*Now* you see what comes of coddling a brat!" she said, turning on Father's Mother in default of anyone else to use as a scapegoat, "*This* is what happens when you let a girl rise above her place. Reading! Figuring! No girl needs to know more than she requires to label her preserves and count her stores or keep the peddlers from cheating her! I told you this would happen, you and your precious Andrean, letting her fill her head with foolish tales!" She turned back to face Talia. "*Now*, girl—when I finish with you—"

But Talia was gone.

She had taken advantage of the distraction of Keldar's momentary tirade to escape. Scampering quickly out the door before any of the Wives realized she was missing, she fled the Steading as fast as she could run. Sobbing hysterically, she had no thought except to get away. With the wind in her face, and sweating with fear, she ran past the barns and the stockade, pure terror giving her feet extra speed. She fled through the fields as the waist-high hay and grain beat against her, and up into the woodlot and through it, following a tangled path through the uncut underbrush. She was seeking the shelter of the hiding place she'd found, the place that no one else knew of.

There was a steep bluff where the woodlot ended high above the Road. Two years ago, Talia had found a place where something had carved out a kind of shallow cave beneath the protruding roots of a tree that grew at the very edge of the bluff. She'd lined it with filched straw and old rugs meant for the rag-bag; she kept her other two books hidden there. She had spent many hours stolen from her chores there, daydreaming, invisible from above or below so long as she stayed quiet and still. She sought this sanctuary now, and scrambling over the edge of the bluff, crept into it. She buried herself in the rugs, crying hysterically, limp with exhaustion, nerves practically afire, ears stretched for the tiniest sound above her.

For no matter how deep her misery, she knew she must keep alert for the sounds of searchers. Before very long, she heard the sound of some of the servants calling her name. When they drew too near, she stifled her sobs in the rugs while her tears fell silently, listening in fear for some sign telling her she'd been discovered. She thought a dozen times that they'd found some sign of her passage, but they seemed to have lost her track. Eventually they went away, and she was free to cry as she would.

Wrapped in pure misery, she hugged her knees to her chest and rocked back and forth, weeping until her eyes were too dry and sore to shed another tear. She felt numb all over, too numb to think properly. Any choice she made seemed worse than the one before it. Should she return and apologize, any punishment she'd ever had before would seem a pleasure to the penance Keldar was likely to devise for her unseemly and insubordinate behavior. It would be Keldar's choice, and her Father's, what would befall her then. Any Husband Keldar would choose now would be—horrid. She'd either be shackled to some drooling old dotard, to be pawed over by night and to be a nursemaid by day—or she'd be given to some brutal, younger man, a cruel one, with instructions to break her to seemly behavior. Keldar would likely pick one as sadistic as Justus, her older brother—she shuddered, as the unbidden memory came to her, of him standing over her with the hot poker in his hand and the look on his face of fierce pleasure—

She forced the memory away, quickly.

But even that fate would be a pleasurable experience compared to what would happen if they decided to offer her as a Temple Servant. The Goddess's Servants had even less freedom and more duties than Her Handmaidens. They lived and died never going beyond the cloister corridor to which they were assigned. And in any case, no matter what future they picked for her, her reading, her escape, would be over. Keldar would see to it that she never saw another book again.

For one moment, she contemplated running away, truly fleeing the Steading and the Holderkin. Then she recalled the faces of the wandering laborers she'd seen at Hiring Fairs; pinched, hungry, desperate for anyone to take them into a Holding. And she'd never seen a woman among them. The "foolish tales" she'd read made one thing very clear, the life of a wanderer was dangerous and sometimes fatal for the unprepared, the defenseless. What preparation had she? She had the clothing she stood up in, the ragged rugs, and nothing else. How could she defend herself? She'd never even been taught how to use a knife. She'd be ready prey.

If only this were a tale—

An unfamiliar voice called her name—a voice full of calm authority, and she found herself answering it, climbing out of her hiding place almost against her will. And there before her, waiting at the top of the bluff—

A Herald; resplendent and proud in her Whites, her Companion a snowy apparition beside her, mane and tail lifting in the gentle breeze like the finest silk. Sunlight haloed and hallowed both of them, making them seem more than mortal. She looked to Talia like the statue of the Lady come to life—only proud, strong and proud, not meek and submissive. Behind the Herald, looking cowed and ashamed, were Keldar and her Father.

"You are Talia?" the Herald asked, and she nodded affirmatively.

She broke out in a smile that dazzled her—it was like a sudden appearance of the sun after rain.

"Blessed is the Lady who led us here!" she exclaimed. "Many the weary months we have searched for you, and always in vain. We had nothing to go on except your name—"

"Led you to me?" she asked, exalted, "But, why?"

"To make you one of us, little sister," she replied, as Keldar shrank into herself and her Father seemed bent on studying the tops of his shoes. "You are to be a Herald, Talia—the gods themselves have decreed it. Look—yonder comes your Companion— "

She looked where the Herald pointed, and saw a graceful white mare with a high, arched neck and a knowing eye pacing deliberately toward her. The Com-

panion was caparisoned all in blue and silver, tiny bells hanging from her reins and bridle. Behind the Companion, at a respectful distance, came all her sibs, the rest of the Wives, and all the servants of the Holding.

With a glad cry, she ran to meet the mare and the Herald helped her to mount up on the Companion's back, while the Hold servants cheered, her sibs stared in sullen respect, and Keldar and her Father stared at her in plain fear, obviously thinking of all the punishments they'd meted out to HER and expecting the same now that she was the one in power—

The sound of hoofbeats on the Road broke into her desperate daydream. For one panicked moment she thought it was another searcher, but then she realized that her Father's horses sounded nothing like this. These hoofbeats had a chime like bells on the hard surface. As the sound drew nearer, it was joined by another; the sound of real bells, of bridle bells. Only one kind of horse wore bridle bells every day, and not just on Festival Days—the magical steed of legend, a Herald's Companion.

Talia had never seen a real Herald, though she'd daydreamed about them constantly. The realization that she was finally going to see one of her dreams in actual fact startled her out of her fantasy and her tears completely. The distraction was too tempting to resist. For just this one moment she would forget her troubles, her hopeless position, and snatch a tiny bit of magic for herself, to treasure all her days. She leaned out of her cave, stretching as far out as she could, thinking of nothing except to catch a glimpse—and leaned out too far.

She lost her balance, and her flailing hands

caught nothing but air. She tumbled end over end down the bluff, banging painfully into roots and rocks. The wind was knocked out of her before she was halfway down, and nothing she collided with seemed to slow her descent any. She was totally unable to stop her headlong tumble until she landed on the hard surface of the Road itself, with a force that set sparks to dancing in front of her eyes and left her half-stunned.

When the grayness cleared away from her vision and she could get a breath again, she found herself sprawled face downward on the Road. Her hands were scraped, her sides bruised, her knees full of gravel, and her eyes full of dirt. When she turned her head to the side, blinking tears away, she found she was gazing at four silver hooves.

She gave a strangled gasp and scrambled painfully to her feet. Regarding her with a gentle curiosity was a—well, a Herald's Companion was hardly what one would call a "horse." They transcended horses in the way that panthers transcend alleycats, or angels transcend men. Talia had read and heard plenty of descriptions of the Companions before, but she was still totally unprepared for the close-hand reality.

The riderless Companion was in full formal array, his trappings silver and sky-blue, his reins hung with silver bridle bells. No horse in Talia's experience had that slender, yet muscular grace or could match the way he seemed to fly without taking a single step. He was white—Companions were always white—but nothing on earth could possibly match that glowing, living, radiant white. And his eyes—

When Talia finally had the courage to look into those sapphire eyes, she lost track of the world—

* * *

She was lost in blue more vast than a sea and darker than sky and full of welcome so heart-filling it left no room for doubt.

Yes—at last—you. I Choose you. Out of all the world, out of all the seeking, I have found you, young sister of my heart! You are mine and I am yours—and never again will there be loneliness—

It was a feeling more than words; a shock and a delight. A breathless joy so deep it was almost pain; a joining. A losing and a finding; a loosing and a binding. Flight and freedom. And love and acceptance past all words to tell of the wonder of it—and she answered that love with all her soul.

Now forget, little one. Forget until you are ready to remember again.

Blinking, she came back to herself, with a feeling that something tremendous had happened, though she didn't know quite what. She shook her head—there had been—it was—but whatever had happened had receded just out of memory, though she had the odd feeling it might come back when she least expected it to. But for now there was a soft nose nudging her chest, and the Companion was whickering gently at her.

It was as though someone were putting loving arms about her, and urging her to cry all her unhappiness out. She flung both her arms around his neck and wept unrestrainedly into his silky mane. The feeling of being held and comforted intensified as soon as she touched him, and she lost herself in the unfamiliar but welcome sensation. Unlike her lone crying in her cave, this session of tears brought peace in its wake, and before too long she was able to dry her eyes on a corner of her tunic and take heed of her surroundings again.

She let go of his neck with reluctance, and took another long look at him. For one wild moment, she was tempted to leap into his empty saddle. She had a vision of herself riding away, far away; *anywhere*, so long as it was away from here and she was with him. The temptation was so great it left her shaking. Then practicality reasserted itself. Where could she go? And besides—

"You've run away from someone, haven't you?" she said quietly to the Companion, who only blew into her jerkin in answer. "I can't have you, you could only belong to a Herald. I'll—" she gulped. There was a huge lump in her throat and tears threatened again at the idea of parting with him. Never, ever in her short life had she wanted anything as much as the way she wanted to—to—be his, and he hers! "I'll have to take you back to whoever you belong to."

A new thought occurred to her, and for the first time that afternoon, hope brightened her for a moment as she saw a way out of her dilemma. "Maybe—maybe they'll be grateful. Maybe they'll let me work for them. They must need *someone* to do their cooking and sewing and things. I'd do anything for Heralds " The soft blue eyes seemed to agree that this was a good idea. "They're bound to be nicer than Keldar—they're so kind and wise in all the tales. I bet they'd let me read when I wasn't working. I'd get to see Heralds all the time—" Tears lumped her throat again, "—maybe they'd let me see you, once in a while."

The Companion only whickered again, and

stretching his neck out, nudged her with his velvet nose toward his saddle, maneuvering for her to mount.

"*Me?*" she squeaked. "I couldn't—" Suddenly, the reality of what *he* was and what *she* was came home to her. All very well to dream of leaping on his back; but in cold, sober reflection the very idea that she, grubby and ordinary, should sit in the saddle of a Companion shocked her.

The enormous, vivid blue eyes looked back at her with a trace of impatience. One hoof stamped with a certain imperiousness, and he shook his mane at her. His whole manner said as clearly as speech that he thought her scruples were ridiculous. After all, who was going to see her? And now that she thought about it, it was quite possible that he had come from a goodly distance away; if she insisted on walking, it was likely to take forever to return him.

"Are you sure you don't mind? That it's all right?" She spoke in a timid voice, unmindful of the incongruity of asking a horse for advice.

He tossed his head impatiently, and the bridle bells rang. There was little doubt that he felt she was being excessively silly.

"You're right," she said in sudden decision, and mounted.

Talia was no stranger to riding. She'd done so every chance she could, often sneaking rides when no one was looking. She'd ridden every horse of an age to bear her weight, broken or not, saddled or bareback. She was the oldest of the littles on the Holding, and hence the only one considered responsible enough to be sent to other Elders with messages or to the village on errands. She was

usually a-horseback at least once a week legiti-
mately. She was generally found sneaking rides at
least three or four times that often.

But riding a Companion was nothing like any
riding she'd ever done. His pace was so smooth a
true little could have stayed in his saddle without
falling, and if she'd closed her eyes she'd never
have guessed he was more than ambling along.
Her Father's beasts had to be goaded constantly to
maintain more than a walk; of his own volition the
Companion had moved into a canter, and it was
faster than the fastest gallop she'd ever coaxed out
of any of *them*. The sweet air flowed past her like
the water of the river, and it blew her hair back
out of her face. The intoxication of it drove all
thought of anything else clean out of her mind. It
was as if the wind rushing past them had swept all
her unhappiness right out of her and left it behind in an untidy heap in the center of the Road.

If this was a daydream, she hoped she'd die in
the middle of it and never have to wake to the
dreary world again.

Two

Within a single candlemark they were farther from her Father's Holding than Talia had ever been before. The Road here ran parallel to the River; on one side of it was the steep bluff crowned with trees and brush, on the other was a gentler drop-off down to the River. The River here was wide and very slow; Talia could see glimpses of the farther bank through the trees that grew at her edge of it. These trees were huge willows that made a living screen with their drooping branches. There was no sign of any human habitation. All she could hear was birdsong and the sounds of insects in the branches overhead and to either side. All she could see were the trees and the occasional glimpse of the River, and the Road stretching on ahead. Although she couldn't be entirely sure, Talia had a notion that the lands of the Holderkin were now all behind her.

The sun was still relatively high, and its warmth was very pleasant, not harsh as it would be later in the summer. The Road's surface was of some material she had never seen before, since she had never actually dared to venture down to the Road itself even once in her life, and there was little or no dust. The scent of green growing things on the breeze was like wine to her, and she drank in every bit of her experience greedily. At any moment now she might come upon the Herald this Companion rightfully belonged to; her adventure would be over, and it wasn't likely she'd ever get to ride a Companion again. Every moment was precious and must be stored away in her memory against the future.

As candlemarks passed and no Herald—in fact, nothing more than a squirrel or two—came into view, Talia began to fall into a kind of trance; the steady pace of the Companion and the Road stretching ahead of her was hypnotic. Something comforting just at the edge of her awareness lulled her into tranquillity. She was lost in this trance for some time, and only came back to herself when the setting sun struck her full in the eyes. Her anxieties and fears had somehow disappeared while she'd ridden unmindful of her surroundings. Now there was only a calm, and a feeling of rightness about this journey—and a tentative feeling of excitement. But night was coming on fast, and she and the Companion were still alone together on the Road.

The shape of the landscape had changed while she rode unaware. The double drop-off had leveled off, very gradually, so gradually that she hadn't noticed it. Now the woods and fields to her right were level with the surface of the Road, and the Road itself was only a foot or two above the lapping surface of the water. The River was a scant two horse-lengths away from the verge of the Road. The land had flattened out so much that Talia knew for certain she was no longer even close to the lands belonging to the Holderfolk that lay on the Border of the Kingdom.

"Are we going to travel all night?" she asked the Companion, who cocked his ears back to catch her words. He whuffed, shook his head, and slowed to a walk. Now she could hear the sounds that birds make only when they're preparing to roost; quiet, sleepy little chirrups and half-calls. The Companion seemed to be looking for something on the woodward side of the Road; at least that was the impression Talia got. Just as the setting sun began to dye his white coat a bright scarlet, he seemed to spot what he was looking for. With no warning, he sped up and trotted right off the Road and down a path into the woods.

"Where are you going?" she cried.

He just shook his head and kept to the path. The trees were far too thick on either side for her to even think of trying to jump off. The underbrush was thick and full of shadows that made her fears reawaken. She had no idea what might be lurking in the growth beneath the trees. There could be thorns there, or stenchbeetles, or worse. Biting her lip in vexation and worry, she could only cling to the saddle and wait.

The path abruptly widened into a clearing, and in the center of the clearing was a small building; only a single room, and windowless, but with a chimney. It was very clearly well-maintained, and just as clearly vacant. With a surge of relief, Talia recognized it from her reading as a Herald's Waystation.

"I'm sorry," she said contritely to the ears that were swiveled back to catch her words, "You *did* know what you were doing, didn't you?"

The Companion only slowed to a stop, pivoted neatly before the door of the Waystation, shook his forelock out of his eyes and waited for her to dismount.

The tales she'd read were a great help here; Talia knew exactly what she'd find and approximately where to find it. She swung her leg carefully over the Companion's back and slid slowly to the ground. Moving quickly (she discovered with a touch of dismay) wasn't possible. She'd never spent this much time in a saddle before, and her legs were feeling very stiff, and a little sore and shaky.

She knew that her first duty was to see to the needs of the Companion. She unsaddled him quickly, and noticed with a start of surprise as she removed the bridle that it had no bit, being little more than an elaborate hackamore. There was no way that it could "control" him, not unless his Herald had the strength of arm to wrench his head around by main force. It was a most peculiar piece of tack—and what it implied was even more peculiar.

She stacked the tack carefully by the door of the Waystation, then lifted the latch and peered around inside. There was just enough daylight left for her to locate what she was looking for; a tinderbox on a shelf just inside the door.

She laid tinder and cautiously lit a very small fire in the fireplace; just enough to give light to see. With the interior of the Waystation illuminated, Talia was able to locate her second requirement; rags to clean the tack, and a currycomb to groom the Companion.

He stood far more placidly than any of her Father's horses while she groomed every last speck of sweat and dust from his coat. When she'd clearly finished with him he cantered to the center of the clearing for a brisk roll in the grass. She giggled to see him drop his dignity and act so very horselike, particularly after the way he'd been acting up until this point—almost as if it was *he* that was taking *her* to someone. She cleaned the tack just as carefully as she'd cleaned him, with a sensuous enjoyment of the leathery scent. She put it just inside the door where the dew wouldn't reach it. There had been two buckets next to the pile of rags; in the blue dusk she hurried down to the river with them while she could still see. The Companion came with her, weeds whisking his legs and hers, following her like a puppy, and drank his fill while she filled the buckets.

The delightful feel of the cool water around her feet reminded her how grubby and sticky she was. There had been first her run through the woods, followed by the fall down the bank, then the long ride to ensure that she needed a bath. And part of the regime of any Holdchild was an almost painful devotion to cleanliness. Talia was more used to feeling scoured than dirty, and fastidiously preferred the former sensation.

"You may be a Companion," she told the watching stallion, "but you still smell like a horse, and now so do I. Do you think it would be safe to bathe here?"

The Companion whickered, then took a few steps away from her and pawed with his hoof at the edge of the water, nodding his head as if to be certain she caught his meaning. She went to where he was standing, and peered through the gathering darkness down into the waterweeds.

"Oh!" she cried delightedly, "Soaproot! It must be all right then; Heralds wouldn't plant soaproot where it wasn't safe to bathe."

Without another thought, she stripped down to the bare skin. She started to pile her clothing on the bank, but changed her mind, and took it into the water with her. It would probably dry wrinkled, but wrinkles were better than dirt.

The water was sunwarmed, like silk against her bare skin, and the bottom here was sandy rather than muddy. She splashed and swam like a young otter, enjoying the sensation of being able to skinswim like a little without wondering what Keldar would do if she caught her. It occurred to Talia that her bridges were all burned now, for certain sure. No female of marriageable age gone overnight without leave would ever be accepted back into the Holding as anything but a drudge, and that only if the Husband and Firstwife were feeling magnanimous. For one moment Talia felt frightened by the idea, for after her performance of this afternoon no one at the Holding was likely to feel generosity on her behalf—but then her eyes fell on the luminous white form of the Companion waiting for her on the bank, and she decided that she should make up her mind not to care, not even a little bit.

When she'd scrubbed herself and her clothing with clean sand and soaproot and the air was beginning to feel chilly, she decided she'd had enough. The Companion continued to follow her all the way back to the shelter, and once they'd reached their goal, he nudged her toward the door with his nose and whickered in entreaty. There was no doubt in Talia's mind as to what he wanted, and it no longer seemed odd to be taking her direction from him.

"Greedy!" she chuckled, "Want your supper, do you? *That* should teach you not to run away, Rolan!"

She paused then, and frowned a little in concentration. "Now where did I get that name?" she wondered aloud. She gazed at the moonlight-dappled Companion, who stood easily, ears cocked forward, watching her. "From you? Is that your name? Rolan?"

For a moment she felt disoriented, as if seeing through someone else's eyes. It almost seemed as if she and something else were briefly joined as one—it was uncanny, and yet not at all frightening. Then the moment passed.

"Well, I suppose I have to call you *something*, no matter where the name came from. Just let me put my things up to dry and go back for the buckets, Rolan. Then I'll get supper for both of us."

She poured a generous measure of grain for him, then took a fire-blackened pot she'd seen earlier to make a grain-and-fruit porridge for herself. Rolan finished his own portion before her porridge was done and moved closer to lie in the grass an arm's length off from her with every sign of content. Insects sang in the woods all around them, and leaves rustled slightly. The firelight shone on Rolan's coat as she leaned up against the Waystation wall, feeling oddly happy.

"What I don't understand," she said to him, "Is why you ran away. Companions aren't supposed to do that sort of thing, are they?"

Rolan simply opened his eyes wide at her and looked wise.

"I hope you know where we're going because I certainly don't. Still, we're bound to meet a Herald sometime, and I'm sure he'll know what to do with you."

The porridge looked and smelled done; she pulled the pot out of the fire with a branch and began to eat it with her fingers as soon as it had cooled enough.

"It really is strange, you coming along when you did," she told him, "I expect I'd have been found before dark or gotten resigned to the situation and gone back to the Holding myself." She regarded him with speculative eyes. "I don't suppose— you didn't come to *rescue* me, did you? No, that's ridiculous. I'm not a Herald, I'm just Holderkin; just strange Talia. Why would you want to rescue me? Besides, if you'd meant to rescue me, you would have brought your Herald along, wouldn't you?" she sighed, a little sadly. "I wish *I* was your Herald. I'd like to live like this always."

Rolan's eyes were closed, and his head nodded. Now that her stomach was comfortably full, Talia found her own head beginning to nod. The woods were very dark, the ground beneath her was very hard, and the interior of the Waystation looked very inviting to a girl who'd seldom spent a night out under the sky, and never alone.

"Well, if you're going to go to sleep, I'd better do the same."

She banked the fire, covering the pot of porridge with the coals and ashes to keep the rest of it warm for breakfast, then pulled up armfuls of the long grass to use to fill the bedbox. It didn't take very long; once she'd settled, Rolan moved to lie across the door, almost like a guard dog. It seemed

to her that she'd no sooner tumbled into it, than
she was fast asleep.

She woke to the sound of birdsong with Rolan
standing in the Waystation beside the bedbox nudging her shoulder. For one moment she couldn't
remember exactly where she was, confused with
sleep; then with full awareness it all came back
with a rush. She jumped out of her nest of sweet-
smelling grasses to hug Rolan's neck, overwhelmed
with thankfulness that it hadn't all been a dream.

She ate her breakfast quickly, then cleaned herself and the shelter to the best of her ability. She
buried the ashes of the dead fire with a little
twinge of guilt; she knew that etiquette demanded
that she replace the wood she'd used, but without
an axe, that simply wasn't possible. She'd have felt
a lot guiltier had it been Midwinter instead of
Midsummer, and she'd really used very little of
what seemed to be a plentiful supply. Once all was
in as good order as she'd found it, she saddled
Rolan and they trotted back to the Road.

The morning passed swiftly. Not only was every
moment with Rolan a delight and a treasure, but
now there was more to see as well. The dense
woods began to give way to cultivated fields; in
the distance she saw stock grazing, and once or
twice a cottage, shaded by trees and cooled by ivy.
Then, just after the sun crossed overhead, the
Road curved and dove down into a village, set in a
small valley.

Talia couldn't help but stare about her with
amazed eyes; this village was very different from
the one she'd lived near all her life. The Holderfolk
wore nothing but somber colors, nothing gayer
than a dull saffron; but here it seemed that every-

one had a touch of bird-bright color about him. Even the shabbiest had at least a scarf or hair ribbon of scarlet or blue. Some (the look of them showing they were prosperous folk who needn't worry about soiling their clothing with work) were dressed entirely in colors. Even the houses were festive with bright designs on their whitewashed walls, and the shutters were painted to match. Those houses looked extremely odd to Talia—why, they couldn't have held more than one man, his Firstwife, and a few littles! There was obviously no room at all for Underwives and *their* littles. Talia wondered if each Wife had her own house, then giggled at the unseemly (but amusing) notion of the Husband running from house to house in the night, intent on doing his duty with each of his Wives.

The village itself, besides looking prosperous and well-cared-for, was also unenclosed; a startling sight to one who was used to seeing walls and stockades around inhabited places.

She reined in Rolan at the sight of a man standing beside a small hut positioned just at the verge of the Road where it first entered the village proper. He looked as if he must be some sort of guard or official; he was dressed in garments of a bright blue that matched, from boots to hat. He had a quiver of short arrows on his back, and Talia saw a crossbow leaning beside him against the wall of the hut.

The sight of him alarmed her no small amount— in her experience, men (especially men in obvious positions of authority) were creatures to be feared. They held the power of life and death over the members of their families; they decreed the rewards of the obedient and the punishments of the rebellious. How many times had the Elders or her Father deemed it necessary that she be beaten or sent into isolation for far, far less than she'd done in the past two days? Too many times to count easily, for certain sure. There was no indication that this stranger might not order the same punishments for her now; or worse, send her back to the Holding. Yet she was going to have to speak to *someone;* she'd been searching for nearly a day now and hadn't found any clue to where this Companion belonged. He seemed to have a friendly, open face, and she took her courage in hand to address him.

"P-pray excuse me, sir," she said politely, stuttering a little, "but have you seen a Herald who's lost his Companion?"

Her question seemed to startle him, and he approached the two of them slowly, as if trying not to frighten her (leaving his crossbow behind, Talia noted with relief).

"No indeed, young miss," he replied, "Why ask you?"

"I found this Companion alone on the Road yesterday," she answered hesitantly, still not sure she hadn't done wrong despite the fact that it didn't seem he was going to take her into custody or hail her before a Council of Elders just yet, "And it seemed to me I should take him back to whoever he belongs with."

He measured her with his eyes; she found his scrutiny unnerving. "Where are you from, child?" he asked at last.

"Sensholding, near Cordor. Back that way." She

waved vaguely back down the Road in the direction she'd come.

"Ah, Holderfolk," he said, as if that explained something to him, "Well, young miss, there's only one thing you can do if you find a lone Companion. You have to return him to the Herald's Collegium yourself."

"*Me?*" her voice broke with alarm. "The Collegium? By myself?"

He nodded, and she gulped. "Is it very far?" she asked in a near-whisper.

"By ordinary horse, three weeks or more, depending on the weather. You're riding a Companion, though, and a little thing like you would be hardly more than a feather to him. You should get there in eight or nine days, perhaps a bit more."

"Eight—or nine—days?" she faltered, looking self-consciously down at her wrinkled, travel-stained clothing. In eight or nine days, she'd look like a tramp. They'd probably shoot her on sight, for thieving Rolan away!

His eyes crinkled at the corners as he smiled, seeming to read her thoughts. "Now, don't you worry, young miss. The Queen makes provisions for circumstances like these. Just wait right here."

She didn't have much choice; Rolan seemed to be rooted to the ground. The man returned in short order with a pair of saddlebags, a brown wool cloak draped over one arm, and a small piece of metal in his hand. "Goodwife Hardaxe has a girl a bit older than you; there's a couple of changes of clothing she's outgrown in the lefthand bag."

She attempted to voice a protest but he interrupted her. "No argument, young miss. I told you the Queen herself makes provisions for this sort of thing. We help you, and we get half taxes next year, the whole village. The right hand bag's got some odds 'n ends in it; firestarter, comb and brush, things you'll need if your Companion can't find a Waystation. Don't be afraid to use what's in the Waystations either; that's what they're there for."

He tossed the bags over Rolan's back, fastening them securely to the back of the saddle. "This cloak's good oiled wool; it should keep the rain off you, and this time of year it ought to be enough to keep you warm if the weather turns nasty. It's more than a bit big, but that's all to the good. Means less of you will hang outside it. Ah, here comes the Innmaster."

A pleasant-faced, plump man came puffing up. He had a waterskin, a small pouch, and a dun-colored frieze bag with him. The wonderful meaty odors rising from the bag made Talia's mouth water, and her stomach reminded her forcibly that it had been a long time since breakfast.

"I saw you didn't have a belt-pouch, so I left word with Daro that you might be needing one," the first man said, "People are always leaving things behind at the Inn."

"I just filled this bag with good spring water," the plump Innmaster said, slinging it on one of the many snaffles adorning the saddle before she could say anything, "And there's an eating knife and a spoon in the pouch. Put it on now, there's a good girl; I've got more left-behind eating tools than you could ever imagine! And these pasties ought to stay sound for longer than it'll take you to eat 'em, if I know the appetite of a growing child!" He handed her the bag, and wiped his hands on his apron, smiling. "Now you make sure you tell people how good our baking is! I have to get back to my custom." And he puffed off before she could thank him.

"See this?" the first man said, holding up a little scrap of engraved brass. "When you get to the Collegium, give this chit to the person who asks you for it. This tells them that we helped you along the way." He handed it to her, and she placed it carefully in her new belt pouch. "If you need anything, just ask people dressed the way I am, and they'll be sure to help you. We're part of the Army, the Roadguards."

Talia was all but incoherent with surprise at her good fortune. Not only had she not been punished or even scolded for her actions, not only had she not been sent back home, but it seemed that she was actually being rewarded with the opportunity to go where she'd never dared to dream she'd be allowed! "Th-th-ank you! B-b-right Lady, it just doesn't seem like enough just to *say* thank you—"

The guard chuckled, his eyes disappearing in the smile-crinkles. "Young miss, it's *us* who'll remember you with thanks, come tax-time! Anything else you need?"

Rolan seemed to think it was time they were on their way again, and began moving impatiently off. "No, nothing," she called over her shoulder as he waved a casual farewell.

Rolan quickly resumed his normal pace and the village fell rapidly behind them, so quickly that Talia had only just realized that she didn't even know the name of the place or her benefactor when it was gone from view.

"Oh, well," she said to Rolan as she bit hungrily into a lightly spiced meat pie, "I'm not likely to forget the baking of Darowife. Even Isrel never made anything that tasted like *this*, not even for feastdays!"

She looked with curiousity at the brass "chit." It bore a number, and the word "Sweetsprings."

"Sweetsprings?" she mused. "That must be the town. I wish I knew what was going on! I've never read or heard anything about Companions running away before, but he acted like it happens all the time."

She passed through another village near to suppertime. This one was much smaller than Sweetsprings had been; mostly a collection of houses and huts around a blacksmith's forge. It was apparently too small to warrant one of the blue-clad Guards, but the people seemed just as friendly. They waved at her as she cantered past, bridle bells ringing, and didn't seem to find anything at all disturbing in the sight of a slightly grubby girl atop a Herald's Companion. Talia could not help contrasting their friendliness with the reaction she'd have gotten from Holderfolk. At best, her own people would have stared, then coldly turned their backs on such unseemly behavior from a girl-child. At worst, they'd have tried to stop her; tried to pull her from Rolan's back to incarcerate as a thief.

Once again, as night was about to fall, Rolan found a Waystation. The Road and the River had parted company not long since, but this shelter boasted a well, so they didn't lack water. Talia discovered among the odds and ends the guard had assembled for her a little box of soft, home-made soap and a washcloth, as well as a curry-comb and brush for Rolan. When the moon rose, both of them were much cleaner.

She decided (somewhat reluctantly) to save the pies for her midday meals and manage with por-ridge for the rest. Once again she fed the two of them, and fell soundly asleep in spite of the rela-tive discomfort of the primitive Waystation.

On the third day of the journey, Talia was suffi-ciently used to the novelty of riding Companion-back that she found her mind drifting to other things. The position of the sun would remind her that at home she'd have been at some particular task, and she found herself wondering what the Holding was making of her disappearance. There wasn't anyone in her extended family she was really close to anymore, not since Andrean had been killed in a raid and they'd sent Vrisa as Underwife to old man Fletcher. Of all her kin, only those two had ever seemed to really love her—even Father's Mother hadn't cared enough for her to stand up for her when she'd done something that truly enraged Keldar. Only those two had dared to brave the Firstwife's anger. Vris acted covertly, smuggling forbidden meals when punishment included doing without dinner. And-rean had been more open, demanding she be allowed to do something or coaxing Father to forgive her sooner. It had been at Andrean's insis-tence that she was allowed to continue her read-ing, for as Second son, his words had carried weight. And she and Vrisa had been closer than sibs; almost like twins in spite of the difference in their ages.

Tears stung her eyes at the thought of Andrean— so gentle with her, protective; always with a smile and a joke to share. He had been with her such a short time—he'd been killed when she was only nine. She could still remember him clearly, looming over her like a sheltering giant. He'd been so kind and patient—so ready to teach her anything she wanted to learn. He was everyone's favorite— except for Keldar. Truly the Goddess must have wanted him with Her, to take him so young—but Talia had needed him, too. They'd scolded her for crying at his wake, but it had been herself she had been crying for.

And poor Vris; she'd been terrified at the prospect of Marriage to old Fletcher, and it seemed she had been right to be so fearful. The few times Talia had seen her at Gatherings, she'd been pale and taut-looking, and as silent as one of the Lady's Handmaidens. All the sparkle had been snuffed out of her, and nothing was left but the ashes.

Talia shuddered—Vris' fate could so easily have been her own. The Companion's timely arrival seemed little less than miraculous in that light.

As she rode, she found her hands itching for something to do. Never since she could remember had there ever been a time when her hands hadn't been filled with some task. Even her reading was only allowed so long as she was occupied with some necessary job at the same time. To have empty hands seemed unnatural.

She filled her time with trying to take in as much of the changing landscape around her as she could, attempting to make some kind of men-

tal map. Small villages appeared with greater frequency the farther she went toward the capital.
The apparent lack of concern people showed over
her appearance had her baffled. One could almost suppose that the sight of a strange adolescent riding a Herald's Companion was relatively
commonplace. The only answer seemed to be as
the Guard had hinted, that this sort of thing happened all the time. But why hadn't her tales made
any mention of this? Companions were clearly of
a high order of intelligence; look at the way he'd
been caring for both of them all along this journey. Her first thought, that he'd run away like a
common farmbeast, was obviously incorrect. At
this point there wasn't much doubt in her mind as
to which of the two of them was truly in charge.
The tales were all true, then—Companions *were*
creatures of an intellect at the least equaling that
of their Heralds. She weighed the little she knew
of Companions against her experiences of the past
three days. It wasn't enough to help her. The
Holderkin held themselves aloof from the Heralds, forbidding the littles to speak of them, and
dealing with them only when they must. Only the
Elders had any contact with them. And the little
illicit gossip she'd heard had concerned only the
Heralds and their rumored licentiousness, not the
Companions.

But if you had to draw conclusions—Rolan must
have chosen to have her accompany him, for
there was no question that he could have returned
to the Collegium perfectly well on his own. And if
that were the case—could he have purposefully
selected her for some reason? Perhaps even arrived at the Holding with the express *intention* of

acquiring her and escorting her off to the capital?
That was almost *too* like a fable. Talia simply
couldn't believe that something like that was possible. Not for her—for some mage-gifted youth like
Vanyel perhaps, but for a plain little girl of
Holderkin? No one in his right mind would even
consider such a possibility.

Yet—the questions remained. Why had he appeared when he had; why had he inveigled her
into his saddle, and why, of all whys, was he carrying her off to the one place she wanted to go
more than anywhere else on the earth or all five
Heavens? The puzzle was almost enough to make
her forget her idle hands.

When the sixth day of her journey arrived, she'd
finished the last of the meat pies, and had decided
to make a test of the instructions the guard had
given her. Perhaps she would learn more from
the next Guard, now that she knew that there was
far more going on than she had any hope of
puzzling out for herself.

The next village—perhaps—would hold the
answers.

Three

Toward nooning she found they were approaching the outskirts of a very good-sized village. It lay in a little valley, well-watered and green with trees. Like the others Talia had seen, the shops and houses were colorfully painted with bold trim and shutters in blues, reds, and yellows. The bright colors contrasted cheerfully with the white plaster of the walls and the gold of fresh thatching. The scene was so unlike a faded gray Holding that it might well be in another land altogether. In the distance Talia could clearly see another guard-shelter; it appeared diminutive in contrast to the two- and three-storied buildings that stood near it. This was the first such shelter she had seen since early morning—it appeared that as she drew closer to the center of Valdemar, the overt presence of the Roadguard decreased. It seemed that this was the logical place for her to attempt to learn what this mystery was about and to reprovision herself at the same time.

The guard-shelter was placed in the deep shade of an enormous tree that completely overshadowed the road. Of all the buildings around, it alone was not brightly painted; rather, it was of plain wood, stained a dark brown. As they neared, Talia saw movement in the shadows, but the bright sun prevented her from seeing the Guard clearly at first. Her mouth fell open in amazement when she saw that the Guard who emerged from the shade was a woman—and one who wore a uniform identical in every respect to the first Guard's. For one bewildered moment she thought that she must *surely* be mistaken—certainly the idea was preposterous. She shook her head to clear her eyes of sun-dazzle, and looked again. The Guard *was* a woman. Impossible as it seemed, there was no mistaking the fact that *women* seemed to be part of the Army as well as men.

Before she could collect herself, the Guard had walked briskly to where they had halted and was standing at Rolan's head.

"Welladay!" she exclaimed before Talia could think what to say, "This *is* Rolan, isn't it?" She patted his neck as he nuzzled her graying black hair; she laughed, and slapped his nose lightly, then bent to examine some marks that Talia had noticed earlier on the saddle. "It certainly is! You've been a long time out, milord," she continued, clearly speaking to the horse. "I certainly hope it's been worth it."

Rolan lipped her sleeve playfully, and she laughed again.

"Now," the Guard turned her attention to Talia, squinting a little in the noon sun, "What can I do for you, young miss?"

Talia's confusion was doubled; however could she have guessed this Companion's name? And "Rolan" was hardly common—to have thought of it purely by accident all on her own—it seemed to hint at a great deal more than coincidence. "His name really *is* Rolan?" she blurted—then hung her head, blushing furiously at her own rudeness. "I'm sorry," she said to the pommel of the saddle. "I don't understand what's been happening to me. The—the Guard in Sweetsprings said other Guards could help me—"

"Sweetsprings!" the woman was plainly surprised. "You're a long way from home, childing!"

"I—guess I am," Talia replied faintly, watching the Guard out of the corner of her eye.

The Guard studied Talia as well, and the girl thought she must be appraising what she saw. Talia was wearing her original clothing, after doing her best to wash the worst of the travel stains from it, and keep it from drying with too many wrinkles in it. The loaned outfits had been of a heavier weight than was comfortable, riding all day in the sun—and at any rate, she hadn't felt quite at ease in them. Once everything had been worn once, it had seemed better to try and clean her own gear and return to it. Now she was glad she had; the Guard seemed to recognize exactly what she was just by the cut of it.

"Holderfolk, aren't you?" there was ready sympathy in her voice. "Huh. I've heard a bit about them—I'll bet you *are* confused, you poor thing. You must feel all adrift. Well, you'll find out what this is all about soon enough—trust me, they'll set you right at the Collegium. I'd try and explain, but it's against the rules for *me* to tell you if you don't already know, which is probably just as well— you'd probably end up more confused than ever. As to how I knew this was Rolan, well everybody on Roadguard duty knew he'd gone out; all his tack's marked with his sigil, just like every Companion—see?" She pointed to the marks she'd looked at, carved into the leather of the saddle skirting. Now that Talia knew what those marks meant, she could see they were a contracted version of Rolan's name. "Now, how can I serve you?"

"I'm afraid I need some provisioning." Talia said apologetically, half expecting a reproof. "They gave me some lovely meat pies—I did try to make them last, but—"

"How long ago was that?" the woman interrupted.

"Four days—" Talia replied, shrinking away a little.

"Four *days*? Hellfire! You mean you've been stretching your food for that long? What've you been eating, that dried horsecrap they keep in the Waystations?"

Talia's expression must have said plainly that that was exactly what she'd been doing, as the Guard's mouth twisted a little, and she tightened her lips in annoyance.

"Rolan," she said sternly, a no-nonsense tone in her voice. "You are letting this poor childing off your back for an hour, you hear me? You know damn well you can make up the time, and she needs a decent meal inside her before she comes down with flux, or something worse! *Then* where would you be?"

Rolan snorted and laid his ears back, but he didn't move off when the woman reached up to hand Talia out of the saddle. Talia slid down, feeling awkward under the eyes of the Guard, gawky and untidy—and once off Rolan, uneasy. Rolan followed close on their heels as the Guard led Talia by the hand to the Inn at the center of the village.

"I suppose the Guard back at Sweetsprings was a male, hm?" she asked wryly, and the woman nodded a bit at Talia's shy assent. "Just like a man! Never once thinks you might be more frightened by all this than excited, never once thinks you might not know the rules. Totally forgets that you may be Chosen but you're also just a child. And you're no better, Rolan!" she added over her shoulder, "Men!"

The Companion only tossed his head and made a sound that sounded suspiciously like a chuckle.

The inn was a prosperous place, with tables placed outside in the shade of a huge goldenoak that grew in the very center of its courtyard. There were a fair number of folk eating and drinking at those tables already. The Guard sat Talia down at one of these tables that was still unoccupied, and bullied the serving maid into bringing an enormous meal. She ordered Talia in tones that brooked no disagreement to "tuck into that food." Talia did so, suddenly realizing how hungry she'd been the past few days, while the Guard vanished somewhere.

She returned just as Talia finished the last crumb, carrying the saddlebags that had been fastened to Rolan's saddle and which now fairly bulged at the seams.

She sat down beside Talia, straddling the bench, and laid the bags between them "I've replaced your clothing. It's Holderfolk style and colors; some of the younglings around here wear that sort of thing for heavy work. I know you'll feel more comfortable in that kind of outfit, and this way people will know when they look at you that you're not used to being out in the big world; hopefully, they'll realize that you're going to be confused."

Talia started to protest that this wasn't necessary, but the stern look the guard gave her made her fall silent again.

"There's enough changes there to get you to the Collegium without you having to wash it yourself. Innkeeper's bringing you some wayfood. I told him no wine; that right?" At Talia's affirmative nod she continued, "Don't stint yourself; you're still a-growing and you don't want to be falling ill. Don't eat that crap they keep at the Waystations. That's supposed to be for the Companions and dire emergencies, no matter what that lazy lout at Sweetsprings told you. I'll tell you, the emergency would have to be pretty *damn* dire before *I'd* stomach that stuff! You stop every day for a hot nooning, unless there's no towns. That's an order! Here's your townchit," she said, handing another scrap of brass to Talia, who put it safely in her pouch. "Frankly, if it weren't for the damn rules, I'd keep you here overnight so's I'd know you'd gotten a hot bath and a proper bed, but—never mind. You'll have to stop once more for wayfood. Try Kettlesmith. The Dayguard there's an old friend of mine; she knows about Holderfolk and she knows children; she'll make sure you're all right. Ready to go?"

Talia nodded dumbly. This woman had all the brisk efficiency of Keldar with none of Keldar's coldness—she had taken charge of everything so quickly that Talia's head spun. And it seemed, at least, that she was concerned that Talia was all alone on the Road. Having someone concerned for her well-being was a strange sensation. Talia might almost have suspected an ulterior motive except that the Guard was so open and honest. If there was anything to be wary of in her manner, Talia couldn't read it.

"Good enough; off you get." She gave Talia a gentle shove toward the edge of the court where Rolan was waiting, surrounded by children. They were all vying for the chance to pet him or feed him a choice tidbit, and he seemed to Talia's eyes to be wearing a very smug, self-satisfied expression.

The Guardswoman gave Talia a boost into the saddle, refastened the saddlebags to the cantle and the bags brought by the Innkeeper to the snaffles at the front skirting, and gave Rolan a genial smack on the rump to send them on their way.

It wasn't until they were far down the Road that Talia realized that she hadn't yet had a single one of her questions answered.

At least—not directly. Indirectly though—now that she thought about it, there had been some information there. The Guardswoman had mentioned "rules" about journeys like this; that implied that they were commonplace. And she'd spoken to Rolan as she would have to a person— that implied that Rolan *was* as remarkable as legends claimed, and that his actions involving Talia were planned and intentional.

So—that meant that there was something that the Companion intended for her to be doing. But *what?*

To have only bits of information was as maddening as having only half a book! But some of that information was beginning to make a pattern.

All right; it was time to try putting more of this together. The three books Talia owned always (now that she thought about it) referred to Companions as having some kind of magical abilities; a mystical bond with their Heralds. There had been an implication, especially in Vanyel's tale, that Companions could communicate sensibly with their Heralds and vice versa. The Guard had spoken to Rolan as if he were a person—actually as if he had taken charge of Talia. That bore out the feeling that Talia had had ever since the first day—that it was Rolan who knew where they should be going and what they should be doing.

Rolan had given every evidence of understanding what the Guard had said to him. For that matter, he seemed to react to everything Talia said in the same way. *He* was the one who found the Waystations every night; *he* was the one who plainly guarded her. He was the one who knew the way back to the Collegium—the Guard had said as much.

It followed that he'd really had a purpose in being where she had encountered him—the Guard had said he'd been out a long time—and that purpose involved her. There was no getting around it. The question was—why?

Was it—dared she think—he might have been looking for someone to be tested as a Herald-candidate?

She had no notion of how Heralds actually *became* Heralds—except that they had to undergo strenuous training at the Collegium. Only Vanyel's tale had mentioned early on that he nearly hadn't had the courage to take up the task—the tale had made no mention of how he'd been picked. And all she knew of Heralds from Hold gossip was that they were supposedly monsters of moral depravity; wanton and loose, indulging in sensuous, luxurious, orgiastic behavior. She had suspected most of this was spite and sheer envy, especially since Heralds gave short shrift to Hold ideas of a woman's inferiority and proper place in life, and they answered to no authority but that of the Monarch and each other. That there were women in the Guard had come as a surprise, but since her first book had been the quest of Sun and Shadow, Talia had long been aware that there were women as Heralds who held equal position with the men. That freedom was one of the reasons she'd longed to become one.

Did she dare to dream that might happen now?

Just when Talia thought she might be getting used to the surprises of her journey, she was taken unawares again. The guard at Kettlesmith was not only another woman, but was one bearing obvious battlescars, with a peg of wood replacing one leg from the knee down. She told Talia, quite offhandedly, that she'd lost the rest of the leg to a wound she'd taken in the last war. The idea of a woman being in battle was so foreign to Talia's experience that she was in a half daze all through her meal and until she reached the outskirts of town afterward. It was only meeting with the Herald that shocked her out of it.

The Road led down into a wooded valley, still and cool. The trees were mostly pines, and Rolan's hooves crushed the needles that had collected on the Road's surface so that they traveled in a cloud of crisp scent. They were well inside the wood itself and out of sight of habitation within a few moments. Finally, in the heart of the wood the Road they'd been on met with another—there was a crossroads there. Talia didn't even notice that there was someone approaching on the other road under the shadows of the trees until an exclamation of startlement jarred her out of her trance.

She looked up, starting out of her daze. Facing her she saw, not more than four or five paces away and his astonishment written plain on his face, a white-clad man on a cloud-white mare. It was a Herald, a real Herald, mounted on *his* Companion.

Talia bit her lip, suddenly feeling a chill of fear. Even after all she'd been told, she still wasn't entirely sure she was doing right. *Now* she was for it; there was no disguising that Rolan was a Companion and that she wasn't any kind of a Herald. If she was to find herself in trouble, this encounter would bring it. She was conscious of an odd little disappointment, though, under all her apprehension; somehow it didn't seem quite proper for a Herald to be so—homely.

For the young man now approaching was just that. Carrying himself with all the authority of his office, poised, collected, yes. Obviously sure of himself, and every inch the Herald, but still—almost ugly. He certainly was nothing like the beautiful Vanyel or the angelic Sunsinger of the tales.

His voice made up for it, though.

"By the Hand of the Lady! Rolan, as sure as I stand here!" The words were melodious and unexpectedly deep. "By all the gods, you've finally Chosen!"

"Th-they told me to take him back to the Collegium, m'lord," Talia stuttered with nervousness, keeping her eyes down as was proper for a girl speaking to a man of rank, and waiting for the axe to fall. "I didn't know what else to do, and they all seemed so sure—"

"Whoa! You're doing the right thing, exactly right," he cut her torrent of explanation short. "You mean you don't know? No, of course you don't, or you wouldn't be acting like I'd caught you with your hand in my beltpouch."

Talia looked up for a second, bewildered by his words. He didn't speak anything like the Heralds in her tales, either. He had almost sounded like Andrean for a moment.

She longed to see if his eyes looked like Andrean's, too, but glanced hastily back down to the pommel when he tried to meet her gaze.

He chuckled, and out of the corner of her eye she could see that his expression was of gentle good humor. "It's quite all right. You're doing exactly as you should. Keep straight on the road you're on, and you'll be at the capital before dinner; anyone there can direct you to the Collegium. Hellfire, Rolan knows the way better than anyone else—you won't get lost. I wish I could tell you what's going on, but it's against the rules. You have to be told the whole of it at the Collegium—otherwise you'd be getting all kinds of stories about what all this means, and you'd be taking days to get straightened out afterward."

"But—" She was longing for someone, anyone, to explain this whole mess to her. It was like being caught in some kind of enormous game, only she was the only one that didn't know the rules and was stumbling from square to square without knowing why or where she was going. If *anyone* knew the whole truth, it would obviously be a Herald. And the kindness in his eyes made her long to throw the whole tangle in his hands. How anyone so homely could put her in mind of Andrean, she had no idea—but he did, and she found herself drawn to him as she'd not been to any male since her brother's death.

"No buts! You'll find out everything you need to know at the Collegium! Off with you!" With that, he rode close enough to reach out and smack Rolan's rump heartily, surprising the Companion enough that he jumped and broke into a canter, leaving the Herald far behind. Talia was so busy regaining her balance that she didn't notice the Herald and his own Companion galloping off into the trees, on a course that would eventually bring them back onto the road considerably ahead of Talia.

By the time she'd gotten over her startlement, the road was becoming crowded with other wayfarers, both going in her direction and in the opposite; other riders, walkers, carts drawn by various beasts, pack animals. But although she craned her neck in every direction, there was no sign of other Heralds.

The crowd on the road was not quite like any other crowd Talia had ever found herself among. For one thing, it was loud. Holderfolk kept their voices restrained at all times; even the Harvest Fair gatherings at the height of bidding excitement hardly generated more than a buzz. For another, all these people wore their emotions, their personalities, plain to be seen on their faces. The faces of well-schooled Holderfolk were closed, giving nothing away, and unlikely to display anything that would reveal their true feelings to one of their fellow creatures.

The other travelers took little special notice of her for the most part. Rolan threaded his way among them with delicate precision, making far better time than most of their fellow wayfarers, although keeping a good pace didn't really seem to be a prime consideration for most of them. Talia was so involved in people-watching that she forgot to watch for the city.

Then they topped a rise, and there it was.

It was so enormous that Talia froze in fright at the sight of it. Once again it was just as well that it was Rolan who plainly had charge of their journeying, or Talia would have turned him back along the way they'd come, bolting back to the familiarity of the Hold.

It sat in a river valley below them, and the view was excellent from the hilltop they'd just mounted. From here it could be seen that it had originally been a walled city, much as the Hold villages were but on a much bigger scale. With the passage of time and increased security, however, the city had been allowed to spread beyond the walls, spilling over them like water from the basin of a fountain. And like water, the spillage had followed certain channels; in this case, the roads.

Within the walls, houses crowded together so thickly that all Talia could see were roofs. Within the first wall there seemed to be a second wall, enclosing a few large buildings and a great deal of green, open space with trees in it. Outside the walls were more buildings, from single-storied huts to massive windowless places that could have held every structure at Sensholding within their walls. These clustered all around the first wall, then trailed out in long arms that followed the paths of the roads and the river. Talia's eyes were drawn irresistibly back to that inner space of green and trees and a stone edifice that towered over all the rest. This—this surely was the Palace and the Collegium—but before Talia could be certain that this was indeed the case, Rolan's steady pace had brought them down past the point where the view was so clear.

As they came closer to the area where the city dwellings began, Talia found herself assaulted on all sides by sound and noise. Hawkers were everywhere, crying their wares; shopkeepers had people stationed by the doors, screaming at the tops of their lungs, extolling the virtues of the goods within the shops. Children played noisily in and around the crowd, often skirting perilously close to the hooves of the horses, donkeys, and oxen that crowded the street. Neighbors screeched gossip to each other over the noise of the crowd; from the vicinity of inns came voices loud in argument or song. Talia's head reeled, her ears rang, and her fear grew.

And the smells! She was assaulted by odor as she was by sound. Meat cooking, bread baking, smoke, dung, spices, sweat of man and beast, hot metal, spilled beer—her poor, country-bred nose was as overwhelmed as her ears.

They came to the gate in the first wall; there were guards there, but they didn't hinder her passage though they looked at her with expressions she couldn't quite read; curiosity, and something else. The wall they passed under frightened her even more; it was as tall as the rooftop of the Temple back home. She felt terribly small and insignificant, and the weight of it crushed her spirit entirely.

The noise and tumult, if anything, was worse inside. Here the houses were multi-storied, and crowded so closely together that their eaves touched. Everything began to blur into a confused muddle of sound, sight, and scent. Talia huddled in Rolan's saddle, unaware that she was drawing pitying looks from the passersby, with her eyes so wide with fear in her pinched, white face. It was just as well that Rolan knew exactly where to go, for she was so frightened that she would never have been able to ask directions even of a child.

It seemed an age before Rolan paused before a gate in the second, inner wall. The gate was small, only large enough to admit a single rider, and closed, and the guard here looked her over curiously. Unlike the lighter uniform of the others, this man was clad in midnight blue with silver trimmings. He opened the gate and came forward as soon as he saw them, and Rolan waited for his approach. He smiled encouragingly at Talia, then drew close enough to read the little marks on Rolan's saddle, and gave an exclamation of glee.

"Rolan!" he cried with delight, seeming to forget momentarily about Talia's existence. "Finally! We were beginning to think you'd never find someone! There was even a bet on that you'd jumped the Border! The Collegium's been in a fine pother since you left—"

He finally seemed to see Talia, nerves strung bowstring-taut and white-faced.

"Your ordeal is almost over, childing," he said with real sympathy even as she shrank away from him. "Come down now, and I'll see that you get to where you need to go."

He aided her down out of the saddle as if she'd been a princess; no sooner had she set her feet on the ground than another uniformed person came to lead Rolan away. Talia watched them vanish with an aching heart, wondering if she'd ever see him again. She wished with sudden violence that she'd followed her first impulse and ridden him far away. Whatever was to happen to her? How could she have dreamed that she'd be of any significance to folk who lived in a place like *this*?

The guard led her into the gray stone, multistoried building at the end of the path they walked. It was totally unlike any structure Talia was familiar with. Her heart was in her shoes as they entered a pair of massive, brass-inlaid wooden doors. Never had she seen anything to equal the work in those doors, and that was just the beginning of the wonders. She was feeling worse by the minute as she took in the grandness of her surroundings. The furnishings alone in just one of the many rooms they passed would have exceeded the combined wealth of the entire Holding. Not even the Temple High Sanctuary was this impressive. She would have bolted given a moment to herself, except that after the first few minutes she was well and truly lost.

At last he brought her to a room much smaller than many of the ones they'd passed; about the size of a large pantry, though no less rich than the rest of the building.

"Someone will be with you in just a few moments, youngling," he said kindly, relieving her of her townchits, "You're among friends here, never doubt it. We've been waiting for you, you know! You and Rolan were a welcome sight to these eyes." When she didn't respond, he patted her carefully on the head. "Don't worry, no one is going to harm you—why, I have little ones nearly your age myself! Make yourself comfortable while I let the proper people know you're here."

Make herself comfortable? How, in a room like this?

She finally chose a leather-padded chair as the one she was least likely to damage and sat on it gingerly. In the silence of the unoccupied room, she began to lose her fear, but her discomfort grew as the fear faded. Surrounded by all this luxury, she was acutely aware of the fact that she was sticky, damp with nervousness, smelt faintly of horse, and was dressed in the kind of fabrics they probably made grain bags out of here. She was also painfully aware that she was only thirteen years old. When she'd been with Rolan, none of that had seemed to matter, but now—oh, *now* she was all too aware of her shortcomings. How had she ever dared to dream she might become a Herald? Never—never—only people born and bred to surroundings like these could aspire to such a position. The Guard had probably gone for some underservant to give her a bit of silver and send her on her way—if she was lucky, it would be someone she could talk into giving her a job.

A miniature whirlwind burst into the room, interrupting her thought.

"Oh!" said the girl, a little of about seven with chestnut hair, blue eyes, and a rather disagreeable expression on an otherwise pretty face, "What are *you* doing here?"

For the first time since she'd seen the city, Talia felt back on secure ground. Littles were one thing she *could* handle!

"I'm waiting, like I was told," she replied.

"Aren't you going to kneel?" the child asked imperiously.

Talia hid a smile. It was amazing how so simple a thing as having to deal with an obviously spoiled child made her feel so very much more confident.

"Kneel?" she asked with mock-astonishment. "Why should I kneel?"

The child was becoming red-faced with temper. "You're in the Presence of the Heir to the Throne!" she replied haughtily, the capital letters audible, her nose in the air and her expression disdainful.

"Really? Where?" Talia looked around her with an innocent face that covered inner mischief newly aroused by the child's pretensions. This little was about to receive the treatment her bad manners deserved. If she *was* the Heir—well, someone was obviously not doing his job in training her. And if she wasn't, she deserved it for lying. "I don't see anyone like that."

"Me! Me!" the girl shouted, stamping her foot, frustrated and angry. *"I'm* the Heir!"

"Oh, I don't think so," Talia said, thoroughly

enjoying herself. "You're nothing but a little having a temper tantrum; one that fibs a lot. I've read all about the Heirs. The Heir is always polite and gracious, and treats the lowest scullery maid like she was the Queen's own self. You act like you'd treat the Queen like the lowest scullery maid. You can't possibly be the Heir. Maybe I should call a guard and tell him there's an imposter in here."

The child's mouth opened and closed wordlessly with frustration and rage.

"Maybe you're a fish," Talia added ingenuously, "You certainly look like one."

The girl shrieked in anger, and drew back one balled-up fist.

"I wouldn't," Talia said warningly, "I hit back."

The child's eyes widened in surprise, then her face grew even redder with rage. "I—how—oh!"

"You said that already."

At that the girl gave an ear-piercing squeal, pushed over a small table that stood nearby, and ran out of the room before it hit the ground. Talia had expected her to do something of the kind and had sprung to the table's rescue, catching it before it was damaged and righting it with a sigh of exasperation.

A dry chuckle came from behind Talia, who turned to see a curtain pushed aside, and a tall, handsome woman in Herald's Whites step into the room. Though she wore a long skirt with the thigh-length tunic instead of breeches, and the materials were clearly fine velvet and silk, she was no different in appearance from other Heralds Talia had seen or heard about. Her face was triangular and strong rather than pretty; her hair was bound in a knot at the nape of her neck and was the same golden color as raival leaves in the fall. She had very penetrating, intelligent blue eyes the same intense sapphire blue as a Companion's.

Talia started to scramble to her feet, but the woman gestured that she should remain seated.

"Stay where you are, youngling," she said, as Talia resumed her place and continued to watch her shyly. "You've had a long and tiring ride—you deserve to sit on something that isn't moving for a while!"

The woman studied the child seated obediently before her and liked what she saw. There had been competence in the way that she had handled the Heir's rudeness and temper; there had been enough mischief there to suggest a lively sense of humor, but at the same time this child had been clever without being cruel. That boded very well indeed for her future success.

"Well, so you're Talia. I hope you don't mind the fact that I was eavesdropping, but I wanted to see how you'd handle her," she said, with a hint of apology.

"With a hairbrush to her behind, if I had charge of her," Talia replied, almost automatically. The incident and the woman's obvious approval had put some of her fears to rest; and if Keldar exuded an air that always made Talia feel nervous and incompetent, this woman had the very opposite effect on her.

"She's had precious little of that," the woman sighed, "and I fear she's overdue for a good share of it."

She examined Talia more closely and was even more encouraged by what she read in the child's face and manner. There was intelligence and curiosity in her large brown eyes, and her expression was that of a child blessed with an unfailingly sweet and patient nature. The woman guessed that she was probably a bit older than she appeared to be; perhaps around thirteen or fourteen. The heart-shaped face crowned by tousled brown curls was very appealing. The sturdily built, well-muscled body showed that this child was no stranger to hard work. With every observation it seemed as if Rolan had supplied the Collegium with the precise answer to all of their hopes and prayers.

"Well, that's tomorrow's problem," she replied, "I am told you're the one Rolan brought back—is that correct? Has anyone told you anything yet?"

Talia was encouraged by the understanding in the woman's face. The encouragement she found there, and the unfeigned interest, and most of all the reassurance, caused words to boil up out of her without her even thinking about them.

"No! Everybody seems to know what's going on but me!" she blurted, "And nobody wants to *explain* anything!"

The woman seated herself with a careless grace. "Well, now someone will. Why don't you tell me about what's happened to you—from the beginning. I'll try to help you understand."

Talia found herself pouring out the whole tale, from the time Keldar called her into the house till this very moment. Before she'd finished, she was fighting back tears. All the doubts that had occurred to her were coming back—she had nothing to count on except the dubious possibility of their gratitude. And she fully realized just what kind of a hopeless situation she was in if the Heralds chose to turn her out.

"Please—you must know someone—someone—"

"In charge?"

"Yes. Can't you please find me something to do here?" Talia begged shamelessly. "I'll do anything—mend, wash, scrub floors—" She stopped, afraid the tears would come if she went on. How had she *ever* dared to dream she might join these magical people? They were as much above her as the stars.

"Dirk was right. You haven't a clue to what's happened to you, have you?" the woman said, half to herself. Then she looked up, and Talia averted her own eyes from the intensity of her gaze. "Did you really mean what you said to the Firstwife, that you wanted to be a Herald?"

"Yes. Oh yes!" Talia was studying the hands clenched in her lap. "More than anything—I know it's not possible, but—I didn't know any better, then. No one ever told me what this place was like, and I don't think—I don't think I could have pictured it anyway. Sensholding isn't anything like this. I never could have guessed what I was asking. Please—please forgive me—I didn't mean any disrespect."

"Forgive?" the woman was astonished. "Child, forgive *what*? It's no disrespect to dream of becoming a Herald—though it's not like the tales, you know. It's work that is both dull and dangerous; if not one, then the other. Half the Heralds never live to reach old age. And it's a life where you find you have very little time for yourself. It's a wonder that anyone *wants* the job, much less dreams of it as her heart's desire. A Herald has to always consider her duty above all else, even her own well-being."

"That doesn't matter!" Talia cried, looking up.

"Why not? What does matter?"

"I'm not sure." She groped for the words to express what until now she'd only felt. "It's that Heralds *do* things instead of complaining about them, things that put peoples' lives back together, even if it's only settling a quarrel about a cow. And—" she faltered, "there's the Companion—"

Tears began to flow despite her resolution as she remembered with bright vividness the days on the road, and how, for once in her life, she hadn't been lonely. It might have been imagination, and yet—it had seemed, at least, that Rolan had cared for her. Dared she think—loved her? There was no doubt in her mind that she had loved him. And now he was gone, no doubt taken to the Herald he *truly* belonged with.

"Oh my poor child," the woman reached out instinctively and gathered Talia to her, to let her sob on her shoulder.

Talia tried to pull away, fighting back the tears, even though she longed to relax on that comforting shoulder. "I'm all over dirt," she sobbed, "And you're in Whites. I'll get you all grubby."

"There are more important things in life than dirt," the woman replied, holding her firmly, exactly as Vris had done more than once. There was something almost as comforting about her as there had been about Rolan—or Vris, or Andrean. Talia's reticence evaporated, and she cried herself out.

When Talia was again in control of herself, the woman gave her a handkerchief to repair the damages with, and said, "It's fairly obvious that, for some reason, you were never told of how Heralds are chosen."

"Aren't they just born into it, like being Eldest Son? I mean—all this—"

"'All this' means nothing—if you haven't the right makings. It *is* true that Heralds are born to the job, since no one can *learn* to be a Herald, but blood doesn't matter. No, the Companions Choose them."

And it all came flooding back—that bright, joyful moment when she'd first looked into Rolan's eyes. "I Choose you," he'd said in her mind. She remembered it all now. . . .

The woman smiled at Talia's gasp, as all the little bits of the mystery suddenly assumed their rightful pattern. "It usually happens that they don't have to go very far. It's a rather odd thing, but for various reasons anyone who is of the proper material to be a Herald finds his or her way to the city, the Court, or the Collegium more often than not. Sometimes, though, the Companions have to go seeking their Heralds themselves. There's one Companion that *always* does this; tell me, in the tales you read, did you ever come across the title 'The Monarch's Own Herald'?"

"Ye-es," Talia replied doubtfully, still a little dazed with the revelation and the newly awakened memories, "But I couldn't make out what it meant."

"It's a position of very special trust. It takes a very extraordinary person to fill it. Everyone needs someone to trust utterly, someone who would never offer false counsel, someone who could be a true friend in all senses of the word. The Monarch needs such a person more than anyone else because she is so surrounded by those who have nothing but their own interests at heart. This is what the 'Queen's Own' really is; the very fact of the Queen's Own's existence is one of the reasons this Kingdom has had so little internal strife over the years. When a ruler knows that there is at least one person who can be utterly trusted and yet will always tell her the truth, it tends to make her more confident, more honest with herself, less selfish—and altogether a better ruler. The position of Queen's Own is a lifetime one, and the person to fill that position is always Chosen by the Companion of the last Herald to hold it. When that Herald dies, the Companion leaves the Collegium to search the Kingdom for a successor. In the past reigns that hasn't taken more than a day or two, and quite often he Chooses someone who is already a Herald or nearly ready to be made one. This time, though, it was different. When Herald Talamir died, his Companion was gone for nearly two months, something that hasn't happened in a very long time."

Talia was so wrapped up in the story the woman was telling that she forgot her apprehensions. "Why?" she asked simply.

The woman pondered Talia's simple question for a long time before answering it. The child deserved the best answer she could give, and an honest one.

"Well, we think it has something to do with the current situation," she replied after long thought. "The Heir has been badly spoiled—that's partly the Queen's fault: she allowed too much of her time to be taken up with politics and things that seemed important at the time, but in the long run, were not. The child's nursemaid is from outKingdom and has given the girl a very exaggerated idea of her own importance. It's not going to be an easy task to make the brat into the kind of woman that deserves to sit on the Throne. Talamir's Companion had to roam far to find someone equal to it."

"He *did* find someone, didn't he?" Talia asked anxiously.

"He certainly did. He brought her to us today."

She watched Talia's reaction carefully, knowing it would tell her a great deal about the girl.

The child was completely incredulous. *"Me?* But—but—I don't know *anything*—I'm just a low-born farmgirl—I don't fit—I can't talk right—I don't look right—I'm not anything you'd want—"

"You know how to handle a spoiled child. Talia, I will admit I was hoping for someone a little older, but—well, the Companions don't make mistakes. You'll be close enough to Elspeth in age that you can be her *real* friend, once you've tamed the brat. As for not fitting in—she's been too much cosseted by courtiers as it is; she could use a good dose of farm sense. Yes, and a good dose of country spanking if it comes to that! And for the future—if I'd had someone that I'd have felt easy in confiding in—gossiping with—I expect I'd never have wedded her father." She sighed.

"You—her father—you're the *Queen?*" Talia jumped to her feet, her eyes horrified, and the Queen did her best to stifle a smile at the look of utter dismay she wore. "I've been getting the *Queen* all grubby?" She would have fallen to her knees, except that the Queen prevented it, insisting that she return to her seat beside her.

"Talia, dear, the Queen is only the Queen in the

Throne Room," she replied. "Anywhere else, I'm just another Herald. And I'm a mother who needs your help very badly. I've bungled somewhere, and I haven't the skill to put things right. I think from what I've seen just in the past hour that you have, despite your tender years."

She hoped that the child could read the entreaty in her eyes.

"No one can force you to this. If you honestly don't feel equal to the task of being Queen's Own to a woman old enough to have mothered you and to a spoiled little monster, we'll find someplace else here where you can be happy. I'll admit to you that this is a job *I* wouldn't want under any circumstances. You can say no, and we'll send Rolan out again. But—I think his judgment was right when he Chose you. Will you be a Herald, Talia, and Queen's Own?"

Talia gulped nervously, still not certain that she wasn't victim of a terrible mistake. She opened her mouth intending to say no, but once again her heart betrayed her.

"Yes!" she heard herself saying, "Oh, yes!"

The Queen sighed as though a heavy burden had been lifted from her shoulders. "Thank you, Talia. Trust me, you won't have to bear this alone for a long, long time. You have too much you need to learn, so there will be many willing and able to help you. The most important thing is that you become Elspeth's friend, so that you can start to guide her. I may set my Heralds hard tasks, but I try not to make them impossible." She smiled, a smile bright with relief. "Is there anything else I can tell you?"

"Could I—" she swallowed a lump in her throat. "Could I see Rolan? Once in a while?"

"See him? Bright Havens, child, he's *your* Companion now; if you really wanted to, you could sleep in his stall!"

"I can? He is? It's really all real?"

It was too much like a tale. At any moment now, Talia expected to find herself waking in her bed back in the attic of the Steading. This couldn't be real. It had to be that she was dreaming. Yet, would a dream have included the feeling of being slightly grubby, and the hard edge of the chair that was digging just the tiniest bit into her leg?

She was forced to conclude that this was no dream. Suddenly she felt dizzy and half-drunk with compounded relief and elation. She was going to be a Herald—she really was going to be a Herald, like Vanyel and Shadowdancer and all the others of her tales and legends! And not just any Herald at that, but the highest ranking Herald in the entire Kingdom.

Best not to think about that for a moment. It was too much to really comprehend completely.

She raised her eyes to meet the Queen's, dropping her Holderkin reserve and letting her happiness show plainly.

"Yes Talia. It's quite real," the Queen's eyes softened with amusement at the naked joy on the child's face. This girl was so self-possessed that it was quite easy to forget that she was only thirteen—until she herself reminded you. Like now, when she was all ecstatic child. It would not be hard to care for this Talia in the least. Especially not at moments like this.

Then she made the switch again, back to miniature adult. "Where do I start? What do I need to do?"

"You start now," the Queen pulled a bellrope behind her to call the Dean of the Collegium, who had been impatiently awaiting the results of this interview. "As soon as Dean Elcarth gets here. He'll get you settled at the Collegium. As for what you need to do; you learn, Talia. And please," her eyes were very sober. "Learn as quickly as you can. I—*we*—need you more than you can guess."

Four

The Queen's summons was answered immediately. Talia hadn't the faintest notion of what to expect, but her first glimpse of the diminutive man in Herald's Whites that the Queen introduced as the Dean of Herald's Collegium gave her a feeling of intense relief. Dean Elcarth was a brisk, birdlike, elderly man, scarcely taller than Talia. The wary unease she usually felt around men evaporated when she saw him; he was so like a snow-wren (complete with the gray cap of hair to match a wren's gray crown) that it was impossible to be afraid of him.

"So," he said, surveying Talia with his head tilted slightly to one side, his round, black eyes bright with intellect. "This is our new Herald-in-training. I think you'll do well here, child; and I'll be the first to tell you that I'm never wrong." He chuckled and Talia responded with a tentative smile.

He nodded slightly to the Queen. "Well, with your permission, Selenay—"

"I leave her in your capable hands," the Queen replied.

"Excellent. Come along with me, youngling. I'll

show you about; perhaps find someone to help get you settled in among us."

He led her out the door and down the wood-paneled hall. Talia obediently fell in beside him; she was glad that he was nearly as small as she was, otherwise she'd never have been able to keep up with him. The pace he set forced her to take two steps for every one of his just to match him.

She watched him carefully, despite her earlier judgment. She had had too many nasty surprises in her life to wish another, especially not here, alone among strangers.

He saw her wary, covert gaze and made note of it. Elcarth had been Dean of Herald's Collegium for decades. He had had plenty of practice in that time in assessing the newly-Chosen, and he hadn't missed a single nuance of Talia's behavior. The way she'd shrunk into herself before she'd gotten a good look at him told him more than she could possibly have guessed. The way she had blindly obeyed him told him even more. He mentally shook his head. She was obviously unaccustomed to taking the initiative. Something would have to be done about that. And this wild-animal shyness spoke of abuse; mental and emotional, and perhaps physical abuse as well. Fortunately, she may have had her spirit bent but it wasn't broken; Rolan would never have Chosen her otherwise. He made another internal note; to discuss the Holderfolk with the Queen. That this child had been left in ignorance of Companion's Choice was criminal. And young Dirk had been right—the child was so withrawn and reticent it was scarcely to be believed. Women did not seem to evoke the reaction nearly so strongly as men—it almost seemed as if she expected blows and abuse from a man as a matter of course. It would take a very long time indeed before a strange man could win her trust. He made swift revision of his original plans; until she was comfortable with what life here meant, it would be best for her mentors to be mostly female. Only Herald Teren was likely to be unthreatening enough that she'd lose her apprehension in his presence.

Elcarth questioned Talia closely as they walked, keeping his tone carefully light and projecting a calming aura at her as he did so. The answers he got were highly satisfactory; he'd feared the child would be at best functionally illiterate. In reading and writing, at least, she was at a comparable level with most of the youngsters Chosen at her age, and she had an incredible thirst for knowledge. So far as academics went, he was confident that all that would be needed would be to give her access to information and teaching, and she would do the rest without external prodding.

In only one area was she frighteningly deficient; she seemed to know little or nothing of self-defense and weaponry. This was more than simply unfortunate; she'd have to learn to protect herself, and quickly. There were many in the Heraldic Circle who doubted that Talamir's death had been happenstance; he shared those doubts. A child, alone, knowing nothing of self-defense—against those who had been able to make the death of an experienced Herald seem due to simple old age, she was no opponent at all. She was so vulnerable—so very vulnerable; such a fragile creature to carry all their hopes. Weaponsmaster Alberich was the *only* instructor capable of teaching her at any speed, and Alberich was likely to frighten her on appearance alone! He made yet another mental note to speak with the Weapons-master as soon as he'd left her in good hands. Alberich was no fool; warned how shy she was, he would know how to treat her.

Meanwhile—Elcarth continued his questions, even more alert to nuances of behavior than he had been before. There was no reaction she made that escaped him.

Talia for her part was more than a little puzzled at Dean Elcarth's questioning, for it seemed to follow no pattern that she could see. He flitted from subject to subject so rapidly that she had no time to think about her answers, and certainly was unable to anticipate his questions. Yet the answers she gave him seemed to please him; once or twice he'd seemed *very* satisfied by what she told him.

They traversed long wood-paneled, tapestried corridors; only the few that had exterior windows and gave Talia a glimpse of sun and trees allowed her any clue even of what direction they were taking. They passed at length through a pair of massive double doors. "We're in the Collegium Wing now; Herald's Collegium, that is," Elcarth said, "There are two other Collegia here associated with the Palace—Bardic Collegium and Healer's Collegium. Ours is the largest, but that is in part because most of the academic classrooms are here, and we save space that way. Healer's has its own separate building; so does Bardic. The House of Healing is part of Healer's Collegium; you may have heard of it. Now, down this corridor are the classrooms; the first floor is entirely classrooms. The door at the far end leads to the court in front of the stables, and the training grounds beyond that. Behind us, on the other side of the doors we just passed through, are the private quarters of the Kingdom's Heralds."

"Are *all* of them here?" Talia asked, overwhelmed by the thought of all those Heralds in one place.

"Well, no. Most of them are out on their circuits. But all of them have at least one room here, some shared, some not, and those on duty permanently at the palace or the Collegium have several, as do those who have retired from active duty if they decide to stay here with us. There's a staircase behind this door here; there's another in the middle of the building and a third next to the door at the end. We'll go upstairs now, to the students' quarters."

The wood-paneled staircase wasn't as narrow as the ones at the Holding, and a little window halfway up lit the stairs clearly. There was a door on the second landing, and the Dean opened it for her.

"This is the dormitory section," he said. Like the hall below them, it was paneled in some kind of dark wood, sanded smooth, but not polished. The doors here were much closer together than they had been in the hall below, and the hall itself seemed oddly foreshortened.

"As you can see, this hall is a bit less than half the size of the one downstairs, since on the other side of that wall is the common room where all meals are served, and on the other side of that is the boys' section. We're standing in the girls' side now. The third floor is one room, the Library and study area. The Library is entirely for the use of students and Heralds; you can go there any time you don't have classes or other tasks to do," Elcarth smiled encouragingly as Talia's eyes lit. "Just try to see that you spend a *little* time in eating and sleeping!"

Just then a small boy, wearing a uniform much like the Guard had worn, but in light blue instead of midnight blue, came running up to Elcarth. He was trailed at a distance by a richly-dressed but harried-looking middle-aged man. This was the first person *not* wearing some kind of uniform that Talia had seen since she'd arrived.

"Havens, what is it *now*?" Elcarth muttered under his breath as the boy pounded up to them.

"Dean Elcarth, sir, it's the Provost-Marshal, sir," the boy said in a breathless treble.

"I can see that, Levand. What's happened this time? Fire, flood, or rioting in the streets?"

"Some of all three, m'lord Herald," the Provost-Marshal had plodded within hearing distance and spoke for himself, as Talia tried to make herself invisible back against the wall. "You know the Lady-fountain in Tailor's Court? The one that used to vent down a culvert to Breakneedle Street?"

"Your choice of words fills me with foreboding, m'lord," Elcarth replied with a sigh. " 'Used to'?"

"Someone chose to divert it, m'lord Herald. Into the cellar gathering-room of Jon Hapkin's Virgin and Stars Tavern. Which is, as you know—"

"The third-year Bardic students' favored place of illicit recreation; yes, I know. This rather smacks of the Unaffiliates, doesn't it? The plumb-line and compass set—"

"Partly, m'lord."

"You fill me with dread. Say on."

"The Bardic students took exception to gettin'

their feet wet, m'lord Herald, and took exception very strongly."

"And went hunting the perpetrators, no doubt?"

"Aye, m'lord. I'm told that drum-beaters make fine cudgels, and there's a few among 'em that lately fancy walking about with carved staffs."

"Well, that covers the flood and the rioting in the streets. What about the fire?"

"Set by the Bardic students, m'lord. In the alley off Fivepenny. Seems the ones they blamed for the water had holed up in the Griffin's Egg and wouldn't come out, and someone gave them the notion to smoke 'em out. They lit a trash-fire and fed the smoke in through the back door."

"Lord—" Elcarth passed his hand over his eyes, looking to Talia as if he had a headache coming on. "Why take this up with me, my lord? So far you need to speak to the parents and patrons of the Unaffiliates involved, and the Dean of Bardic."

"The which I've done, m'lord Herald. *That's* been taken care of."

"There's more? Lady save me—"

"When all the hue and cry was over, and the gentlemen and ladies separated from one another, it was discovered that they'd had their purses lifted, one and all. The purses were found, intact, hanging from the trees in the Cloister gardens; the Lady's priestesses never saw anyone put them there, of course, but several of the combatants remembered someone in the thick of all the pummeling that had been wearing Heraldic student Grays."

"Needless to say—"

"Aye, m'lord Herald. Only one student you've got that's able to pull that prank."

"Lord-Dark and Lady-Bright," Elcarth muttered,

rubbing one temple. "Hold on a moment, my lord Provost-Marshal. I have another bit of business I'll have to delegate, and I'll be right with you."

Elcarth looked around, and spied Talia shrunk inconspicuously as possible in the corner. "Child, this is unbearably rude of me, but I'll have to find you another guide for the moment," he said, putting his hand gently behind her shoulders and propelling her forward a little. The door to the common room opened, and a small group of young women, all dressed identically in gray, stepped into the hall.

"And there," Elcarth said with satisfaction, "Is just the person I was needing. Sherrill!"

One of the young women, a tall, slender brunette with a narrow face and hazel eyes, turned at the sound of her name being called, smiled, and made her way toward them.

"Sir?" she said, then looked curiously at Talia.

"This is the young lady Rolan brought in," Elcarth replied. "She's from one of those Border settlements that might just as well be outKingdom, and she's very confused. She'll need lots of help in adjusting. Unfortunately, the Provost-Marshal has some other business I need to handle. Would you—"

"Take her off your hands? Surely! Is she as badly off as *I* was?" The young woman's smile was infectious, and Talia returned it tentatively.

"Seriously, yes—worse, in some ways," the Dean replied.

"Bright Havens, that bad? Poor baby!" The young woman gave Talia another encouraging smile. "Well, we'll see what we can do for her. Uh, sir—is the 'business' Skif again?"

"It looks that way."

"Oh, Havens. Doesn't he ever learn?"

"He does. He never does the same trick twice," Elcarth replied, fighting down a chuckle. "It isn't too bad this time. He's not the main perpetrator, apparently; he's more of a loose end. I think I can get him off easily."

"Well, I hope so; I like the little monkey."

"Don't we all? Except possibly Lord Orthallen. You will take good care of young Talia, won't you? I'm counting on you, since the Provost-Marshall is beginning to look impatient."

"Yes, sir," she grinned. As she turned toward Talia, the grin became sympathetic. "The Dean knows I was in the same predicament as you are now when I first came. My people are fisherfolk on Lake Evendim, and all I knew was fish. You should have seen the saddlesores I came in with—and I couldn't even read and write!"

"I can read—and write and figure, too," Talia said shyly.

"See? You're three better than I was to start with! Dean—" she recaptured Elcarth's attention from wherever it had been wandering, "Basic Orientation with Teren tomorrow, sir?"

"Naturally; we've been holding the class until Rolan returned. I'll arrange a schedule for her and leave it with Teren. And tomorrow I want you to take her over to the training grounds and let Alberich decide what he wants to do with her."

Sherrill looked from Talia to the Dean, a little surprised that the girl was being put into Alberich's class so quickly, and caught Elcarth's silent signal that he wished to talk more with her later. She nodded briefly and Elcarth bid them both farewell, hurrying off with the harried Provost-Marshal.

She took a good look at the latest (and most important) of the Chosen. The poor little thing seemed exhausted, shy, and rather worried, and was most certainly bewildered by all that had been happening to her. Sherrill was surprised by a sudden surge of maternal feelings toward the child.

"Well, Talia, the first thing we need to do is find you a room and get you your uniforms and supplies," she said, hoping her casual tone would put the girl at ease. "How old are you, anyway?"

"Thirteen," Talia replied softly, so softly Sherrill could hardly hear her.

"That old? You don't look it," she said, leading the way. "I'll tell you what, though, it's not so bad being small; there aren't that many Chosen that are your size, and at least you can count on getting uniforms that aren't half patches!"

"Uniforms?"

"Like my outfit—take a good look. It's identical to a Herald's except that it's silvery gray instead of Herald's White, and the materials are a bit different. You see, wearing uniforms puts us all on an equal footing, and it makes us easy to identify as Heralds-in-training. Bardic and Healer's Collegia do the same; full Bards wear scarlet, and the trainees wear red-brown; Healers have their Healer's Green, and the Healers-in-training wear pale green. We wear gray until we've earned our Whites. There are some students that don't belong to any of the Collegia; they wear uniforms too, but they're pale blue. Officially they're called the Unaffiliates; we call 'em the Blues. There's all kinds—people learning to be something more than just simple clerks, ones that have talents for building things, highborns whose parents think they ought to have something to do besides choose new horses and clothing."

She frowned for a moment in sudden thought, wondering how much to tell the girl about the Blues. Should she frighten the child, perhaps needlessly, or should she leave her in ignorance of the intrigues going on all around her? It was hard to judge when the girl seemed determined to show an impassive face to the world. Sherrill knew she hadn't the ability of Elcarth to "read" someone, and this Talia might just as well have been a rock for all that *she* could judge of what might be going on behind those big eyes.

She decided on a middle course. "You might want to watch out for them," she warned, "Both Bardic and Healer's Collegia are pretty careful about who they accept for training, and anyone in Grays has been Chosen by a Companion, but the unaffiliated students have no selection criteria applied to them. All that's required is that they keep passing the courses they choose. A good half of the ones from the Court circles are no better than well-born bullies, and there's one or two of them that are *really* nasty-minded. In your place, I'd try and stick close to other Grays in public places." She stopped, and opened one of the doors at the very end of the hall. "Now, this will be your room."

The little room revealed had scarcely enough space for the furniture—bed, desk, chair, bookcase, and wardrobe. It was obvious that to Talia, however, it seemed palatial. No doubt she'd shared at least a bed with other girls and very possibly had never had even a corner of a room to call her own before this. Sherrill slipped a card with Talia's name printed on it into a holder on the door, and smiled at her expression. She sympathized completely; before she'd been carried off to the Collegium by her own Companion, she'd spent most of her life packed together with the rest of her family like salt-fish in a barrel. Her summers had been spent on the boat, with nowhere to go for any kind of privacy, the winters were spent in a one-room longhouse with not only her own family but the families of both her uncles as well. She sometimes wondered now how anyone managed to ignore the press of people long enough to ensure that the family name was carried on!

"Do you like it?" she asked, trying to elicit some response from the child.

Talia was overwhelmed. She'd slept all her life in a bed shared with two of her sisters in the barracks-like attic of the Housestead. This room—now all her own!—seemed incredibly luxurious in comparison. Sherrill seemed to understand, and let her contemplate this wealth of privacy for a long moment.

"Oh, yes!" she replied at last, "It's—wonderful!"

It was more than wonderful; it was a long-wished-for haven, a place she could retreat to where no one else could go. Talia hadn't missed the fact that there was a bolt on the inside of the door. If she wanted to, she could lock the whole world out.

"Good! Now we go see the Housekeeper," Sherrill said, interrupting Talia's reverie before she had a chance to really get used to the idea of having her own room. "She'll get your supplies and put you down on the duty roster."

"What's that?"

"A question at last! I was beginning to wonder what had happened to your tongue!" Sherrill teased gently, and Talia flushed a little. "It's the tradition of the three Collegia that everyone share the work, so there are no servants anywhere around here. In fact, the only people in the Collegia that aren't students and teachers are the Cook and the Housekeeper. We all take turns doing something every day. The chores never take that long to do, and it really drives home to the 'gently-born' that we're all equals here. If you're sick, you're excused, of course. I suspect they'd even have us doing all the cooking if they weren't sure that we'd probably poison each other by accident!"

Sherrill chuckled; Talia laughed hesitantly, then offered, "I can cook. Some."

"Good. Make sure to tell Housekeeper. She'll probably put you down as Cook's helper most of the time, since most of us don't know one end of a chicken from the other."

She chuckled again as she recalled something. "There's a Herald that just got his Whites a month or so ago, his name is Kris, who was one of the 'gently-born' and pretty well sheltered when he first came here. First time he was Cook's helper, Cook gave him a chicken and told him to dress and stuff it. He hadn't been the kind that does any hunting (scholarly, you know) so Cook had to tell him how to slit the chicken for cleaning. He did it, then looked inside and said 'I don't need to stuff it, it's already full!' He *still* hasn't lived that one down!"

By this time they'd descended the stairs past the landing on the first floor and had reached the bottom of the staircase. Sherrill knocked twice at the door there, then opened it and entered. Behind the door was a narrow, whitewashed room lit by a window up near the ceiling; Talia reckoned that the window must have been level with the ground outside. This room contained only a desk, behind which sat a matronly, middle-aged woman who smiled at them as they entered.

"Here's the new one, Housekeeper," Sherrill said cheerfully.

The woman measured Talia carefully by eye. "Just about a seven, I'd say. We don't get many Chosen as small as you. Did you bring anything with you, dear?"

Talia shook her head shyly, and Sherrill answered for her. "Just like me, Housekeeper Gaytha; the clothes she stood up in. You're going to have to have a word with Queen Selenay about that— the Companions never give the Chosen any time to pack!"

The Housekeeper smiled and shook her head, then left the room by a door in the wall behind her desk. She returned shortly with a pile of neatly-folded clothing and a lumpy bag.

"Collegium rules are that you wash before every meal and have a hot bath every night," she said, handing half the pile to Talia and half to Sherrill. "Dirty clothing goes down the laundry chute in the bathroom; Sherrill will show you where that is. You change the sheets on your bed once a week; you'll get them with the rest of the girls, and the old ones go in the laundry. If you've been working with your Companion or at arms practice, change your clothing before you eat. There's no shortage of soap and hot water here, and staying clean is very important. Heralds have to be trusted on sight, and who'd trust a slovenly Herald? You can get clean uniforms from me whenever you need them. I know this may not be what you're used to—"

"I had trouble with it," Sherrill put in. "Where I come from you don't wash in the winter since there's no way to heat enough water, and you'd probably get pneumonia from the drafts. I never visit home in the winter anymore—my nose has gotten a lot more sensitive since I left!"

Talia thought of Keldar's thrice-daily inspections, and the cold-water scrubbing with a floor-brush that followed any discovery of a trace of dirt. "I think I'll be all right," she answered softly.

"Good. Now as Sherrill has told you—or should have—you all have small chores to see to every day. What can you do?"

"Anything," Talia replied promptly.

The Housekeeper looked skeptical. "Forgive me, my dear, but that doesn't seem very likely for someone your age."

"She's older than she looks," Sherrill said. "Thirteen."

Talia nodded. "They were going to make me get married, so I ran away. That's when Rolan found me. Keldar said I was ready."

The Housekeeper was plainly shocked. "Married? At *thirteen?*"

"It's pretty common to marry that young on the Borders," Sherrill replied. "They don't wait much longer than that back home. Borderers treat themselves and their children just like they do their stock; breed 'em early and often to get the maximum number of useful offspring. There's no one true way, Housekeeper. Life is hard on the Border; if Borderers were to hold by inKingdom custom, they'd never be able to hold their lands."

"It still seems—barbaric," the Housekeeper said with faint distaste.

"It may well be—but they have to survive. And this kind of upbringing is what produced us a Herald that has a chance of turning the Brat back into a proper Heir. You'll take notice that Rolan didn't pick any of *us.*" Sherrill smiled down at Talia, who was trying not to show her discomfort. "Sorry about talking about you as if you weren't there. Don't let us bother you, little friend. Not all of us have had the benefits of what Housekeeper calls a 'civilized upbringing.' Remember what I told you about not washing in winter? Housekeeper had to hold me down in a tub of hot water and scrub me near raw when I first got here—I was a *real* little barbarian!"

Talia couldn't imagine the immaculate and self-assured Sherrill being held down and scrubbed by anyone—still less could she imagine Sherrill *needing* that kind of treatment.

"Talia, can you cook or sew? Anything of that nature?"

"I can cook, if it's plain stuff," Talia said doubtfully. "Only the Wives did feasts; they were too important to be left to us. My embroidery isn't any good at all, but I can mend and sew clothing and knit. And weave and spin. And I know how to clean just about anything."

The Housekeeper suppressed a chuckle at the exasperated tone of the last sentence. That tone convinced her that Talia probably was capable of what she claimed.

"It's so unusual that our students have as much

experience in homely tasks as you do, that I think
I'll alternate you as cook's helper and in the sewing room. There's never any lack of tears and
worn spots to be mended, and there's generally a
dearth of hands able to mend them. And Mero
will be overjoyed to have me send someone capable of dealing with food for a change." She handed
Talia a sheet of paper after consulting one of the
books on her desk and writing in it. "Here's your
schedule; come see me if it's too hard to fit in
among your classes and we'll change it."

Sherrill led the way back up the stairs to Talia's
new room. Talia examined her new clothing with
a great deal of interest. There were loose linen
shirts, meant to be worn with thigh-length tunics
of a heavier material, something like canvas in
weight, but much softer, and long breeches or
skirts of the same fabric. There were some heavier, woolen versions of the same garments, obviously meant for winter wear, a wool cloak, and
plenty of knitted hose, undergarments, and night-
gowns.

"You'll have to make do with your own boots
for a bit, until we have a chance to get you fitted
properly," Sherrill said apologetically, as she helped
Talia put the clothing away. "That won't be for
another week at least. It's too bad—but there's
nothing worse than badly fitted boots; they're worse
than none at all, and Keren will have your hide if
you dare try riding without boots. Unless it's bareback, of course."

They'd only just finished making up the bed
when a bell sounded in the hall outside.

"That's the warning bell for supper," Sherrill

explained. "Get one of your uniforms, and we'll go get cleaned up and you can change."

The bathing room was terribly crowded. Sherrill showed her where everything was located; the laundry chute, the supplies for moon-days, towels and soap—and despite the press of bodies managed to find both of them basins and enough hot water to give them at least a sketchy wash. Talia felt much more like herself with the grit of riding and the last trace of tears scrubbed away. Sherrill hurried her into her new clothing and off they went to the common room.

Supper proved to be a noisy, cheerful affair. Everyone sat at long communal tables, students and adults alike, and helped themselves from the bowls and plates being brought from a kind of cupboard in the wall. It seemed much too small to have held all that Talia saw emerging from it; Sherrill saw her puzzled look and explained over the noise.

"That's a hoist from the kitchen; the kitchen is down in the basement where Housekeeper's office and the storerooms are. And don't feel *too* sorry for the servers. They get to eat before we do and Mero always saves them a treat!"

Talia saw several figures in Herald's White interspersed among the student gray.

"The Heralds—are they *all* teachers?" she whispered to Sherrill.

"Only about half of them. The rest—well, there's Heralds just in from the field, a few retired from duty who choose to live here and don't care to eat with the Court, and a couple of ex-students that have just gotten their Whites that haven't been given their internship assignment yet. There's also

three Heralds on permanent assignment to the
Palace; to the Queen—that's Dean Elcarth; to the
Lord Marshal—that's Hedric, and we don't see
him much; and the Seneschal—that's Kyril, and
he teaches, sometimes. They almost always *have* to
eat with the Court. There ordinarily would be a
fourth, too, the Queen's Own, but—" She stopped
abruptly, glancing at Talia out of the corner of
her eye.

"How—what happened to him?" Talia asked in
a small voice, sure that she wasn't going to like the
answer, but wanting badly to know anyway. The
Queen had said—as had her tales—that being a
Herald was dangerous, and there had been something about the way people had spoken about the
former Queen's Own that made her think that
Talamir had probably encountered one of the
dangers.

"Nobody seems to be sure. It *could* have been an
illness, but—" Sherrill was visibly torn between
continuing and keeping quiet.

"But? Sherrill, I *need* to know," she said, staring
entreatingly at her mentor.

Her urgency impressed Sherrill, who decided it
was better that she be warned. "Well, a lot of us
suspect he was poisoned. He was old and frail,
and it wouldn't have taken much to kill him."
Sherrill was grim. "If that's true, it didn't gain the
murderers anything. We think the reason he was
eliminated was because he was about to convince
Selenay to send the Brat out to fosterage with
some family that wasn't likely to give in to her
tantrums. I guess you don't know—the law is that
the Heir also has to be a Herald; if the Brat isn't
Chosen by a Companion, the Queen will either

have to marry again in the hope that another child will prove out or choose an Heir from those in the blood who *are* Chosen. Either way, there would be an awful lot of people maneuvering for power. Poor Selenay! Any of the rest of us could just choose a partner and go ahead and *have* as many children as needful, without bringing a possible consort and political repercussions into it—but there it is, she's the Queen, and it has to be marriage or nothing. It's not a nice situation." Sherrill regarded the tiny, frail-seeming girl at her side with sober eyes. She was beginning to have a good idea why Elcarth wanted Talia weapons-trained so early.

Talia thought Sherrill had a talent for understatement. Her revelations concerning the former Queen's Own frightened Talia enough that the rest of her speech—which rather bore out the Holderkin assertions of the immorality of Heralds—passed almost without notice. "What about the—the people who poisoned Herald T-T-Talamir?" she stuttered a little from nervousness. "Would they—am I—would they try to—hurt me?" As she looked into Sherrill's eyes, watching for the signs that would tell her if the older girl was speaking the truth, she could feel her hands trembling a little.

Sherrill was a little surprised at Talia's instant grasping of the situation—and hastened to reassure her. Those big brown eyes were widened with a fear even Sherrill could read. "They won't dare try that *particular* trick again, not with the suspicions that have been raised. What they probably *will* try and do is to make life unpleasant enough for you that you give up and leave. That's one reason why I warned you about the Blues. They might get orders from their parents to harass you. You should be safe enough with us, and I'm fairly sure you'll be safe with the Bardic and Healer students, too." Sherrill smiled down at Talia, who returned the smile, though a bit uncertainly. "Talia, if *anyone* bothers you and you think you can't handle them, tell me. My friends and I have taken the scales off the Blues a time or two before this."

Maybe. Talia wanted to trust her—desperately wanted to fit in here, but even of her kin only two had ever proved willing to back her against others. Why should a stranger do so? She ate in silence for a while, then decided to change the subject. "How many students are there?"

"About sixty in Healer's, forty in Bardic, and with you, exactly fifty-three in Herald's Collegium. The number of Blues varies; there's never less than twenty, not often more than fifty. I couldn't tell you the exact number right now, you'd have to ask Teren. He's Elcarth's assistant, and you'll have him as your first instructor tomorrow."

"How long does it take to become a Herald?"

"It varies; around five years. Usually we arrive here when we're about your age, most of us get our Whites at eighteen; I'll probably earn mine next year. I've seen younger Chosen, though, and Elcarth wasn't Chosen till he was nearly twenty! And Havens! Elcarth made up for being Chosen so late by being made full Herald in three years! After you get your Whites, there's a year or year and a half internship in the field, partnered by a senior Herald. After that, you're usually assigned out on your own."

Talia thought about this for a while, then asked

worriedly "Sherrill, what—how do I learn what I need to do?"

Talia was so earnest that Sherrill laughed sympathetically. "You'll learn, don't worry. You'll have Orientation class first. We've had four more Chosen in the past month, and they were only waiting for Rolan to come back before starting it. For the rest—you'll be placed in your classes according to where the Dean feels you fit in, which means you may be taking some classes with me, and some with beginners."

Talia smiled suddenly, "In other words, you throw the baby into the River and see if she learns to swim quickly!"

Sherrill laughed again, "We aren't quite that extreme! Are you finished?"

Talia nodded, and they carried their implements to the hoist inside the cupboard. "I've got dishwashing tonight, so I'll have to leave you on your own," Sherrill continued, "Will you be all right alone, or would you like me to find someone to keep you company?"

"I—I'll be all right. I would like awfully to see the Library if you don't think anyone would mind."

"Help yourself, that's what it's there for. Just remember not to wait too long before you take your bath, or all the hot water will be gone. I'll come by for you in the morning."

Sherrill clattered down the stairs and Talia climbed cautiously upward.

Sherrill was grateful that dishwashing took so little time, and equally grateful that Mero let her off early when she told him that the Dean needed to speak with her. Elcarth would not have given her the signal he had—in fact, he would have said what he intended to openly, in front of the child— had he not felt that there were things he needed to discuss with Sherrill that he would rather Talia were not privy to.

As she had pretty much expected, Sherrill found him waiting for her in the cluttered little room attached to his suite that served him as an office of sorts. It was hardly bigger than a closet, and piled high with everything under the sun, but he would never move to anything more spacious, claiming the clutter would "breed" to fill the space if he did so.

"Any problems getting away?" he asked, removing a pile of books and papers from one of the chairs, a comfortable, padded relic as old as Elcarth.

"I had dishwashing—it made a convenient excuse. Right now Talia's probably having raptures over the Library," Sherrill replied with a half-smile, taking her seat as Elcarth perched himself behind a desk heaped with yet more books and papers.

"Good; can I take it as given that you don't mind being her mentor? She needs one rather badly, and you're the only student with the kind of background that's close to her own."

"Poor little thing—no, Dean, I don't mind at all. Although I don't think my background is all that close," Sherrill frowned slightly, thinking about the little that Talia had allowed her to learn. "You know Evendim clans, we're all noise and push, and we're almost incestuously close. I got the feeling she's been sat on so much that now she's afraid of being punished for breathing—*and* I got the feeling nobody's ever bothered to give the poor thing a little love. She holds everything inside; it's hard to read her, and I don't recall much about Holderkin from class."

"There you've hit it. The fact of the matter is that we just don't *know* that much about Holderfolk. They're very secretive; they keep almost totally to themselves and they don't encourage long visits or curiosity from strangers. Until we heard Talia's story, we didn't even know that they don't tell their children about Companion's Choice!"

"They *what?*" Sherrill was shocked.

"It's quite true; she hadn't the vaguest idea of what it meant when Rolan Chose her. I'm fairly certain she still isn't entirely aware of what his true nature is. This is what I need to talk to you about. You're going to be dealing with a child who seems to have had a very alien upbringing. I can make some educated guesses; she seems to be afraid of men, so I can assume she tends to expect punishment from them. That would fit in with what I do know about Holderfolk; their familial life is patriarchal and authoritarian. She seems to be constantly repressing her emotions, and again, that would fit in with what I know of her people. They frown on any sort of demonstrative behavior. At the same time, she always seems to be— almost at war with herself— "

"Holding herself back, sir?" Sherrill offered. "As if she wanted to make overtures, but didn't quite dare? She seems to be wary all the time, that much I can tell you. I doubt that she trusts anyone at this point, except maybe Rolan."

"Exactly. The first moves are always going to have to be yours, and I think she'll continue to tend to keep her feelings very much to herself,"

Elcarth replied. "It's going to be up to you to discover if there's anything bothering her because she'll never tell you on her own."

"Gods," Sherrill shook her head. "Just the opposite of my people. I don't know, sir; I'm more used to dealing with folk who shout their minds and hearts to the world. I'm not sure I'm good enough to read the signs of trouble, assuming she'll give me anything to read."

"Do your best, that's all I ask. At least you both came from Border Sectors; that will be a bond."

"Why are you turning her over to Alberich so early?" Sherrill asked curiously. "I realize why she'd best learn self-defense as soon as possible, but I should think, with the kinds of insecurities she seems to have, that he would be the *last* person you'd want to expose her to. I mean, Jeri would be a much less threatening figure to deal with."

"I wish there were some other way, but she knows absolutely *nothing* about self-defense; I know that Jeri is very good, but she isn't the kind of experienced teacher Alberich is. He's the only one likely to be able to teach her with the speed that's necessary. If a mob of troublemakers should corner her—or, Bright Lady forbid it, someone should decide that a knife in the dark solves the problem of the new Queen's Own turning up. . . ."

He let the sentence trail into silence.

"And I can't be with her all the time. Well, I hope he gentles his usual routine with her, or she may drop dead of fright on the practice field and save an assassin the trouble." Sherrill's tone was jocular, but her eyes held no amusement.

"I've already spoken with him, and he's not as unsympathetic as you might think. He was my year-mate, you know. I have reason to believe he'll be quite soft-handed with her."

"Alberich, soft-handed? Really? Tell my bruises that some time, sir."

"Better bruises now than a fatal wound later, no?" Elcarth grinned crookedly. "I could wish one of Talia's year-mates was another girl; I could wish we had someone more likely to understand what she won't let us see. You're the closest I could come. Well, that's all I have to tell you. It isn't much—"

"But it's a start. Take heart, Dean. Companions don't Choose badly, and look how long it took Rolan to find her. She'll manage. And I'll manage. Heralds always do."

At the head of the staircase Talia opened a door that led into a single enormous room filled with bookshelves. There were cubicles containing desks and chairs at the ends of the rows of shelves along the walls. She had been expecting perhaps twice or three times the number of books in her Father's library—twenty—but nothing prepared her for this. There were hundreds of books here; more than she ever dreamed existed, all colors, and all sizes. It was more than a dream come true—it was a vision of heaven.

Dusk had fallen while they'd been eating, and lanterns had been lit at intervals along the walls. Talia peeked into the nearest cubicle and saw that there were candles on the desk, and a permanent holder affixed to one side of it.

She heard footsteps approaching from the farther end of the library, and she turned to see who it could be, hoping for someone she knew.

"Hello!" said a cheerful tenor. "You're new here, aren't you? I'm Kris."

The young man who stepped into the circle of light cast by the lantern was in Whites and as incredibly beautiful as the Herald Talia had met outside the city had been homely. His features were so perfect they didn't seem to be real, every raven hair was neatly in place, and his sky-blue eyes would have been the envy of any Court beauty. Talia immediately felt as awkward and ungainly as a young calf—and more than a little afraid as well. Dealing with her older sib Justus had taught her that beauty could hide an evil nature. Only the fact that he was a Herald—and there simply *wasn't* any such thing as an evil Herald—kept her from bolting outright.

"Yes," she replied softly, blushing a little and staring at her boot-tops. "I'm Talia."

"Have you been up here before?"

She shook her head, beginning to relax a little.

"Well," he said, "The rules are very simple. You can read anything you want, but you can't take the book out of the Library, and you have to put it back exactly where you found it when you're done. That's pretty easy, isn't it?"

Talia could tell by his patronizing tone of voice that he was feeling just slightly superior. Yet he seemed to be friendly enough, and there hadn't been anything in his manner to indicate that he was ill-tempered. The patronization annoyed her, and she decided it was safe to get a little of her own back.

"Y-yes," she said softly. "As simple as stuffing a chicken."

"Ouch!" he laughed, clapping one hand to his

forehead. "Stung! Isn't there *anybody* that hasn't heard that story? I deserved that—I shouldn't have talked down to you. Well, enjoy yourself, Talia. You'll like it here, I hope."

He turned with a parting grin and exited through the door she'd just used, and she heard his footsteps descending the staircase.

She wandered through the forest of bookcases, losing all track of time, too overwhelmed by the sheer numbers to even begin to make a choice. Gradually, however, she began to notice that the books were arranged by category, and within each category, by title. Once she'd made that identification, she began perusing the bookcases with more purpose, trying to identify what groups there were, and where they were, and marking the locations of particular books that sounded interesting. By the time she had it all clear in her mind, she found herself yawning.

She made her way to her own room, found one of her new bedgowns, and sought the bathing-room. Sensholding had possessed the relatively new indoor latrines, so those hadn't surprised her any when Sherrill had shown them to her. However, all hot water for bathing back at the Holding had needed to be carried in pots from the kitchen. Here at the Collegium there were several charcoal-fired copper vessels for heating water, each at least the size of one of the tubs, with pipes at the bottom to take the hot water to the tubs and a pump to refill them with cold water from the top. This arrangement positively enchanted her; being neither little nor adult, she'd rarely ever gotten a really hot bath. The littlest littles were always bathed first, and the adults waited until later when all the kettles of water had been filled and heated a second time. Those who were too old to be bathed but too young to stay up late and bathe with the adults had to make do with whatever was left after cleaning the babies—which wasn't often much, or very warm.

There were several girls and young women there already, and all the bathtubs were in use. Talia took her turn at the pump, after being hailed by "you must be the new one" and shyly giving her own name.

"I'm glad you turned out to be a girl," one of the ones near her own age said, pumping water vigorously. "The boys outnumber us by too many as it is. Every single one of the other new ones has been a boy! That's why our side's smaller."

"Well, my sister's at Healer's, and it's the opposite there," a voice replied out of the steam.

"Besides, it's quality that counts, not quantity," the second bather's voice was half covered by vigorous splashing. "And it's quite obvious that we women have the quality."

The rest giggled, and Talia smiled tentatively.

"Sherrill told me there were fifty-three of us," she replied after a moment, reveling in the fact that she was one of the fifty-three. "How many of each are there?"

"Thirty-five colts and eighteen fillies," replied the girl at the pump. "And I'm referring to the human foals, not the Companions. It wasn't quite so bad until those four new boys came in, but now they outnumber us by almost two to one."

"Jeri, you're betraying your youth," said the young woman who was climbing out of the nearest tub. "You may not be old enough to appreciate odds like that, but Nerrissa and I *are*. In my part of the Kingdom, women slightly outnumber the men, and I like it much better the other way 'round. I'd much rather be the one being courted than the one doing the courting. Whoever's next, I'm done."

"Is it like that where you're from, Talia?" Jeri asked, looking at her curiously as she claimed the now-vacant tub.

"I—I suppose it must be," she said, momentarily distracted from her shyness, mentally trying to count the distribution of the sexes in the Holdings she knew. "I'm Holderkin."

"Where's that?" the young woman called Nerrissa asked, folding a towel around her wet hair.

"East—on the Border," Talia replied, still thinking. "I know it's rather dangerous off the Holdings themselves. More men die every year than women; there are lots of wild animals, and raiders come every winter. I think there's nearly twice as many women as men, at least on the farthest Holdings."

"Havens! You must be knee-deep in old maids."

"Oh, no—if you don't go to the Goddess, you *have* to get married. My father had eleven wives, and nine are still living."

"You can have my tub, Talia," Nerrissa emerged from the steam. "Why do females *have* to get married?"

"W-why women can't Hold a Steading, or speak in Council or—anything important. It wouldn't be seemly," Talia said in astonishment.

"So-ho! That must be why they never send female Heralds to the lower Eastern Border. They wouldn't be listened to. Talia, it's very different here. It's going to take a lot of getting used to, and it's going to seem strange for a long while. We reckon a person's importance by what they are, not by what sex they are," Nerrissa told her. "There's no such thing as 'seemly' or 'unseemly.' Just doing the job you're given."

Talia nodded thoughtfully, immersed in her tub. "I-it's hard to think this way. It j-just doesn't seem natural. I-I-I think *I* like it. Most of my Father's wives would hate it, though. Keldar for sure, and Isrel would be miserable without someone to give her orders."

"Nessa, the child doesn't need a lecture at this time of night!" the first woman called from the doorway. "Honestly, they should make you a teacher when you go into Whites, I've never heard anyone make so many speeches! Come *on*, or you'll be here all night!"

"All right, all right!" Nerrissa replied, laughing a little. "Pleasant dreams, little one."

Talia finished her bath and found her room, feeling drained to the point of numbness. It seemed very odd to be climbing into a bed that had no one in it but herself. Her mind whirled in circles—this entire adventure hardly seemed real. In less than two weeks she'd gone from being the scorned scapegrace of Sensholding to a Herald-in-training; it seemed impossible. She kept returning to the astonishing moment when she'd realized what all that had occurred to her truly meant, holding the memory as wonderingly and gently as a new kitten, until sleep began to overpower her.

But her very last thoughts as she drifted off to

sleep were of Nerrissa's words, and the sudden decision that she *did* like it here.

Now if only all this was half as wonderful as it appeared on the surface—and if only they would let her fit in.

Five

She woke to Sherrill's light tap on the wall and pulled on her unfamiliar uniform before opening her door.

"It's about time, sleepy!" Sherrill said genially, looking altogether *too* awake for sunrise. "The waking-bell rang ages ago, didn't you hear it? If we don't hurry, there won't be anything left but cold porridge." Without looking to see if Talia was following, she turned and headed for the door of the common-room.

Sherrill had exaggerated the "danger," as Talia found when they entered the double-doors. There was still plenty left to eat—an almost bewildering variety for Talia, who expected little besides the aforementioned porridge, bread and milk, and perhaps a little fruit. And there were plenty of other students who trailed in after them, rubbing sleepy eyes or complaining cheerfully to one another.

After breakfast, a somewhat more subdued meal than supper had been, and punctuated more by yawns than conversation, Sherrill led her to the first floor and out the door at the far end of the corridor. Talia recalled that the Dean had told her this door led to a court and the stables beyond it. They crossed a wide, paved courtyard that lay between the two buildings, with the sun casting long shadows on the bedewed paving-stones before them, and Talia lingered a little, hoping wistfully to see Rolan.

"Talia, come catch up!" Sherrill called back over her shoulder, squinting against the sunlight. "Or don't you want to see your Companion this morning?"

Startled, she ran to overtake Sherrill. "Aren't the Companions in the stables?" she asked breathlessly.

"In the stables? With the regular horses? Bright Havens, they'd disown us! The Companions have their own place—we call it Companion's Field—and an open building so they can come and go as they like. On a beautiful morning like this, they're all probably out in their Field."

They'd come to a tall wooden fence surrounding a park-like area full of trees, and Talia thought that this must have been the green place she'd seen within the walls when she'd first caught sight of the capital. Sherrill climbed up on the fence, as agile as any of Talia's brothers, put her fingers in her mouth, and whistled shrilly like a boy. When Talia joined her, she could see tiny white shapes moving off in the distance, under the trees. Two of these detached themselves from the rest and began trotting toward them.

"I don't mindcall at all well—not unless I'm scared stiff," Sherrill said, a little shamefacedly, "Ylsa says I'm blocked—so I have to whistle for Silkswift. She doesn't seem to mind any."

Talia had no difficulty in recognizing which of

the two Companions approaching was Rolan, and her joy at seeing him again was such that she didn't once wonder what Sherrill had meant by "mindcalling" and "being blocked." With a cry of happiness she jumped off the fence to land beside Rolan and spent several jubilant minutes caressing him and whispering joyous nonsense into his ear. He was even more of a magical creature than she remembered him being. Someone had tended him well last night, for he had been groomed until he nearly glowed. His coat and mane were softer than the finest fabric she'd ever touched, and he was as beautiful as one of the Moon-steeds that drew the Lady's chariot. He nuzzled her with something she no longer doubted was love, whuffing softly at her, and the feeling of total well-being and confidence she'd had when with him on the road returned. While she was with him, she feared nothing, doubted nothing. . . .

"I hate to say this, but we *do* have an appointment with Master Alberich," Sherrill said at last, reluctantly. "Talia, it's part of your training to spend a lot of time with your Companion—you'll see him again this afternoon. You have to—from now on tending him and grooming him will be all up to you. They may be incredible darlings, but they don't have hands; they need us as much as we need them. So you'll get back to him before supper—and we really do have to be going."

Rolan nudged her toward the fence, then shook his forelock as if in admonishment. When she continued to hesitate, he gave her a good shove with his nose and snorted at her.

"All right," she replied, "I'll be good and go. But I'm coming back, classes or not!"

Sherrill took her to a long, low building just beyond the stables; inside it was all but bare—smooth, worn wooden floors and a few benches, with storage cabinets built into the walls. Between the cabinets were a few full-length mirrors, and the place was lit from windows that were high up on the walls, near the ceiling. There they found the man Sherrill introduced as Alberich, the Weaponsmaster. He alone of all the instructors was not wearing Whites, rather, he was dressed in old, supple leather; part armor, part clothing, and of a dark gray color like old ashes, darker than Student Grays.

"I thought all the instructors were Heralds," Talia whispered to her guide as they approached him.

"All but one—but Alberich *is* a Herald; he's just a law unto himself. He never wears Whites unless he's being official."

The Weaponsmaster frightened Talia into near speechlessness when he turned to face them. He was tall, lean, and dark; his face was seamed with scars, and he looked as though he never smiled. Thick streaks of white ran through his abundant black hair, and his eyes were an agate-gray and very penetrating. As his sober stare held her pinned in place, Talia decided that now she knew how a mouse felt in the gaze of a hawk.

"So, " he said at last. "You are how old? Thirteen? What physical training have you, child? Know you any weaponry? Tactics? Eh?"

She hardly knew how to answer—she really couldn't make out what he was asking of her. Physical training? Did playing games count? Was the sling she'd used to keep wolves off the sheep a weapon?

At last he gave her a wooden practice knife, and stood with his arms crossed, still looking fierce and hawklike.

"Come you, then. Come at me—"

She still hadn't the faintest notion what he wanted of her, and stood stonelike, arms stiffly at her sides, feeling clumsy and ridiculous.

"What ails you? I told you to attack me! Is it that women do not fight among your people?" he asked, his speech heavily accented, his brows drawing together into an intimidating frown. "Have you no weapons skill at all?"

"I can shoot a bow, a little," she said in a small and shamed voice. "One of my brothers showed me. He wasn't supposed to, but I begged him so hard—and I guess I'm all right with a sling."

She thought with misery that she seemed to have gotten into the wrong again. It seemed that nothing she'd ever learned was appropriate here— except, perhaps her housekeeping skills. And she'd never once read a tale that praised a Herald's ability at peeling roots!

She waited, cringing, for him to dismiss her back to the building in disgust. He did nothing of the sort.

"At least you have sense not to pretend to what you have not," he replied thoughtfully. "I think it is too late to teach you the sword. Fortunately, you are not likely to need to use one. Bow, of necessity, and knife, and hand-to-hand. That should suffice your needs. Return one hour after the nooning." Then he did dismiss her, after staring at her long and broodingly.

Talia was very subdued and discouraged by this encounter; Sherrill managed to see this even though she tried to mask it. "Don't feel badly," she said, and Talia could clearly hear the encouragement in her voice. "You actually got off pretty easily. When he first saw me, he threw his hands up in the air and growled, 'Hopeless! Hopeless! Let her throw nets and dead fish to defend herself!' At least he thinks you're worth working with. He left *me* to one of his assistants for months!"

"But—why d-d-did he say that ab-b-bout the f-fish?" Oh, that hateful stutter! No matter how confident she tried to appear, it always gave her away!

"Because I spent half my life on a boat and the other half in very crowded conditions; the last thing you want to do on a slippery deck or a floor thick with babies is run! I had to learn how to move freely, something you've always known."

"It d-d-didn't seem as if he th-thought I was worth anything."

"He didn't scream at you—that's a wonder in itself. He didn't tell you to get yourself back home and raise babies, either. I think maybe you won him a little by being honest about how little you know—an awful lot of new students try to pretend they're more expert than they are, and he generally does his best to make fools of them in front of everybody by way of punishment."

By now they'd reached the Collegium building again. Sherrill held the door open for Talia and stopped outside the first classroom door on the right. "Here's where the rest of the new ones are. I'll meet you for lunch." With that, Sherrill vanished down the hall, leaving Talia to face the next ordeal alone.

She tugged the door open and tried to slip inside unobtrusively, but felt more like creeping inside than anything else when she felt everyone's eyes on her. There seemed to be at least a dozen people there. There were no other girls. The boys were mostly her own age, and though they made her feel rather shy, didn't arouse her unease; but the one who stood at the head of the classroom was one of those fearful creatures of ultimate authority, an adult male. As such, he made her wary immediately. She had to keep reminding herself that he was a Herald—and no Herald would *ever* do anything to harm anyone except an enemy of the Queen and Kingdom.

"Be welcome, youngling," he said, perching casually on the front edge of his desk. "Boys, this is your fifth year-mate; her name is Talia. Talia, the red-haired fellow is Davan, the tall one is Griffon, the twins are Drake and Edric—and I can't tell them apart yet." He winked at them, and the twin boys grinned back, obviously very much at ease with him. "Maybe I should ask Alberich to give one of you a black eye—then at least I'd know which of you was which until it faded."

Talia slipped shyly into an unoccupied seat and took a closer look at her teacher. Like Alberich, he was lean, but his brownish hair was only beginning to gray, and he had none of the Weapons-master's hawkishness about him. He put her more in mind of a hunting hound, all eagerness, good nature, and energy. His eyes were hound-brown, and just as friendly. And there was something about him—once again she was reminded of

Andrean; she wanted to trust him—something within her was prompting her to do so, and she was a little surprised at herself.

"Well, now that you're here, I think we're ready to start. First, let me explain what this class is all about. I'm here to help you understand what being a Herald really means; not the hero tales, nor the horror stories, nor the wild rumors of drunken debauchery—" he wriggled his eyebrows, and the twins giggled. "But rather what our job really involves. Davan is probably the only one of you who knows—or thinks he knows—what being a Herald is all about. That's because both of his parents are Heralds themselves. So I'll start Davan with the question I'm going to ask each of you: Davan, what exactly does a Herald do?"

Davan's brow wrinkled in thought. "They dispense the Queen's justice," he finally replied.

"Good enough answer, as far as it goes, but *how* do they do that?"

"Uh, they ride circuit in their assigned areas, going through all the towns and villages, they deliver the new laws of the Kingdom and report on the acts of the Council and Queen. They see that the people understand the laws and act as judges, and sometimes lawgivers when something comes up that isn't covered in Kingdom law or by local custom."

"Bright Havens! You mean those poor people have to wait a year or more to get anything settled?" Teren asked in mock dismay.

"No, no! There's regular judges, too."

"So why not use them?"

Davan couldn't seem to think of a good answer,

but one of the twins was waving his hand over his head. "Herald Teren?"

"Go ahead, whichever you are."

"Drake. Our village was too small to have a judge."

"That's a fair reason. But there's another; sometimes it happens that the feelings of the local people—and that includes the judge—are too worked up for a case to be adjudicated fairly. There's one reason for you. Davan, you have another?"

"Heralds can do the Truth Spell; regular judges have no way of knowing who's lying."

"Good! But that works *only* if someone involved in the case knows what really happened, remember that. All right, Heralds are judges and lawgivers. What else, Drake?"

"They report on what they see on their circuits to the Queen and the Council."

"Why should they do that?"

"So that the Queen knows the true condition of her Kingdom. Sometimes the mayors and headmen don't always tell the whole truth in their Domesday Book reports. Heralds know what's been reported, and how to look for things that don't match."

"Quite true, Edric, your turn."

"They serve as ambassadors to other Kingdoms. While they're there, they can see if there's something wrong the Queen should know about, like maybe an army that's awfully big for a country supposed to be peaceful. Since Heralds can't be bribed, she can always trust what they say."

"That's correct," said Herald Teren, "And there's more; the kind of training a Herald receives here makes it possible for him to note little things that others might miss—things that tell him that there may be more going on than he's being told. Griffon?"

"Heralds are the Queen's messengers. There's no faster, safer way to get a message across the Kingdom than to give it to a Herald, 'cause Companions run faster and for longer than any horse ever born. That's why Heralds are called 'the Arrows of the Queen.' And they act as warleaders in an emergency, until the regular Army can arrive. That's another reason for the name."

"Very good. Talia, your turn."

She had thought hard while the others were giving their answers. "They—make the Kingdom safe," she said softly. "Sometimes they're just what the rest said, and sometimes other things—spies, scouts, sometimes thieves—they do whatever needs doing so that the Queen knows what she needs to know to guard us all. They risk everything for that, for the safety of the Kingdom, and for her."

"And that is why," Teren said slowly, holding each of their eyes in turn, "about half of us don't live to see an honorable old age. Being a Herald is important—the Queen has said that we're the 'glue that holds everything together'—and it can be exciting. For the most part we are very much honored in this Kingdom; but being a Herald can also be a fatal occupation. Hero tales aside, younglings, songs don't help you much when you're looking death in the face and you're all alone. And being alone is another thing you are when you're a Herald. There aren't enough of us, and we get spread very thin. That puts you in the front line in a lot of very dangerous situations."

His eyes clouded a moment. "The danger is in direct proportion to the importance of the job at hand and your own ability to see it through. It's a sad fact that the better a Herald you are, the more likely it is that the Queen will set you risky tasks. I'm sure each of you has had a lazy fit now and again, sloughed some job off; but by the time you've earned your Whites, you will be totally unable to give anything less than your best to whatever is set before you. And when you're in the front line—well, that white uniform makes a pretty obvious target. I'm telling you all this now because this is your last chance to leave the Collegium. No one will think any the less of you for it. Well? Anyone want out?"

Talia cleared her throat.

"Yes, Talia?"

"I never got to finish the tale of Herald Vanyel, sir. The tale said at the beginning that he nearly didn't become a Herald at all because he was afraid—but he decided it was something he had to do anyway, that the job needed doing and he was the one chosen to do it. The last I read he was trapped by the Dark Servants, like he'd seen happening in a vision years before. What happened to him?"

"He died. The Dark Servants hacked him to pieces before help could arrive—yet he held them back long enough that his King was able to bring up an army in time to repel their invasion. But he still died, alone, and all the songs in the world won't change that. Now I want you to think about that for a moment—really think hard. Does that frighten you? Any of you could be asked to pay Vanyel's price. The Queen will weep that she had to send you, but that won't stop her from doing it. Want to leave?"

"No, sir," Talia's voice was very small, her eyes very large.

"Doesn't the idea frighten you?"

"Yes, sir," she said, softly, biting her lip. "Only somebody awfully stupid wouldn't be—" she stopped, groping for words.

Griffon found the words for her. "We've all heard the tales, sir—the ones with the bad, nasty endings right along with the ones that end with the hero's welcomes and celebrations. And I got here right after Talamir was buried; you think we didn't hear the talk then about poison? My own brother said right out he thought I was crazy to want to be a Herald. When we hear the bad tales, you best bet we get scared! But it's still something we *got* to do, just like Vanyel. Maybe you can't be made a Herald, maybe you got to be born one, and all this teaching you give us does is show us how to do better 'n easier the things we know we got to do anyway. Whatever. It's like bein' likker-cravin' or something. You still got to do it, no choice; couldn't stop, don't want to." He sat down with a thump, only then realizing he'd risen to his feet making his speech.

Herald Teren's tense expression eased. "I take it that you all agree with Griffon?"

They nodded, very much sobered.

"Then I can only say that once again, as always, the Companions seem to have Chosen aright. Griffon, you have unexpected depths of eloquence in you. I think you ought to consider seriously taking Logic and Oration—you could be very useful as a diplomat."

Griffon blushed, and looked down at his hands, murmuring a disclaimer.

"Now, having obliquely touched on the subject—you all know that it is the Companions that choose new Heralds, but do any of you know *how* they do it?"

They looked at one another in puzzled silence. Teren chuckled. "Nor do I. Nor does anyone. A few—the most sensitive to the bond that forms between a Herald and his Companion—have described that first encounter as 'a feeling that I was being measured.' But *what* it is that they measure, no one knows. All that we do know is that after a Companion has Chosen, there exists a kind of mind-to-mind link between him and his Herald that is similar, but not identical, to the kind of mind-link that exists between twins," he said, sharing a grin with Drake and Edric. "You'll learn more about that bond later, and how to use it. For now, it's enough for you to know that it *does* exist—so if you feel something between you and your Companion, you know that you're not imagining it or going mad. As you get older, you may develop one of the Gifts—what outsiders call 'Herald's magic.' You'll learn more about those later as well—but if you *thought* your Companion spoke to you when he Chose you, you were right. He did. No matter if you never have more than a touch of a Gift, your Companion will always speak to you in your heart at that moment—even if he never does so again. It wasn't something you dreamed. And if you have the right Gift, one day you'll learn to speak back."

Talia breathed an unconscious sigh of relief,

not noticing that all the others except Davan were doing the same.

"And there's another thing about them that you should know," Teren continued, "Never, ever, for one moment doubt that they are something considerably more than animals. Any tale you've ever heard is no more than a pale reflection of their reality. Now, to elaborate on that, do any of you know where the Companions first came from?"

Davan nodded. "My parents told me, sir."

"Then tell the rest of us, if you would."

"It goes right back to before this Kingdom ever existed," Davan began. Talia gave him every bit of her attention, for this tale was all new to her. "It happened there was a good man who was living in a land with a bad King, 'way off to the East, right past any of our neighbors. His name was Baron Valdemar; he lived on his own Kingdom's western border. His King was the kind who took what he wanted and never paid any attention when his lands and people suffered, and most of his nobles were like minded. For a while Baron Valdemar was able to at least protect his own people from the King; that was because he was a wizard as well as a Baron, and his lady was a sorceress—old magic, the kind that's gone now, not Herald's magic. But the day finally came when there wasn't any way of stopping him short of outright rebellion. Baron Valdemar knew, though, that rebellion wasn't the answer either; he couldn't hold out against all the might the King could bring against him for very long at all. There were plenty of his neighbors who would be only too pleased to help the King destroy him for a share in his lands and goods after. So he did the only thing he could do;

he fled away into the West, taking with him every last one of his people as were minded to follow. He led them on until he was sure there wasn't anybody following; then right here where we're sitting he stopped, and founded a whole new Kingdom, and those who'd come with him made him the King of it." Davan paused for a moment to think, "There was a whole lot about all the hardships they went through, and I can't remember that part too good."

"You're doing fine, Davan. You'll all get more detail later in your History classes; just go on with what you do remember."

"Well, 'ventually they got this city built; they all started to have a pretty good life by the time King Valdemar was an old man. Right then is when he took the time to notice how old he was getting, and to think about the future. He hadn't exactly had much time for thinking before this, 'cause there was too much to do, if you take my meaning. Anyway, what he thought was, 'I know *I'm* a good ruler, and a good man; I'm pretty sure my son will be the same—but what about my son's children, and theirs? How can I make certain that whoever takes this throne will be good for the people who support it?' "

"A good question. So what did he do?"

"Well, he waited till Midsummer's Day; he went out into the grove that stands in the middle of what we call Companion's Field now, and he asked every god he'd ever heard of to help him. An' Mama told me in the version she'd read, it said he cast a special spell, too, 'cause remember, he was a magician—a *real* magician, not just Gifted. She says there used to be lots of real magicians down where he came from, and that there used to be lots here, too, but that Vanyel was the last Herald-mage."

"That's the tradition; go on."

"Well, he started out at dawn; it wasn't till sunset that he got an answer. Everything went kind of light all over, like when you get too much sun on snow, and all he could hear was the sound of hoofbeats—hoofbeats that sounded just like bells. When the light cleared away, there were three horses standing in front of him; horses with coats the color of moonshine and eyes like pieces of the sky. Old Valdemar hadn't ever seen anything like them before in his life. And when he came up close to them, one of them looked him straight into the eyes—well, that's all there was to it. Ardatha told him her name in his mind and bound them together—"

"And the first Companion had Chosen."

"Right then his chief Herald—and a Herald was just a sort of mouthpiece for the King back then, didn't do a tenth of what Heralds do today—came looking for him. The second Companion—Kyrith—Chose *him*. The King's son, the Heir that was, he'd come along, and Steladar Chose him. When they all were in a mind to be thinking again, 'twas the King decided that the title of Herald should be made to mean more than it did, since only one person can be King or Heir, but there could be lots of Heralds."

"And King Valdemar, Prince Restil, and Herald Beltran began the work of making the Heralds into what they are now, starting with decreeing that the Heir must also be a Herald. The work wasn't easy, and it took the lifelong toil of several

Kings and Queens, but it was with those three that it first began. By the time Valdemar died, there were twenty-one Heralds, including himself, his Heir, and his Heir's second son. You have a good memory, Davan, thank you," Teren concluded.

"Where did all those Companions come from?" Edrik wanted to know.

"At first they all came from the Grove in the middle of what we now call Companion's Field, like the first three; other than that, no one knew. After a while, though, the mares began foaling, and now all Companions with a single exception are born right here at the Collegium. That exception is the Companion to the Monarch's Own Herald," his glance flickered from Edrik to Talia and back again, so quickly she couldn't be certain she'd seen his eyes move. "*That* Companion appears from the Grove just as the originals did. He is always a stallion, and he never seems to age. He always gives his name to his Herald; the others may or may not do so, and may allow their Heralds to pick a name for them. If he is killed—and many have been—another appears from the Grove to take his place. If the Monarch's Own Herald is still living, that is the Herald he Chooses; if not, he stays only long enough to be caparisoned and goes out to seek the next in line. It is usually someone already a Herald or about to receive Whites that he Chooses, but that is not always the case."

"Talamir was Queen's Own, wasn't he, sir?"

"Yes, he was. His Companion was Rolan," Teren replied, nodding.

"Then that makes Talia Queen's Own, doesn't it?"

"Yes, it does. It's an important position. Are any of you jealous of her?"

Drake shook his head vehemently. "Ha!" he said. "We've seen the Br—, I mean the Princess. I wouldn't want any part of the job!" The rest nodded agreement.

Teren half smiled. "Watch your tongues carefully, younglings. We can call Elspeth the Brat among ourselves—the Queen calls her that, in fact—but make sure nobody from the Court overhears you. Some people would be only too happy to use that to make trouble. You're right; Talia is going to have a tough job. She'll need our help with it, all of us, because there are people at Court who would like very much to see her fail. Only Talia can do her job—but the rest of us can help her by making certain that no one makes it more difficult for her than it is already. Right, gentlemen?"

The boys nodded agreement; but Talia, determined not to be any kind of a burden on the Collegium or those in it, and still not quite ready to believe in the trustworthiness of strangers, pledged silently to manage on her own, no matter what.

A bell rang twice in the corridor outside. "Which of you is Cook's helper today?" Teren asked.

Talia raised her hand a little.

"For future reference, all of you, that's the signal for the helpers; the servers go on three rings, and the meal is served on four. Off with you, youngling. Gentlemen, if you left your rooms in a mess, you'd better rectify the situation; there's inspection after lunch. I'll see you here tomorrow morning."

Teran directed Talia to use the door and staircase near the door leading out to the courtyard. Instead of letting out into the Housekeeper's office, this one led her to a huge kitchen—and much to her surprise, the cook was a balding, moon-faced man. She was too surprised to find a man in charge of the kitchen to even think to be afraid of him, and his easy, gentle manner kept her from being alarmed, despite his sex.

He ignored what seemed to be chaos swirling around him to question her as to her abilities, his smile broadening with each of her answers.

"Finally!" he said, round face beaming. "Someone who knows what to do with food besides eat it!" He gave her charge over the vegetables.

While she peeled and chopped them, she peered about her, curiously. This place didn't seem all that different from the kitchen of a Hold house; even the ovens were in the same place. That was at first—then she began to notice small things; pumps to bring water to the huge sinks, another one of the copper boilers to heat the water, pipes leading from the sinks to carry the waste away. There was an almost fanatical precision about the placement of pots and pans and tools and the scrupulous cleanliness of the place—Keldar would surely have approved. She was surprised to see that all the ovens were in use; there wasn't much noticeable heat coming from them. They must have been insulated with far better care than the ones in the Holding. Or perhaps—as she considered it, it occurred to her that they actually extended out beyond the outer wall. Perhaps that had something to do with it.

She soon saw that what had seemed like chaos was in fact as carefully orchestrated as any general's field maneuvers. No one was allowed to stand idle for more than a moment or two, and yet the Cook had gauged his helpers' abilities and stamina perfectly. They usually tired just as their tasks were completed, and one by one were sent to rest at a trestle table. Then, just as tired hands had recovered and tired legs were ready to move again, the dishes began coming out of the cupboard and the pots off the stove and out of the oven, and they began transporting the filled dishes to the hoist. When the last of them had vanished upward, they turned to find their table laid ready with tableware and food.

Talia edged over onto a corner, and discovered her seatmate was Jeri. "I *like* this job," Jeri said, filling her bowl and Talia's with stew. "Mero always saves the best for us."

The cook grinned broadly, even his eyes smiled. "How else to insure that you work and not shirk?" he asked, passing hot bread and butter. "Besides, doesn't the Book of One say 'Do not keep the ox who threshes your grain from filling his belly as he works'?"

"What's the 'Book of One'?" Talia whispered.

"Mero's from Three Rivers—there's a group up there that believes there's only one god," Jeri replied. "I know it sounds strange, but they must be all right; 'cause Mero's awfully nice."

It seemed more than very strange to Talia, and she knew what the Elders would have said. Yet there was no denying the warmth and kindness of this man; he went out of his way to coax Talia into helping herself when she seemed too shy to dive in the way the others were. What Nerrissa had said last night was beginning to be something more than words.

But before she could begin to grasp this more than dimly, the Cook produced a hot berry pie from the oven with a flourish worthy of a conjurer, and all other thoughts were banished. Abstract thought takes a poor second place to berry pies when you're only thirteen.

They were just finishing when the dishwashing crew arrived, and the Cook banished them all back upstairs. Remembering what Herald Teren had said about room inspections, Talia made haste to straighten hers before anyone could see the state she'd left it in that morning. She changed quickly into one of her older and more worn outfits for working with the Armsmaster before hurrying out to the practice yard.

By now the sun was high; the trees that ringed the practice yard gave very welcome shade. The "yard" itself was nothing more than a square of scuffed, yellowed grass, with benches along two sides of it, and a small well behind the benches. Just beyond the trees was a cleared area with archery targets at one end; there were racks of bows and arrows at the other end. As Talia watched, two of the students picked up several bows in succession, trying them till they found one to their liking; apparently no one had his own special weapon. She moved hesitantly to the practice yard itself, where the Armsmaster was currently holding forth; he seemed to be dividing his time equally between those who were shooting and the ones practicing hand-to-hand fighting.

She had been filled with dread at the thought of reencountering the fearsome Alberich, but she discovered that afternoon that having served as the butt of her older brother Justus' cruelty had been useful after all. Alberich actually looked mildly pleased when she demonstrated that she knew how to fall without hurting herself and how to use a bow without ruining forearm, fingers, or fletching. So far as proficiency with the bow went, she thought she wasn't much worse than the other students her own age and began to feel a tiny bit more confident. There were a lot more of them than she thought there would be, for mixed among the gray of her own Collegium were uniforms of the pale green of Healer's and the rust-brown of Bardic. It did seem a bit odd, though, that she was the youngest to be receiving training with edged weapons. Most of the students her age were being put to stave-work or hacking away at dummies with clubs that only vaguely resembled practice-blades.

Once again Jeri was there; a familiar face was comforting, and Talia sat next to her when her turn at the targets was over. "Why aren't there any Blues?" she asked curiously.

"Them?" Jeri gave a very unladylike snort. "Most of *them* have their own private arms tutors—at least the ones that aren't learning to be scholars or artificers. The scholars don't need weapons-work— the courtiers wouldn't want to soil themselves among us common folk. Besides, Alberich won't coddle them, and they know it. King or beggar, if you don't lunge right, he's going to smack you good and hard. Oh-oh," she groaned, as Alberich dismissed the boy he'd been working with and nodded at her, "Looks like it's my turn to get smacked."

She bounced to her feet to take her stance opposite Alberich with her practice blade in hand. Talia watched her enviously, wishing *she* could move like Jeri did.

"Don't let Jer fool you, young 'un," chuckled an older boy, who Talia judged to be about sixteen. "Her blood's as blue as the Queen's is. If she hadn't been Chosen, she'd be a Countess now. She's had a good share of the benefit given by one of those private tutors she was demeaning just now; that's why she's so incredible at her age."

"And why Alberich treats her rougher than the rest of us," put in another, a short, slim boy near Talia's own age, with dark brown hair, bushy eyebrows and nearly black eyes, and a narrow, impish face. He had just finished a bout with another student, and dropped down next to Talia, mopping his sweating face with a towel. He winced as Alberich corrected Jeri's footwork by swatting the offending leg with the flat of his blade.

"He doesn't approve of private tutors?" Talia hazarded. "He doesn't like nobles?"

"Starseekers! No!" the second boy exclaimed, "He just expects more out of her, so he rides her harder. I think he may have ideas about making her Armsmistress when he steps down—if she survives his training and her internship!"

"Believe me, with swordwork that good, by the time she gets her Whites the only way to take Jeri down will be with an army," the first replied.

"Well Coroc, if anyone would know, you would," the second admitted, watching him step forward to replace Jeri. "His father's the Lord Marshal, so he's been seeing the best swordwork in the Kingdom since he was born," he told Talia.

Talia's eyes widened. "The Lord Marshal's son?"

Her compatriot grinned, hanging his towel around his neck. "Whole new world in here, isn't it? On your right, the Lord Marshal's son, on your left, a Countess—and here we sit, a former thief and beggar—" he bowed mockingly "that's yours truly, of course—and—a "what are you, anyway?"

"Holderkin."

"Farmgirl, then. Hard to believe, isn't it? Like one of those mad tales we used to listen to. You're Talia, right?"

She nodded, wondering how he knew.

"I'm Skif—if you were with the Dean when the Provost-Marshal came by, you probably heard plenty about me! It's not fair, I know; we all know who you are just because you're the only female face we don't recognize, but you have fifty-two names and faces to learn! And as if that wasn't bad enough, everything you've been seeing probably runs against all you've been taught at home, and you're all in a muddle most of the time." He reached out too quickly for her to flinch away and tousled her hair with a grin of sympathy. "As they kept telling me all during *my* first year, 'this, too, shall pass.' We're all glad you're with us, and we all most fervently wish you luck with the Royal Brat. Now it's *my* turn to get whacked on by Master Alberich—with luck I'll get a set of bruises to match the last batch he gave me. Take heart," he ended, rising, "you follow me."

Despite his own words, Skif seemed to give a good accounting of himself with the Armsmaster. Talia, in spite of her lack of experience in weaponry, saw that Alberich was drilling him in a style radically different to the styles Coroc and Jeri had

used. Skif's weapon was a short, heavy blade, as
opposed to Jeri's lighter rapier or Coroc's longsword. His bout seemed to include as much gym-
nastics as bladework, and seemed to depend on
avoiding his opponent's weapon rather than coun-
tering it in any way. He bounced about with the
agility of a squirrel—nevertheless, Armsmaster
Alberich eventually "killed" him.

Skif "died" dramatically, eliciting a round of
applause at his theatrics; then rose, grinning, to
present Alberich with his own gloves—which Skif
had filched from Alberich's belt some time during
the practice bout. Alberich received them with a
sigh that said wordlessly that this was not the first
time Skif had pulled this trick, then turned to
motion Talia to take his place. She came forward
with a great deal of trepidation.

"You were watching Skif closely?" Alberich asked.
"Good. This is the style I wish you to learn. It has
nothing of grace, but much of cunning; and I
think it will do you more good to know the ways
of avoiding the blade of the assassin in the arras
than the duelist on the field of honor. So. We
begin."

He tutored her with far more patience than she
had expected, having witnessed his outbursts of
temper over some of his pupils' mistakes. He favored her with none of the sarcastic comments he
had heaped on the others, nor did he administer
any corrective slaps with the flat of his practice
blade. Perhaps it was her imagination, but he almost seemed to be treating her with a kind of
rough sympathy—certainly he paid far more attention to the level of her spirits and energy than
he had any of the others—for just when she was

quite sure she could no longer keep her rubbery knees from giving way with exhaustion, he smiled briefly at her (an unexpected sight that left her dumb) and said, "Enough. You do well, better than I had expected. Rest for a moment, then go to work with your Companion when you are cool."

She rested just long enough to cool down without stiffening up, then ran to Companion's Field with an eagerness that matched the reluctance with which she had gone to arms practice.

As she approached the fence, she saw that Rolan had anticipated her arrival; she scrambled up the rough boards and swung from the top of the fence to his back without bothering to saddle him, and they set off across the field at a full gallop. It was intoxicating beyond belief; though she'd urged the farmbeasts to an illicit gallop many times, there was no comparison to Rolan's speed or smooth pace.

The Field proved to be far more than that— almost a park, full of trees and dells and with streams running all through it. It was so large that when they were most of the way across it, the people near the fence on the Collegium side looked hardly bigger than bugs. At the far edge of the Field they wheeled and returned at top speed to the fence. She leaned into his neck, feeling so at one with him that it seemed as if it were her own feet flying below them. She gripped a double handful of the mane whipping about her face and whispered, "Don't stop, loverling! We can take it! Jump!"

She felt him gather himself beneath her as the fence loomed immediately in front of them—she shifted her weight without thinking—and they were airborne, the fence flashing underneath his tucked-up hooves. It was over in a heartbeat, as he landed as easily as a bird, his hooves chiming on the paved court on the other side.

As she combed her own hair out of her eyes with her fingers, she heard a hearty laugh. "And I thought I'd have to coax you into the saddle with a ladder!" a rough voice said behind her. "Looks like you might be able to teach me a trick or two, my young centaur!"

Rolan pivoted without Talia's prompting so that they could face the owner of the voice; a tall, thin woman of indeterminate age, with short, graying brown hair and intelligent gray eyes, who was clad entirely in white leather.

The woman chuckled and strode toward them, then walked around them with her hands clasped behind her back, surveying them from all sides. "No doubt about it, you have a very pretty seat, young Talia. You're a natural. Well, you've shown me what you can do bareback, so let's see what you can do in the saddle, shall we?"

Herald Keren (who proved to be Teren's twin sister—which explained the grins he'd traded with Drake and Edric) was openly pleased at having so adept a pupil. She told Talia after the first hour that she intended Talia to learn everything she herself knew before too very long. What Keren could do with a horse was incredible and what she could do with her Companion was nothing short of phenomenal.

"Before you've got your Whites, m'dear," she told Talia on parting, "you'll be able to duplicate anything you can do afoot on the back of your Companion. You're going to be a credit to both of us; I feel it in my bones. When I'm done with you, the only way anyone will be able to get you off Rolan's back unwilling will be dead."

Talia, much to her own surprise, felt the same instinctive liking for Keren as she had for her twin. It was disturbing; almost frightening. Her instincts were all telling her to trust these people— but everything she'd ever learned urged her to keep her distance until she could truly be *sure* of them. After all, she'd been hurt and betrayed time and time again by her own blood-kin. How could she expect better treatment from strangers? And yet, and yet—something deep inside kept telling her that her fears were needless. She wished she knew which inner prompting to trust.

Keren called a halt to the drilling when the sun was westering, insisting that both she and Rolan were tired—or should have been. "Just go out into the Field together for a while. Ride if you like, walk if you prefer, but be together—the bond that's to build between you has a good start, but it needs nurturing. Don't *try* to do anything, just enjoy each other's company. That'll be enough."

Talia obeyed happily; she climbed over the fence and walked dreamily beside Rolan, thoughts drifting. There was no explaining why, but at this moment she could feel none of the tenseness and anxiety that had been a part of her for as long as she could remember. For now, at least, she was held securely in a place where she *belonged*; and with that certain knowledge came another trickle of confidence. Being with the Companion erased all her doubts and stilled all her fears. She didn't come to herself until she heard the double bell for the Cook's helpers sound across the field.

She swung up on his bare back and they trotted to the enormous tack shed near the middle of the Field. Keren showed her where to find Rolan's gear; she groomed him hurriedly, but still with care, and flew back to her room, having scarcely time to wash and change before sliding into a vacant place at dinner.

She'd thought she would be too excited to sleep, but to her own surprise found herself nodding over her plate. She had barely enough energy to take the prescribed bath—and was grateful that there was little competition for the tubs this early in the evening, for if she'd had to wait in the steamy room for long, she'd have fallen asleep on her feet.

This time she had no thoughts at all, for she was asleep when her head touched the pillow.

Six

Every day for the next week Talia followed the same schedule; she woke just after sunrise to the sound of the waking bell—which she'd somehow slept through her first morning. She would either bundle herself hastily into her uniform and run downstairs to help with breakfast, or spend a more leisurely hour in getting both herself and her room ready before the meal. After breakfast came the Orientation class, and other classes were added every other day as the time spent there was shortened. Her afternoons were given over to Master Alberich in self-defense class, equitation with Herald Keren, and, of course, in building her bond with Rolan. On the days she wasn't helping with breakfast or lunch she spent long hours with several others mending a seemingly endless pile of gray uniforms.

At the end of the week Herald Teren dismissed them for the last time, but asked Talia to remain behind as the others filed out. She tensed without realizing it, her outward relaxation draining away as she waited, biting nervously at a hangnail, to hear the reason why he wanted to speak to her.

She watched him covertly as he leaned a little

on his desk, not meeting his eyes except by accident. He looked worried and slightly unhappy, and in her experience that sort of expression on an adult face meant trouble for her.

Teren was uncomfortable with the situation he found himself in now; this poor, confused child was having more than enough problems in trying to come to terms with the Collegium and her new role, without having to cope with trouble from her family as well. He mentally cursed their cruelty, who could send a message so coldly calculated to destroy what little stability the child had gained.

"Talia—" he began; then hesitated, seeing her start from raw nervousness. "Childing, there's nothing for you to be afraid of—I've just got some rather unpleasant news for you that I thought you would rather receive alone. It's word from your family."

"My family?" she repeated, her expression surprised and puzzled.

"We sent a messenger to them, just as we do with every child Chosen, telling them what had happened to you. Now usually no matter how angry they are, the honor of being Chosen seems to make every parent forgive whatever disobedience had occurred, and we thought that would happen for you, too."

Now at last she was looking directly at him, instead of from underneath downcast lashes. He was uneasy beneath her stare, and oddly at a loss for words. "Talia, I wish things had gone as we'd expected; I can't tell you how sorry I am—this is all the reply they gave us."

He fumbled in his tunic pocket and pulled out a much-folded bit of paper and handed it to her.

She opened it, smoothing out the creases unthinkingly, while Teren waited in apprehensive anticipation for her reaction to what it held.

Sensholding has no daughter Talia, it read. The half-literate scrawl bore her Father's mark.

She didn't realize that she was weeping until a single hot tear splashed on the paper, blurring the ink. She regained control of herself immediately, swallowing down the tears. She hadn't realized until this moment just how much she'd hoped that the Family would accept her because of her newly-won status. She hadn't thought, though, that the Heralds would have told them—she'd expected that it would be she herself that would break the news; perhaps by riding one day into the Holding in the full formal array of Herald's Whites. It was when she had first realized that she really *was* a Herald that she had begun to hope that the achievement would mean forgiveness—even, perhaps, a hint of approval. Holderkin did not condemn *everything* Heralds did and stood for, and even the most critical of them generally admitted that Heralds served an important function. Certainly the Holderkin welcomed their intrusion into their midst when the raiders came over the Border, or a feud needed settling! Perhaps, she'd hoped, her kin would realize now why she'd done things that were a bit unseemly—they'd realize she was only following her own nature. Surely *now* they'd understand. Perhaps they'd welcome her back, and let her have a place to belong.

It was odd, but when she'd chosen to run away, their certain excommunication hadn't seemed so great a price to pay for freedom; but somehow now, after all her hopes for forgiveness had been raised only to be destroyed by this one note—

Never mind; once again she was on her own— and Herald Teren would hardly approve of her sniveling over the situation. "It's all right," she said, handing back the note to the Herald. "I should have expected it." She was proud that her voice trembled only a little, and that she was able to meet his eyes squarely.

Teren was startled and slightly alarmed; not at her reaction to the note, but by her immediate iron-willed suppression of it. This was not a healthy response. She should have allowed herself the weakness of tears; any child her age would have. Instead, she was holding back, turning farther into herself. He tried, tentatively, to call those tears back to the surface where they belonged. Such suppression of natural feelings could only mean deep emotional turmoil later—and would only serve as one more brick in the wall the child had placed between herself and others around her.

"I wish there was something I could do to help." Teren was exceedingly distressed and tried to show that he was as much distressed at the child's denial of her own grief as with the situation itself. "I can't understand why they should have replied like this."

If he could just at least get her to admit that the situation made her unhappy, he would have an opening wedge in getting her to trust him.

"Perhaps if we sent another envoy to them, later—" he offered, trying to hold her gaze.

Talia dropped her eyes and shook her head; there was no return for her, at least not as the triumphal Holderkin Herald. To even her closest kin she would be a total stranger, and "Talia Sensdaughter" had never lived. She had violated the Holy Writ that a girlchild be totally obedient in all things; she was outcaste, and they would *never* change their minds.

"But—"

"I'm going to be late—" Talia winced away from his outheld hand and ran, wishing that Teren had been less sympathetic. He'd brought her tears perilously close to the surface again. She'd wanted, above all other things, to break down and cry on his shoulder. But—no. She didn't dare. When kith and kin could deny her so completely, what might not strangers do, especially if she exposed her weaknesses? And Heralds were supposed to be self-sufficient, self-reliant. She would *not* show that she was unworthy and weak.

Fortunately, the next class—History, which as far as Talia was concerned was no less than one neverending tale—was engrossing enough that she was able to concentrate on it and ignore her unhappiness. Like many of the classes it was structured cyclically, so that a student could drop into it at any point, completing it when the point at which he'd entered came around again. An elderly woman—Herald Werda—taught this class. Today the lecture and the discussion that followed were fascinating; enough to make her forget for a while.

And Geography was nearly as enthralling. All Heralds at the Collegium for more than a few days taught it in turn, covering their own home areas as they came under study. Teren's conclusion of the Orientation class brought him to lead this one for a time, since it was covering the Lake Evendim area.

This class was not just the study of maps, but a study of everything that made up the environment of the area, from the topography and vegetation to the weather. These things were then related to the people who lived there, and how their lives had been shaped; how changes in these factors might affect them. This too was engrossing enough to hold her attention away from her rejection.

Teren made a tentative gesture in her direction when the class was dismissed—Talia pretended not to see it and hurried on to the next, part of the crowd, and yet apart from it.

Following this class was Mathematics; Talia had never been overly fond of figures, but Herald Sylvan seemed to love the precision and intricacies of her subject so much that some of that enthusiasm was bound to be contagious.

Talia's newest class, just before lunch, was something called "Courtly Graces"; she was feeling very uneasy about it. She was certain that she'd look as out of place at Court as a goat. Most especially did she dread it now, when she was so knotted up inside and out of balance. She almost feared meeting the instructor, picturing some stiff-necked, gilded aristo, and anticipating ridicule.

She crept in, and hid herself behind several of her taller classmates before the instructor entered. She slumped into her seat as the buzz of conversation ended, hoping to remain unnoticed.

"Isn't Talia here? I thought she was joining us today," the puzzled voice was very familiar and startled Talia into raising her head.

"Bright Havens, child," Housekeeper Gaytha

smiled, "we ought to put stilts on the bottoms of your boots—you're almost too tiny to see!"

"You're not—" Talia blurted, then blushed.

"I'm not a courtier, as such, and I'm not a Herald either—but before I accepted this position I was Governess to House Ravenscroft; that's why I teach this class," Gaytha explained patiently. "A Governess sees the court from a unique viewpoint; within it, yet invisible. For this reason I can teach you all the manners that smooth the way, and the means of seeing the poison fangs hid by the velvet tongues. Make no mistake about it, if you retain the habit of speaking before thinking, the fangs will be felt!"

The tiny, gentle smile she wore softened the rebuke.

Perhaps Courtly Graces wasn't going to be as horrid as Talia had thought.

In fact, it was rather fascinating; a convoluted, intricate dance of manners—though Talia had cause to wonder more than once if she'd ever truly understand it all, much less feel comfortable treading the measures of it.

A free reading hour spent in the Library followed lunch and that class, and it would have taken drawn daggers to keep her out of that room of wonders. Remembering Davan's tale of the beginnings of the Kingdom, she chose a book from the very front of the section on History.

Today she wasn't Cook's helper, so following her reading hour was an hour spent in the sewing room, a cramped but well-lit room, crowded with tables holding baskets of uniforms in various stages of disrepair. It was here, with her hands full but her mind unoccupied, that she found she could no longer keep her loneliness at bay—especially not with the other students laughing and chattering away about things and people she had no acquaintance with whatsoever. She found a corner partially in shadow and screened by a mound of things to be mended, and took her basket of work there. The misery had to come out sooner or later, and this was a good time and place; one where she wouldn't be noticed. The torn hose acquired a certain salty dampness before the hour was over.

At least today she wasn't forced to deal with the demonic Alberich—he had delegated the ex-thief Skif as her tutor instead. She had found herself warming shyly to the boy during the past week. Skiff seemed to sympathize with her awkwardness, and was endlessly patient with her. Without rebuke, he helped her position her rebellious limbs and slowed his own movements down enough that she could see exactly what she was supposed to be doing. When she looked downhearted, he cheered her with ridiculous stories about the preposterous things he'd supposedly done back in his days as a street-child, beggar, and pickpocket. She responded tentatively to his open friendliness, and he seemed to know when to reach out to her and when to back down.

From there she went to archery practice, and then to Rolan.

Once in her Companion's presence the ache of loneliness vanished. They worked over the obstacle course until they were both tired, then went off to a far corner of the Field to cool off together and to be alone. Again, simply being with him worked some kind of alchemy on her spirits. When she thought about how lonely she'd been even with her two closest kin—and how fulfilled she felt when she was with Rolan—the price she had paid for coming here no longer seemed so high. By the time Rolan was brushed and curried, Talia had very nearly regained her cheer. Whenever she was with him, she knew without doubt that she was loved and that *he* would never leave her friendless.

Either she was growing used to the pace or her endurance was increasing; she was not tired enough to stay indoors after supper, so she decided to explore the gardens that abutted the Collegium grounds.

It was there that she learned why Sherrill had warned her not to confront the unaffiliated students alone.

She was walking the graveled paths between the mathematically-laid-out flowerbeds, as the sun set and the coming dusk seemed to thicken the air and turn it blue. The scent of the roses mingled with that of the nightblooming flowers that were only just beginning to open. She was half daydreaming and didn't notice that there was anyone about until someone spoke.

"Do I smell manure?" a male voice behind her sniffed superciliously. "I really believe that I do!"

"Perhaps the gardeners have manured the flowerbeds?" It was a girl's voice this time, and one with a nasty edge to it.

"Oh, I think not," the first replied. "This smell is most decidedly fresh, and altogether goat-like."

Talia turned, startled; there were four or five adolescents in blue uniforms lounging in the shadow of a hedge.

"Why, what have we here?" the first speaker feigned surprise at seeing her. "I do believe that I've found the source of the odor!"

"No doubt of it," the girl at his side replied, "since it's that wench from the Border. What a pity—they'll allow *anything* into the Collegium these days. Still, you'd think they'd bathe it before letting it roam civilized surroundings."

They watched her with expressions of sly anticipation. Talia had first thought to give them word for word, but thought better of the idea at once. There were five of them, and she was alone—and from what Sherrill had said, they weren't likely to stop with insults, nor to fight fairly.

"My Lady, these creatures are steeped in filth; a hundred baths couldn't wash the smell away," the boy continued maliciously. "Which isn't surprising, considering that they are also steeped in ignorance. I'm given to understand that this one tried to give its Companion back to the Collegium—that it hadn't the faintest idea what it meant to be Chosen."

Talia's ears burned with shame and anger.

"Is it as stupid as it is smelly?" a third asked.

"It must be, since it apparently doesn't realize that we're talking about it."

Tears sprang up, and were as quickly suppressed. There was no way that she would let *this* lot know how their insults had hurt—that would only encourage them. Talia shut her smarting eyes and began to walk away; they moved up on her so quickly that she didn't realize that she was surrounded until a calculated shove sent her sprawling headfirst into a well-watered flowerbed. She wasn't ready for the tumble, and landed hard, getting a face full of dirt and dead leaves.

As laughter faded into the distance, Talia extricated herself. She'd had the breath knocked out of her; the bed had been planted with rose-vines and none of the thorns seemed to be less than an inch long. By the time she got out, her uniform was ruined, and she was scratched and bloody as well as filthy.

Hot, angry tears slipped over her cheeks; she scrubbed them away with the back of a gritty hand and sprinted for the safety of the Collegium, grateful for the cover of gathering darkness.

It was early enough that there was no one in the bathing room; she hastily shoved the ruined clothing down the chute. A long soak changed the angry scratches into cuts she could have picked up in practice and the sound of the running water covered her sniffles as she sobbed, half in anger, half in hurt.

She had no intention of asking Sherrill for help; she couldn't spend all her time in the older girl's company, and the minute she was alone she'd be a target again. Besides, despite what Sherrill had told her, Talia had strong misgivings about her real willingness tolerate the constant presence of a child at her side, day in, day out.

And Talia had had plenty of experience with bullies before this; she knew what to expect. Once they'd started, they wouldn't leave her alone until they'd become bored with the game.

And there was another facet to be considered as well. She pushed her wet hair out of her eyes and regarded the coin-sized scar on the palm of her left hand soberly. How old had she been when

Justus had burned that into her hand with a red-hot poker? Nine? Ten? No matter. When the thing had happened, the adults had believed him and not her, when he'd said she'd done it to herself.

So why should anyone here believe her—she was new, unknown; they were obviously children of ranking courtiers. Given the circumstances, who'd be thought the liar? Better to remain silent. They'd had their fun; perhaps they'd become bored soon if she didn't react, and leave her alone.

Her hope was in vain.

The very next day she discovered that someone had purloined her History notes; the day following, a shove from behind sent her blundering to her knees, bruising both knees and elbows on the floor of the corridor. When she collected her books and her wits, there was no one to be seen that could have shoved her—although she could faintly hear giggles from somewhere in the crowd about her.

Two days later she was pelted with stones by unseen assailants as she was running to weapons class alone. The day after that, she discovered that someone had upended a full bottle of ink over her books, and there was no sign that anyone had been near them but herself. That had been a nearly unbearable humiliation—to be thought to have been so careless with a *book*.

She began to acquire a certain reputation for awkwardness, as she was shoved or tripped at least once a week; more often than that if she dared to go anywhere outside the Collegium.

And there was persecution of a nonphysical nature as well.

She began receiving anonymous notes; notes

that appeared mysteriously in her pockets or books, notes that picked her shaky self-confidence to tiny pieces. It got to the point where the mere sight of one would bring her to the edge of tears, and she couldn't show them to anyone because the words faded within moments after she'd read them, leaving only common bits of unmarked paper.

And she didn't dare to confide in anyone else—for there was no evidence to her mind that the perpetrators were confined to the Blues. Granted, if things were as they seemed, it was wildly unlikely that any of her fellow trainees was part of the group tormenting her—but Justus had hidden his sadism behind an angelic expression and a smiling face. Things were not always as they seemed. No, it was better to bear things alone—at least there was always Rolan.

But Keren had seen that *something* was wrong. She'd already had her twin's report on the note Talia had received from her family; a session with Elcarth had convinced her that *she* might be just the person to get the child to emerge from her shell of isolation. *She* had seen no evidences of clumsiness when she'd worked with Talia, and the reports of constant accidents sat ill with the evidence of her own eyes. There was something amiss, badly amiss.

As a child Keren had schooled herself to develop incredible patience—had been known to sit for hours with a handful of breadcrumbs, scarcely moving an eyelash, until the birds fed from her hand. She used that same kind of patient stalking with Talia now; dropping a word here, a subtle encouragement there. If there was someone persecuting the child, soon or late Keren would find out about it.

There were times she cursed the protocol of those Gifted with thought-sensing; if not for those constraints, she could have read plainly what was bothering the child—or if she couldn't, there were others who could have penetrated *any* shield. But the protocols were there to protect; one simply didn't ruthlessly strip away the inner thoughts of anyone, no matter how well-meaning one's intentions were. If the child had accidentally let something slip, it would be another case entirely. Unfortunately, she was entirely too well walled off. Nor was there any likelihood that someone more talented than Keren would "hear" something; Talia's reticence was being interpreted as a desire for privacy, and was being respected as such. Those who can hear thoughts tend to be fanatical about privacy, whether their own or others; a good thing under most circumstances but a distinct handicap for Keren in this case.

Although Talia hadn't consciously noted Keren's solicitude, the attention was making itself felt. She was on the verge of telling the riding-instructor about the notes, at least, when she began receiving another set—

Do go and tell someone about this, bumpkin, these notes said, *it will so entertaining to watch you try and explain why you haven't got anything but blank scraps of paper. They'll think you're mad. They might be right, you know. . . .*

That frightened her—the specter of madness had haunted her ever since she'd gotten the first of the letters. After all, how could letters vanish from off the paper after they were read? And if they only *thought* she were mad—they might turn her out of the Collegium, and then where could she go? It wasn't worth the risk. She confided in no one and wept in private.

Then, just as her nerves were at the breaking point, the three months of Midwinter revelry began at Court and the persecution ceased abruptly.

When several days passed without even a note, Talia began to hope; when a week went by, she dared to relax her guard a little. By the end of the first month free of pursuit, she decided that they'd grown tired of her non-reaction and found some other game.

She threw herself into her life at the Collegium then with such unrestrained enthusiasm that before Midwinter Festival she began to feel as if she'd come to belong there. Her Family's rejection no longer ached with the same intensity.

The Collegium suspended classes for the two weeks of the Festival; those students that didn't return to their own homes for the holiday generally visited with friends or relatives near the capital. It was only Talia who had nowhere to go; she had kept so much to herself that no one realized this in the rush of preparations.

The first day of the holiday found her wandering the empty halls, listening to her footsteps echo, feeling very small and lonely, and wondering if even the Library would be able to fill the empty hours.

As she listened to the sound of her own passing echo eerily in the hallways, another, fainter sound came to her ears—the sound of a harp being played somewhere beyond the doors that closed off the Heralds' private quarters from the rest of the Collegium.

Curiosity and loneliness moved her to follow the sound to its source. She pushed open one of the double doors with a faint creak, and let the harp-notes lead her down long corridors to the very end of the Herald's wing, and a corner overlooking the Palace Temple. It was quiet here. Most of the rooms were singles, occupied by Heralds currently out on Field duty. The place was easily as empty as the Collegium wing. The harp sounded sweet and a little lonely amid all the silence. Talia stood, just out of sight of a half-open door on the ground floor, and lost all track of time in the enchantment of the music.

She sighed when the harp-song ended.

"Come in please, whoever you are," a soft, age-roughened voice called from within the room, "There's no need for you to stand about in a dreary hall when I could do with some company."

The invitation sounded quite genuine; Talia mastered her reluctance and shyly pushed the door open a bit farther.

Sunlight poured in the windows of the tiny room on the other side, reflecting from paneled walls the color of honey and a few pieces of furniture of wood and fabric only a shade or so darker. A brightly burning fire on the hearth gave off the scent of applewood and added to the atmosphere of light and warmth. Seated beside the fire was an elderly man—older than anyone Talia had ever met before, surely, for his silver hair matched the white of his tunic. But his gentle, still-handsome face and gray eyes held only welcome, and the creases that wreathed his mouth and eyes were those that came of much smiling rather than frowning. His brow was broad, his mouth firm, his chin cleft rather appealingly, and his whole demeanor was kind. He held a harp braced against one leg. Talia's eyes widened to see that the other, like that of the village guard she had met, was missing from the knee down.

He followed her gaze and smiled.

"I am more fortunate than a good many," he said, "for it was only a leg I lost to the Tedrel mercenaries and the King's service, and not my life. What keeps a youngling like you here in these gloomy halls at Festival time?"

Perhaps it was his superficial resemblance to her Father's Mother; perhaps it was simply that he was so openly welcoming of her; perhaps it was just that she was so desperately lonely—he made Talia trust him with all her heart, and she spoke to him as candidly as she would have to Rolan.

"I haven't anywhere to go, sir," she said in a near-whisper.

"Have you no friends willing to share holiday and hearth with you?" he frowned. "That seems most unHeraldlike."

"I—I didn't tell anyone that I was staying. I really don't know anybody very well; my family doesn't want me anymore, and— and—"

"And you didn't want anyone to know; perhaps ask you to come with them not because they wanted you, but because they felt sorry for you?" he guessed shrewdly.

She nodded, hanging her head a trifle.

"You look to be about thirteen; this must be your first Midwinter here or the entire Collegium would know you had nowhere to spend it. There's only one newly-Chosen that fits that description, so you must be Talia. Am I right?"

She nodded shyly.

"Well, there's no loss without a little gain," he replied. "I, too, have nowhere to spend my Festival. I could spend it with the Court, but the crowding is not to my taste. My kith and kin have long since vanished into time—my friends are either gone or busy elsewhere. Shall we keep the holiday together? I am called Jadus."

"I—would like that sir. Very much.' She raised her eyes and smiled back at him.

"Excellent! Then come and make yourself comfortable; there's room next to the fire—chair, cushion, whichever you prefer."

A keen sensitivity alerted him to the depths of Talia's shyness, and he made a show of tuning his harp as she hesitantly placed a fat pillow of amber velvet on the hearth and curled up on it like a kitten. His Gift was thought-sensing, and while he would never even dream of prying into her mind, there were nuances and shadings to her thoughts and behavior that told him he would have to tread carefully with her. He was by nature a gentle man, but with Talia he knew he would have to be at his gentlest, for the least ill-nature on his part would frighten her out of all proportion to reality.

"I'm glad that my playing lured you to my door, Talia."

"It was so very beautiful—" she said wistfully. "I've never heard music like that before."

He chuckled. "My overweening pride thanks you, youngling, but the hard truth is that any Master Bard would make me sound the half-amateur that I truly am. Still—honesty forces me to admit that I have at least *some* Talent, else they'd never have admitted me to Bardic Collegium in the first place."

"*Bardic* Collegium, sir?" Talia said, confused.

"Yes, I know. *Now* I am a Herald, complete with Companion, who is even now sunning her old bones and watching the silly foals frolic in the snow—but when I first arrived here, it was to be admitted to Bardic Collegium. I had been there for three years, with two more to go; I was sitting in the garden, attempting to compose a set-theme piece for an assignment, when something drew me down to Companion's Field. And *she* came, and proceeded to merrily turn my life inside out. I was even resentful at the time, but now I wouldn't exchange a moment of my life for the coronet of the Laureate."

Talia watched the strong, supple fingers that caressed the silken wood of the harp almost absently.

"You didn't give up the music, though."

"Oh, no—one doesn't forsake *that* sweet mistress lightly after one has tasted of her charms," he smiled, "And perhaps Fortunea did me a favor; I've never needed to please a fickle crowd or ungrateful master, I've sung and played for the entertainment of only myself and my friends. Music has served me as a disguise as well, since Bards are welcome nearly everywhere, inKingdom or out. And even now, when my voice has long since gone the way of my leg, I can charm a tune from My Lady to keep me company. Or to lure company to my door."

He wrinkled his nose at her, and she returned his smile with growing confidence.

He looked at her appraisingly, taken with a sudden thought. "Talia, youngling, can *you* sing?"

"I don't know, sir," she confessed, "I'm—I *was*—Holderkin. They don't hold with music; only hymns, mostly, and then just the priests and Handmaidens."

"Holderkin, Holderkin—" he muttered, obviously trying to remember something. "Ah! Surely you know the little sheep-calming song, the one that goes, 'Silly sheep, go to sleep'?"

He plucked a simple melody.

She nodded. "Yes sir—but *that* isn't music, though, is it?"

"Even a speech can be music in the right hands. Would you sing it for me, please?"

She began very hesitantly, singing so softly as to be barely audible above the voice of the harp, but she began to gain confidence and volume before long. The harp in counterpoint behind the melody fascinated her; soon she was so engrossed in the patterns the music made that she lost all trace of self-consciousness.

"I thought so," Jadus said with self-satisfaction as she finished, "I thought you had a touch of Talent when I listened to you speak. You'll never give a major Bard competition, little one, but you definitely have—or will have, rather—a quite good singing voice. Would you be willing to give an old man a great deal of pleasure by consenting to yet another set of lessons?"

"You mean—music lessons? Teach *me*? But—"

"It would be a shame to waste your Talent; and you do have it, youngling," he smiled, with just a hint of wistfulness. "It would truly be something that I would enjoy sharing with you."

That decided her. "If you think it's worth wasting your time on me—"

He put a finger under her chin, tilting her head up so that she had nowhere to look but his earnest, kindly eyes. "Time spent with you, my dear, will never be wasted. Believe it."

She blushed a brilliant crimson, and he released her.

"Would you be willing to begin now?" he continued, allowing her to regain her composure, "We have all the afternoon before us—and we could begin with the song you just sang."

"If you don't mind—I don't have anything *I* was going to do."

"Mind? Youngling, if you knew how long my hours are, you would never have made that statement."

Jadus felt a bond growing between the two of them—felt without really thinking about it that it was his own "helpless" condition that allowed Talia to feel he wasn't any sort of a threat. He had been allowing himself to drift in a hermit-like half-dream for several years now, allowing the world outside his door to move off without him. It just hadn't seemed worth the effort to try and call it back—until now—

Until now, when another heart as lonely as his had strayed to his door, and brought the world back with her. And as he watched the child at his feet, he knew that this time—for her sake—he would not permit it to drift away again.

Talia learned quickly, as her teachers already knew; music was a whole unknown world for her, and in one way this was all to the good as she had nothing to unlearn. She was so enthralled that she

never even noticed how late it was getting until a
servant arrived to light candles and inquire as to
whether Jadus preferred dinner in his room.

When she would have absented herself, he
insisted that she share dinner with him, saying
that he had had his fill of solitary meals. When the
servant returned, he sent him on another errand,
to search out some songbooks he'd had stored
away. These he presented to Talia over her protests.

"I've not missed them in all the time they've
been stored," he said firmly. "The music and the
memories are safe enough in here—" he tapped
his forehead "—so I have no need of the books
themselves. A Midwinter Gifting, if you like, so
that you can learn fast enough to please your
tyrannical teacher."

She departed only when her singing was punctuated by yawns. She felt almost as if she'd known
the old Herald for as long as she'd been alive, and
that they'd been friends for all of that time. She
felt comfortable and welcome with him, and could
hardly bear to wait for the new dawn and another
day with him.

She rose nearly with the sun. But she feared to
intrude too early and disturb the aged Herald, so
she gulped down a hasty breakfast of bread and
milk from the stores in the Collegium kitchen and
took her energy out to Rolan.

She and he played like the silliest of children,
she tossing snowballs at him and he avoiding them
adroitly or trying to catch them in his teeth. She
felt quite lightheaded with happiness; happier than
she ever remembered being before. Finally he cur-
vetted coaxingly toward her, in a plain invitation
to mount and ride. They galloped together until

the sun was quite high, fairly flying over the Field. This was enough to loosen her taut nerves and spend some of her energy without losing any of her enthusiasm. She tapped on Jadus' door at midmorning with sparkling eyes and flushed cheeks.

By the end of this, the second day of her lessons, the servants had gotten wind of what was going on and could be seen lurking in the vicinity of the Herald's room. Though untrained, Talia's voice was good and her pitch was true; the servants were finding the lessons to be rare entertainment indeed. Now that Midwinter Festival was at its height there was scarcely enough room in the Great Hall for all the nobles come to Court, much less an off-duty servant—but here in this little corner of Herald's Hall there was entertainment in plenty. Before long, had anyone chanced by, they would have seen folk perched quietly like a flock of sparrows in every available nook and cranny. Talia was unaware that they were there, oblivious as she was to everything but her lessoning. Jadus knew, though, his ear long sensitized to the unusual sound of anyone in his out-of-the-way corridor; and he tacitly welcomed their presence. He had spent enough lonely holidays to know how cheering a bit of music could be—and he was showman enough to appreciate having an audience. Besides, knowing they were there made him put a bit more polish on his own performances, and that was all to the good where his new pupil was concerned.

Midwinter Eve itself came before Talia was aware that it was upon them.

That afternoon Jadus had been telling her tales

drawn from his own experiences as a young Herald, when there was a hesitant knock on the half-open door.

"Come," he answered, one eyebrow rising quizzically.

It was the young servant who habitually tended to Jadus' needs. "Your pardon, Herald," he said diffidently, "We—the rest of us, that is—couldn't help but listen to yourself and young Talia all this past week, and we wondered—well, to put it shortly, sir, it's this. You two haven't anywhere to go this Midwinter Eve and you're plainly not wanting to spend it at Court either, or you'd be there now. Would you be caring to share *our* celebration? And, if you could be bothered to sing or play a bit for us, we'd be beholden to you. We entertain ourselves, you see; 'tisn't masterly, but it's fun, and it's homelike."

Jadus broke into a wide smile. "Medren, I do believe that's one of the handsomest offers I've had since I was Chosen! Talia, what think you?"

She nodded speechlessly, amazed that *anyone* would come seeking *her* company.

"Right gladly do we accept—and right gladly will we do our best to help amuse and please you."

Medren's sturdy brown face was wreathed in smiles. "*Many* thanks, m'lord Jadus. We'd have asked you aforetime, but that we thought you wished to be alone. But then when you and the child began the lessoning, well, we bethought maybe we were wrong."

Jadus rested his hand fondly on Talia's head. "I have lived overly much in my memories, I think. It was time someone woke me to the present.

Welladay, will you send someone to fetch us when the time comes?"

Medren nodded. "Second hour after sundown, Herald, and I'll come myself. Do you wish your carry-chair?"

"Oh, I think not. I'll do well enough with my cane and my friends," he replied and smiled at Talia with affection.

Medren was prompt; enthusiastic cries of greeting met them at the door of the Servant's Hall as they entered. The room was approximately three times the size of the Collegium common room, with a fireplace at either end, oil lamps along the walls, and one door leading into the hallway in the middle of one of the longer walls, and another leading to the Palace kitchen in the middle of the other. There were many trestle tables set up in the middle of it, all crowded with off-duty servants. Jadus entered through the hall-door slowly, managing very well with his cane and one hand resting lightly on Talia's shoulder for balance. She held his harp in both arms with great care, feeling honored that he trusted it to her. Tucked into her belt was the little shepherd's pipe he'd given her a few days previous. Jadus' eyes widened and lit from within at the sounds of welcome; he seemed even to stand a bit straighter. The greetings they received were warm and unrestrained, for although she hadn't known it, Talia had long ago won the sympathy of the servants with her stalwart refusal to give in to self-pity out of loneliness. Jadus was another favorite—partially because he never demanded any favors though he'd long since earned the right to demand special treatment, and partially because he had never stood on protocol with anyone, servant or noble.

First there was a feast, prepared at the same time as that being served in the Great Hall; everyone able took his or her turn at waiting on the others. Following the food came the entertainment. As Medren had said, it was not "masterly," but the enjoyment was perhaps more genuine. While several amateur musicians played simple country-dances, the rest sent their feet through their paces. Tiny Talia often ended up being swept completely off the floor by some of her more energetic partners. There were some attempts at juggling and sleight-of-hand, all the more hilarious because the outcomes were so uncertain.

When at last everyone's energy was drained to the point where they were willing to turn their attention to something quieter, Talia and Jadus took their turn.

Jadus first played alone; his skillful fingers wove a spell of silence over the assemblage. There wasn't a sound to be heard as he played but the crackling of the fire on the hearth. The silence that endured for several long moments when he'd finished was a poignant tribute to his abilities.

Before the silence ended, Jadus nudged his young protégé, and Talia joined him on her pipe, playing the melodies she'd learned taking her turn on watch during the long, cold nights of lambing season. The tunes themselves were simple enough, but with Jadus' harp behind them, they took on new complexity and an entirely new voice. There was another eloquent silence when they'd done, followed by wildly enthusiastic applause. Talia's heart was filled with joy at the sight of the new life and light in Jadus' face. She was fiercely glad then that they'd come.

Then Jadus played while Talia sang something he'd picked out of an old book—a comic ballad he remembered from many years agone called "It Was A Dark and Stormy Night." The spontaneous laughter that followed the last line about the lute was so hearty that Talia was soon blushing with pleasure. Now she, too, knew how heady a drink acclaim could be.

The two of them then performed as many requests as they knew, until it grew so late that Talia found herself beginning to nod, and Jadus confessed that his fingers were growing tired. Talia helped him back to his room; she scarcely knew how she found her own bed. She thought before sleep claimed her that without a doubt it was the finest Midwinter Festival she'd ever had.

Seven

After Midwinter's Evening there could have been no firmer friends in all the Collegium and Circle than Talia and the old Herald Jadus. Even after classes began again, she always found the time for music lessons and practice sessions with him every evening. He seemed to take as much joy in her company as she did in his—and not even the fact that her unknown tormentors resumed their games soon after the end of the holidays served to take that happiness out of her heart. It sometimes occurred to her that if it hadn't been for Jadus and Rolan, she'd have thought more than once about giving it all up and running away—though where she'd go, she had no idea. Without those two stalwarts to turn to, her misery would have been deeper than it had been at the Holding at the worst of times.

The signal that "they" were still at her came in the form of another of the anonymous notes. It appeared among her books just before one of her music lessons, and she was hard put to make herself seemly after the spate of tears it caused.

It would have been impossible to hide the fact that she was troubled and upset from Jadus; her red-rimmed eyes gave her away immediately. He insisted, gently but firmly, that she tell him something of what was wrong.

"You know I would never say or do anything against your will, little one—" His voice was soft but held a note of command. The hesitant, wary child that had replaced the cheerful Talia that he had come to know and love was not at all to his liking, "But you aren't happy, and if you're not happy, than neither am I. I wish you would tell me why—and who or what is the cause. You know by now you can trust me, surely?"

She nodded slowly, hands clenched in her lap.

"Then tell me what your problem is. It may even be I can help."

She was reluctant to confide in him, but found herself unable to resist the kindness of his eyes. "Y-y-you have to promise something, please? That you won't tell anyone else?"

He promised that he would not, rather than lose the trust she had given to no one else. The promise was given with great reluctance. "If that is the only way you'll tell me—yes. I promise."

"I-it's like this—" she began, telling him eventually only of the shovings, the destructive tricks, and not of the notes. She feared *those* were too wildly unlikely even for Jadus to believe.

He sensed that there was more to these pranks than she was telling him, and it worried him.

Bound by his promise, though, there was little he could do for her but offer an emotional shelter and proffer some advice. He hoped that that would be enough.

"Don't go anywhere alone—well, you know that already. But try to stay only with people you know;

Sherrill, or Skif, or Jeri. None of those three would ever hurt you. And—here's a thought—try to always be within sight of one of your teachers. I doubt that even the cleverest would dare try anything under the eyes of a Herald. And little one—" He touched her cheek with a gentle hand, eliciting a wan smile. "—*I* am always here for you. No one would dare try anything against you here, and any time you want someone to cry with—well, I have a plenitude of handkerchiefs!"

That actually earned him a tiny chuckle, and Jadus felt amply rewarded as they began the lesson.

"Make friends, child," he urged her before she left him. "The other Herald-students won't bite you. They won't try to hurt you, either, and the more friends you have, the better protected you'll be. Now think—have you ever seen or heard *any* of them do or say anything intended to be cruel?"

"No," she had to admit.

"I know your life wasn't easy at the Hold; I know people often hurt you deliberately. Things are different in the Collegium. You trust me—now I tell you to trust them as well. If nothing else, once you are part of a group, you'll be less of an available target for tricks."

Jadus was proved right—she *was* a less conspicuous target. The pranks began to decrease in frequency immediately.

There was more—though he was bound by his promise to say nothing, Jadus was aided by the fact that some of the teachers and older students, Keren, Teren, and Sherrill among them, had decided that there was something odd and unpleasant afoot and had begun making a habit of keeping an ostentatious eye on her. Keren especially had long since made that decision, and when Talia had begun to show signs of unhappiness again had taken to lurking in the child's vicinity, looking as conspicuous as possible. The perpetrators of her misery soon found it nearly impossible even to slip those mysterious notes among her things without being seen—and being seen was no part of their scheme. Before a month was out they seemed to have given up; Talia's cheerfulness was restored, and Jadus heaved a profound mental sigh of relief.

None of them guessed that there was more afoot than petty harassment.

Collegium and Circle alike had incorrectly assumed that the suspicions surrounding the death of Talamir had frightened the anti-Herald faction off of any serious attempt to rid the Kingdom of the new Queen's Own. The case was otherwise. The harassment had been at the instigation of the parents of some of the nobly-born "unaffiliated" students; courtiers who had everything to lose should Elspeth be salvaged and made Heir in fact as well as presumptive.

These older conspirators had long ago made their decision regarding Talia. If it did not prove possible to induce her to leave the Collegium, she was to be gotten rid of—by any means that came to hand.

Since she had now proven impossible to drive away, the next step was to turn to more permanent measures.

They were only waiting for Talia to make the mistake of being alone to put their new plan into motion—and their chance came on the coldest day of the year.

The sky was overcast; a dull, leaden gray. The

snow was creaky underfoot, and the cold ate its way up from the ground to Talia's feet even through sheepskin boots and three pairs of woolen stockings. The wind was strong and bitter, and Talia had decided to take the longer way from classroom to training salle, past the stables, where there was some relief from the wind's bite.

As she rounded a corner with her thoughts miles away, she suddenly found herself surrounded by Blues. Their faces were far from friendly.

Before she could think to flee, they grabbed for her, trying to pinion her arms and legs.

She was befuddled for only a scant second; she fought back with all the skill she had so far managed to acquire at Alberich's hands. He had taught her a "no holds barred" discipline; she kicked, pulled hair, and bit without compunction—and muffled cries of pain attested to the fact that she was scoring on them, even though they were fairly well protected by bulky winter garments. Oddly enough, it seemed almost as if they had no real intentions of hurting her; as if their intentions were rather to immobilize her for some unknown reason.

She took advantage of this apparent reticence on their part to bolt through a gap between two of them, leaving her cloak behind in the hands of a third.

She almost managed a clean escape—then a flying tackle from behind sent her headfirst into the stable muckpit. The contents were fresh, well-watered, and soft. She was covered from head to toe with the stinking mess, and flailed about, helpless with retching.

"Oh, poor little bumpkin—it's made a mess,"

cooed one of the girls in a sugary voice. "How awful for it!"

"Perhaps it thought it was home," replied a boy, as Talia tried to scrape filth off her face and away from her eyes. "We'd better get it clean—it certainly doesn't know how to clean itself."

They pulled her out and seized her before she could flounder free, knocked her down, and stuffed a piece of rag into her mouth before she could scream for help. They took turns rubbing handfuls of muck into her face and hair, as if in retaliation for the injuries she'd managed to inflict on *them,* then some of them pinioned her arms and others her legs. They hauled her outside where the stuff froze stiff in the icy wind and she couldn't get her eyes open to see. She was still trying to catch her breath after the blow that had knocked her down, and couldn't seem to get any air into her lungs. Right now, full lungs seemed the most important thing in the world—

She was half-carried, half-dragged, acquiring numerous scrapes and bruises from the cobblestones. She couldn't seem to think further than trying to breathe—couldn't guess what they planned next as they dragged her along. They seemed to be hauling her halfway to the Border!

Then, as she felt the road begin to climb, a vague idea of what they planned came to her, and she began to thrash in panic.

"Into your bath, goatling!" the hateful male voice sang out.

She tried to wriggle loose and kicked as hard as she could, but it was all to no avail. They were bigger and stronger than she, and far outnumbered her. She only succeeded in causing their grip to slip a little so that the back of her head cracked against the stone paving, stunning her briefly. That gave them the relief they needed; she felt herself tossed up into the air, landing in the icy waters of the river with a shock that drove what little breath she had from her lungs.

The water closed over her head; she fought for the surface, pulling the rag out of her mouth as she did so, only to have her throat fill with water as she tried to breathe inches too soon. As she reached the air and choked and gasped in the icy wind, she heard someone call out, voice receding into the distance, "Farewell, bumpkin. Give our greetings to Talamir."

Only last week a careless would-be daredevil had died here, trying to cross on the ice instead of the bridge. Talia began to thrash hysterically, remembering that he hadn't lasted more than a few moments in the frigid river. What ice she could reach that didn't break when she grabbed it was too slippery to get a grip on—there was nothing to hold to, and no way she could haul herself up on it. Her sodden clothing, especially those heavy, water-logged sheepskin boots, was pulling her down, the current was tugging her inexorably farther from shore, and she could feel her limbs growing numb and unresponsive.

She couldn't keep her mouth above water for long; she couldn't get enough breath to cry for help. Her mind shrieked in incoherent fear.

Then, like a gift from the gods, a trumpeting neigh split the air and something huge and heavy plunged in beside her. Strong teeth seized her collar and pulled her to within reach of a broad warm, white back that rose beside her like magic.

"Rolan!" she gasped; she tried to make her fingers work enough to grab mane or tail while he maneuvered himself to support as much of her as he could.

For a moment it almost seemed as if it would work.

Then her fingers loosed themselves and she began sliding away from him, dragged by the punishing weight of her clothing and the strong pull of the current. Her mind went numb, as cold as the water. She lost her last tentative hold on his back, and darkness closed over her mind as the water closed over her head. Her lungs filled with water again, but she was beyond caring.

Something jerked at her collar; her head broke the surface and a stubborn spark of life made her cough and gag once again in the painfully icy air.

Then she was being hauled roughly across the ice, and many hands reached to pull her up on the bank where she was pounded and pummeled until she'd coughed all the water out of her lungs. A babble of angry, frightened voices filled her ears as she was wrapped in something heavy and made to drink a fiery liquid that brought tears to her eyes and made her choke. Her vision cleared of the dancing sparks that had taken the place of the darkness when they'd started pounding on her, and she saw she was surrounded by the anxious faces of her teachers and fellow students.

Safe. She fainted.

She half-roused as someone lifted her up to a rider's arms and they galloped to the very doors of the Collegium. The rider vaulted from the saddle still carrying her, and sprinted effortlessly with her up the stairs to the dormitory floor.

She was passed into more hands on the other side of a steamy portal, and those hands stripped her of her soaked, filthy garments quickly and efficiently. Once again she found herself up to her neck in water, but this time it was blessedly hot.

That brought her fully awake again; that, and the fact that she was being scrubbed with strong soap by three other people.

"Wha—" she coughed, her throat raw. "What happened?"

"That's what *we'd* like to know," said Jeri, soaping her hair vigorously. "Ugh—your hair is *full* of this muck! Rolan heard your mindcall for help; he alerted the rest of the Companions, and they roused their Heralds. Then he went after you himself. Lord of Lights! You should have seen the Collegium—it looked like a nest of angry wasps! People came boiling out of everywhere! Most of us got to the riverbank just in time to see you slip off Rolan's back and go under. Keren was just a fraction ahead of everyone else, and she dove right off the saddle after you; Sherrill was right behind her. They managed to pull you out—when I knew you were alive, I came back here to get Housekeeper and start what we'd need to warm you up again. Once they'd gotten the water out of you, Teren brought you here. This tub's filthy. We're going to change. No—" she warned as Talia started to move, "don't try to do anything—let us do the work for you. You've got an awful bump on your head and you might get dizzy and fall."

They lifted her over to a second tub; she still seemed chilled to the bone.

"Are they—all right?" Talia managed to get out.

"Who? Sherrill and Keren? They're fine. Don't you remember? They're from Lake Evendim. This isn't the first ice-rescue they've done. And there were two more riders waiting to bring them here, too. They're both soaking in hot tubs, the same as you."

"They are?" Talia raised her head, as the room spun before her eyes, and tried to look around. The bathing room seemed oddly turned backward, reversed in mirror-image.

"What ha'n'd to th' room?" Her tongue didn't seem to quite want to behave.

"You're on the boys' side, silly," Jeri giggled, "It was closer. Take a good look—you might not get a second chance."

"Hush," Housekeeper Gaytha scolded affectionately. "Talia, I think we've gotten the last of the filth off you. How are you feeling?"

"Still c-cold." There seemed to be an icy core that the heat didn't touch. They drained some of the water and ran in more that was fresh and hotter than before. She finally felt herself stop shivering and began to relax. Then a sudden thought made her struggle to sit up.

"Rolan!"

"He's perfectly all right," Jeri and Housekeeper Gaytha held her firmly in place. "It'll take more than a cold ducking to stop him!"

"The worst was heaving him up onto the bank; he wasn't even chilled, and he's inordinately proud of himself," said the third member of the group, silent until now. "I suppose he has every right to be, since your bond isn't supposed to be strong enough at this stage for you to call one another, even in panic. You're very lucky that wasn't the case for the two of you."

Her sight seemed to be blurring, but Talia finally got a good look at this third person as she moved to within Talia's range of vision to speak to her. The woman was a square-jawed ash-blond, and she wore full Heraldic traveling leathers with the silver arrow of a special messenger on one sleeve.

"I'm sorry we weren't properly introduced, Talia," she smiled. "I'm Herald Ylsa. Keren may have mentioned me?"

Talia nodded, and was immediately sorry. Her head began pounding, and her vision blurred still more. "Keren—was going—t' be waitin' f'r you—" she said with difficulty.

Ylsa saw the glazed look, the fixed pupils of Talia's eyes, and said sharply, "Problems, kitten?"

"I can't—see too well. And m' head hurts."

"Can you tell what's wrong?" Gaytha asked the Herald in an undertone.

The woman frowned a little. "Well, I'm no Healer, but I know the technique. Hold still, kitten," she addressed Talia. "This isn't going to hurt, but it may make your head feel a little odd." She caught Talia's blurring gaze and looked deeply into her eyes—and Talia felt something like a light touch inside her head. It *was* a very odd sensation.

Ylsa placed one hand on Talia's forehead in the lightest of feather-like touches once she'd caught Talia's attention, beginning her probe. She continued to speak in a casual voice, knowing commonplaces would keep Talia from becoming too alarmed if she sensed anything. "I'd only just come through the gate when the alarm went up. Keren's got the tightest bond with that stallion of hers that I've ever witnessed. The two of them were headed for the river before Felara had managed to do more than tell me that there was bad trouble. We took off after them, but we couldn't even manage to keep up. Her mindlink with her brother is almost as strong, and she must have told him what was needed before we even hit the riverbank because he came pounding up with blankets and ropes right after she went in. I knew that she and Dantris were good, but I have *never* seen anyone move like they did—I never even knew you *could* slingshot into a dive from the back of a Companion in full gallop!"

While she spoke, she "read" the child as the Healers she had worked with did. Since she was not formally Healer-trained, she took longer at it—and inadvertently made more contact than she'd intended to.

Talia's head wasn't exactly feeling odd, but the sensation of internal touch was stronger than ever, and she was seeing the strangest things. They came in flashes, confusing and disorienting, as if she were seeing things through someone else's eyes—and what she was seeing concerned Keren and this stranger—intimately. And it was very heavily laden with overtones of complex emotions—

She blushed an embarrassed crimson. Ylsa and Keren—long-time lovers? She didn't even *know* this woman; why should her mind be producing a fantasy like that? She looked up at Ylsa in startled confusion.

Ylsa hastily broke the contact between them when she realized what the child was sensing, and stared at her with wide-eyed respect. First the mindcall to her Companion, and now this! Ylsa *knew* she had one of the strongest shields in the Circle, yet this untrained child had picked out something it might have taken a master to extract. Granted, Ylsa's shields were probably lowered a trifle because of the reading she was doing, but it should have taken someone fully trained to have taken advantage of the fact. This child was certainly far more than her appearance led you to believe.

"Concussion," she said to the others, "And if she had some kind of cold before she went in, it's getting worse by the moment. I think we'd best get her into a warm bed and have a real Healer take her in hand."

And I'd better have a word with Keren as soon as I can! she thought to herself. *If this poor child begins a fever, there's no telling what she's likely to pick up. Anybody that watches her had better have excellent shields— for* her *sake.*

The three of them helped Talia out with care, dried her off, and put her into her warmest bedgown. She wasn't allowed to walk at all; they gave her over to Teren who carried her to her room and tucked her into her bed. It had been warmed, and she was glad of it, for once out of the steam-filled bathing room the air had been very cold and she was shivering by the time they reached her room.

She was having trouble holding to reality. It only seemed that she'd gotten the blankets tucked around her when there was a stranger standing beside her, come out of nowhere, appearing at her bedside as if he'd been conjured. It was a cherubic-faced man whose beardlessness made him

seem absurdly young; he was dressed in Healer's
Green. He held one hand just fractions of an inch
from her forehead and frowned in concentration.

Talia's head was truly beginning to hurt now; it
felt like someone was pressing daggers into her
skull just behind her eyes. The rest of her was
starting to ache, too; her chest rasped when she
breathed and she wanted badly to cough, but knew
it would only set off an explosion in her head if
she did so.

The young Healer took his hand away and said
to someone just outside the door, "Concussion for
certain, though the skull doesn't seem to be broken. And I'm sure you noticed the fever—pneumonia is a real likelihood."

There was a murmur in answer, and the Healer
leaned down so that his face was at Talia's eye
level. "You're going to be a very sick young lady
for a while, youngling," he told her quietly. "It
isn't anything that we can't cure with time and
patience, but it isn't going to be very pleasant. Can
I count on you to cooperate?"

She made a wry face, and whispered, "You wan'
me t' drink p-potions, right? Willowbark tea?"

The Healer chuckled, "I'm afraid that will be
the least of the nasty things we'll ask you to drink.
Can you manage your first dose now?"

She nodded just the tiniest fraction; carefully,
so as not to send her head pounding. The Healer
busied himself at her fireplace for several long
moments, and returned with something green and
foul-looking.

With his aid she drank it as quickly as she could,
trying not to taste it. Whatever it was, it was a great
deal stronger than Keldar's willowbark tea, for she

found the pain in her head beginning to recede, and her alertness as well. With her alertness went her awareness. Before long, she was soundly asleep.

She woke to fire and candle-light. There was someone sitting in the shadows beside her bed; soft harp-notes told her who it was.

"Herald Jadus?" she whispered, her throat too raw and swollen to produce real sound.

"So formal, little friend?" he asked, laying down his harp and leaning forward to place one hand on her hot forehead. "How do you feel?"

"Tired. Cold. Head hurts. Everything hurts!"

"Hungry?"

"Thirsty," she rasped. "Why'r'you here?"

"Thirsty can be remedied if you're willing to take another one of Devan's evil brews first. As to why I'm here, that's easy enough. You need someone to help you while you're ill, and I have plenty of time for my friend Talia." He handed her a mug of the same green potion she'd drunk before, nodding in approval as she downed it as fast as she could, then handed her another mug of broth. "We're taking it in turn to keep an eye on you, so don't concern yourself over me, and don't be surprised to see Ylsa or Keren. Ah, Devan—as you predicted, she's awake."

The same Healer moved into view on silent feet, smiling down at her. "You're a tough little thing, aren't you? Sometimes being a Border brat like we both are has its positive aspects."

Talia blinked owlishly at him over the rim of her mug. "How long—sick?" she croaked.

"A few weeks; perhaps more. And you'll feel worse before you feel better. Comforting, aren't I?"

She managed a weak grin. "Truth better."

"I thought you'd probably prefer it. You may start seeing things when you get more fevered. There will always be someone with you, so don't worry. Beginning to feel sleepy?"

"Mm," she assented.

"Finish that, then get more rest. I'll leave you in Herald Jadus' competent hands," he departed as silently as he'd come.

"Is there anything else you'd like, youngling?" Jadus asked, relief evident in his voice.

Talia surmised vaguely that the Healer's confidence had allayed some worry he'd had. He took the now-empty mug from Talia's heavy fingers.

"Play for me?" she whispered.

"You have only to ask," he replied, sounding inordinately pleased and surprised at the request. She drifted off to sleep followed by harpsong.

Ugly dreams and pain half-woke her; someone—it might have been Ylsa—calmed her panic, and coaxed her to drink more broth and medicine.

She half-woke countless more times, obediently drinking what was put to her lips, letting herself be steered to and from the bathing room and the privy. She was otherwise unaware of her surroundings. She alternately froze and burned, and lived in a dream where people from Hold and Collegium mingled and did the most absurd things.

When her dreams turned evil, they were always chased away by harpsong or comforting hands.

Finally she woke completely to see sunlight streaming in her window. Her head ached abominably; she felt at the back of it, and winced as her fingers encountered a lump.

"Hurts, doesn't it?" the rough voice from the

chair beside the bed was sympathetic. Turning her head carefully, Talia saw that Keren had assumed the position she'd last seen occupied by Jadus. She was lounging carelessly in Talia's chair with her feet up on the desk that stood beside it.

She also had her sword resting unsheathed in her lap.

"You're all right!" Talia croaked with relief.

Keren cocked an eyebrow at her. "You forget, little centaur; *I* went in of my own will. My entry was a bit more controlled than yours was. You're damned lucky to be here, you know. You slipped right under the ice when you lost your hold on Rolan's back. I almost couldn't reach you. One fingerlength more and we'd not have found you till Spring thaw."

Once again, Talia seemed to be seeing things through other eyes—and feeling things as well. She felt a dreadful fear not her own—and saw herself being pulled under the thick sheet of ice that covered most of the river. And she saw what had followed. She spoke before she thought. "You went under the ice after me—" she said in awe "—you could have died!"

Keren nearly choked. "Nets of the Lady, Ylsa was right! I'd best watch what I think around you, youngling. We might share more than either of us want to! To change the subject—yes, since you know already, it was a damned close thing. Good thing for both of us that it was Sherrill that was behind me. Once I'd hooked you, she was able to pull both of us out from under, the more 'specially as I'd had the wit to grab one of Ylsa's spare lead-ropes from her saddle and clip it to my belt on the way to the river. When Sherrill saw *that* trailing out behind me, she grabbed it. Good thing she's been on ice-rescues herself."

"She's all right, too?"

"Oh, she's not as tough an old snake as I am; she caught a cold. Don't feel sorry for her—since we'd put you out of reach, the rest of the trainees made a great fuss over her. She's their heroine; they packed her into bed and waited on her hand and foot till she hadn't so much as a sniffle."

"What do you mean, put me out of reach? Why? And why have you got your sword out? What aren't you telling me?"

Keren shook her head ruefully. "You look so naive—innocent, helpless—but even half-dead with concussion and pneumonia you don't miss much, do you? Ah, little one, there's no use trying to keep it from you. We're guarding you. The ones that threw you in the river were caught; you've got friends in Servant's Hall who spotted them coming in mucky. They swore it was just a 'joke'— some joke!—and all the Queen could legally do was banish them from Court and Collegium. On the surface of it, since there weren't any witnesses to contradict them, she had no choice. Well, I would have had their heads—" Talia could feel the anger that Keren's bland expression concealed "—or rather, their hides; but I'm not the Queen, and there's only so much she could do by the law. Since you managed to survive their little 'joke' she couldn't even call Truth Spell on them."

"One of them told me to give their greetings to Talamir—that was before Rolan came," Talia said quietly.

Keren whistled, and Talia could feel her anger mount. "Damn! I wish we'd been able to tell the

Council *that* when that lot came up on charges! Well, nobody really believed them, so Ylsa, Jadus, and I have been taking it in turn to guard you; Mero's been making all your meals himself and Teren brings 'em straight from his hands."

"Jadus?" Talia looked at Keren's sword doubtfully.

"Don't make the mistake of thinking he's helpless because he's short a leg, lovey. There's been a loaded crossbow within reach the whole time he's been up here, and that cane of his has a swordblade in it. Anybody trying to take him would have had one hell of a surprise."

"Is all this really necessary?" Talia asked, beginning to feel more than a bit frightened.

"The danger's real enough to warrant a few simple precautions. We lose enough of the Circle as it is—we're not about to lose you through carelessness," Keren paused, and then added, (half in anger, half in hurt), "—and next time, youngling, *tell* somebody when there's something wrong! We could have avoided all this—maybe caught whoever was chewing your tail! Heralds *always* stick together, dammit! Did you think we wouldn't believe you?"

"I—yes—" Talia said, and was horrified that her mouth had once again betrayed her. To her further horror, slow tears began to fall, and she was helpless to stop them.

Keren was out of her chair and at her side in a moment, holding her against a firm shoulder, anger turned immediately to concern and a touch of guilt. "Lovey, lovey, I didn't mean to upset you. We want you, we need you—it'd half kill us to lose you. You've got to learn to trust us. We're your family. No, we're more than that. And we'll never, ever desert you. No matter what happens."

"I'm—sorry—" Talia sobbed, trying to bring herself back under control and pulling away from Keren.

"No, you don't. It's time you let some of that out," Keren ordered. "Cry all you want. If my twin's right—and he usually is—you've got a lot of crying to catch up on."

Her care—her sincerity was too much to stand against. Talia yielded with speechless gratitude, as the barriers within her that had been weakened by her friendship with Jadus came crumbling down. Keren held her as if she were her own child, letting her sob herself into dry-eyed exhaustion.

"Feel better?" Keren asked, when the last of the tears were gone.

Talia smiled weakly. "Sort of."

"Except that now your head aches and your eyes are sore. Next time, don't let things build up for so long. That's one of the things friends are for—to help you with troubles. Now—about that 'new' thought-sensing ability of yours—"

"It's real? Then I *am* feeling what you're feeling? And you and Ylsa—" she broke off in confusion. "But where did I get it from? I couldn't do that before!"

"You're still picking up from me? Oh hell!" Keren frowned a little in concentration, and abruptly Talia was no longer awash with confusing emotions. "That better? Good. Oh, this thought-sensing is real, all right, and disconcertingly accurate. Only the Circle knows about Ylsa and me; we couldn't have kept it from them with all the Gifted about, even if we'd wanted to. We're lifebonded; I don't suppose you've heard of that, have you?"

"Like Vanyel and Stefen? Or Sunsinger and Shadowdancer?" Keren's amazed glance flicked over Talia like a spray of cold water, but given Talia's penchant for tales it wasn't overly surprising that she *had* heard of lifebonding. Rare among Heralds, rarer still in the general population, a lifebond was a very special tie, going far beyond the physical.

"Not so dramatic, but yes, like Vanyel and Stefen. Well, I'd guess that either the blow to your head woke your Gift early, or overwhelming fear did. It happens sometimes. Now if you *weren't* Queen's Own, we wouldn't even think about training you to use it for another few years, but you're by definition a special case. Do *you* want it trained?"

"Please—not another set of lessons—" Talia said pathetically.

Keren chuckled. "All right then, lovey, we'll leave things as they are. Maybe when your head heals, it'll go away; I've seen that happen before. But if it starts to get bothersome, you tell one of us, all right?" She paused, and eyed Talia speculatively. "It doesn't disturb you—about Ylsa and me?"

"No," Talia replied, a trifle surprised. "Should it? I mean—there's lots of—um—" she blushed again "—'special friends' on the Holdings."

"Are there?" Keren raised an eyebrow. "I never figured on that, old rocks that they are. Makes sense, I guess—all those Underwives, and damn few of 'em wed for affection," she relaxed visibly. "I won't deny that I'm glad to hear that from you. You've got an old head in a lot of ways, lovey; I'm beginning to think of you as much as my friend as my student, and I'd hate to see anything get in the way of that friendship."

"Me? Your friend?" Talia was visibly startled.

"Surprised? Jadus thinks of you as a friend, too, and he hasn't opened up to anyone in years. There's something about you that I can't pinpoint—you're so much older than your years, sometimes. Maybe it comes of being Queen's Own. Lady knows *I'm* not old enough to have known Talamir as a lad. You seem like someone I've known and trusted for years. Like a little sister. As close, maybe, as my twin—which is damned odd, considering that I've got a niece and nephew nearly your age. I'm not the only one to feel that way. There's Jadus, like I said—and Sherrill, and Skif, and probably more."

Talia digested this with wonder.

Keren shook her head, "Enough of this—how's the skull feel?"

"Awful."

She stood up and examined the lump with gentle, skillful fingers.

"Lovey, luck was all on your side in this. An inch or two lower, or on the temple instead, and you'd have been unconscious or paralyzed when you hit the water. You'd have gone under without a ripple, and we'd never have known what happened to you. Think you can stomach more of that vile green brew? It'll take the ache out, anyway."

Talia nodded slowly, and Keren brought her a mug of the concoction, then returned to her former perch on the chair; feet propped up and sword on her lap.

"How much of my classes have I missed?"

"Not a thing that can't be made up quickly, 'specially since you're excused from chores and Alberich's tender mercies till you're well again. If your eyes play tricks on you, we'll read to you, and everybody in the Collegium wants to loan you their notes. Fair enough?"

Talia was about to answer when a deep, somber-toned bell—one she'd never heard before—began tolling somewhere nearby.

Keren stiffened as her head snapped up on the first peal, "Damn," she said softly, but with venom, "Oh, *damn*."

"What's the matter?" Talia did not like the tense bitterness on Keren's face. "What's happened?"

"That's the Death Bell." Keren stared sightlessly out the window, tears trickling unheeded down her cheeks. "It rings when a Herald dies. It means that the bastards got another one of us. And one of the best. Ah, gods, why did it have to be poor Beltren?"

Eight

Minutes after the bell began its somber tolling, someone tapped on Talia's door; before Keren could answer, Skif stuck his head inside.

Keren lowered the blade she had aimed reflexively at the entrance.

"Keren—" Skif said hesitantly "—your brother sent me. He thought you might want to be with the others. I can watch Talia."

Keren pulled herself together with an obvious effort. "You sure? I know you *think* you're good, youngling—"

Talia didn't even notice Skif's hand moving, but suddenly there was a knife quivering in the wall not an inch from Keren's nose. Both of them stared at it in surprise.

"Huh!" was all the reply Keren made.

"If there had been a fly on your beak, I could have nipped it off without touching you," Skif said soberly, with none of his usual boastfulness. "I know I've got a long way to go in everything else, but not even Alberich can best me with these."

He held up his right hand, with a dagger that matched the first in it. "Anybody who tries forcing their way in here is going to have to get around six inches of steel in his throat."

"I'll take your word for it," Keren rose and sheathed her sword. "You may regret this—because I'll probably arrange for you to share Talia-watch from now on."

"So? I volunteered, but Ylsa wouldn't take me seriously."

"Well, I will." She passed him, waving him into the room. "And youngling? Thanks. You've got a good heart."

Skif just shrugged and pulled his knife out of the wall.

"What's going on?" Talia whispered hoarsely. "What's the Death Bell?"

Skif perched himself cross-legged on the top of her desk; his expression was unwontedly serious. "What do you want answered first?"

"The Bell."

"All right—since I don't know what you know, I'll take it from the beginning. There used to be a little temple in the Grove in Companion's Field; King Valdemar had it put up. It had a bell-tower, but not until just before he died was there a bell in it. The bell was actually installed the day before he died, but the rope to ring it hadn't been hung, and it didn't have a clapper. So you can imagine that when a strange bell was heard tolling before dawn the next morning, people were pretty startled. When they went out to look, they saw what you'd see now if you were to go out to the Field— every Companion here gathered around the tower and staring at it. When they got back to the Palace they learned what the Heralds had already known— that Valdemar was dead. The temple's long gone, but the tower is still there—and every time a Herald dies, the Death Bell tolls."

"And Keren?"

"Every Herald knows when another one dies, and whether or not it was from natural causes. You sort of start to get the sensing of it around about your third year—sooner if your Gift is strong; I haven't got it yet. It hurts, they tell me, like something of yourself has died—the ones with the strongest Gifts may know details of what happened. You always know who, if you're a full Herald, and a little of how, as soon as the Bell begins to ring. Most of 'em find it easier to be together for a while, especially if it was someone you knew really well. That's why Herald Teren sent me—Beltren was one of Keren's year-mates."

There wasn't much Talia could say in reply. She and Skif stared gloomily out the windows for a long time, listening to the Bell; the tolling that sounded like the cold iron was sobbing.

Word on what had actually befallen Beltren did not reach the Collegium for several days. When news came, it was not good. Someone or something had ambushed him, and sent both Beltren and his Companion over the edge of a cliff. There were no clues as to who the murderer was—and if the Queen knew why it had happened, she kept her own council.

The atmosphere became more desolate and oppressive, with every passing day. Talia's newly-awakened sensitivity left her painfully aware of it, and the weakness she was prey to as she recovered did not make bearing the brunt of this easy.

Skif (who, true to Keren's threat, was now sharing guard-duty with the three adults) did his best to cheer her with Collegium gossip and more of his absurd stories, but even he could not completely counteract the effect of the mourning of all those around her.

Finally the Queen gave orders—and the Heralds flew like the arrows they were named for to obey. Talia never did hear details, but the murderer was caught—though not even the news that he had been found and condemned by Queen and Council did anything to ease the atmosphere of pain, for Beltren had been universally held in high regard by the members of the Circle.

The entirety of the Collegium as well as those of the Circle at Court assembled for the memorial service several weeks later. As was all too often the case, there was no body to bury, and the service was held at the single pillar that held the names of all those Heralds who had sacrificed themselves for Monarch and Kingdom.

Talia had only just been allowed to leave her bed, but something impelled her to beg the Healer, Devan, to permit her to attend the memorial. Impressed by the urgency she was obviously feeling, he overrode his own better judgment and agreed that she should be allowed to go. She had not confided how strongly she was being affected by the mourning about her to anyone yet; she had been hoping that Keren had been right and it would go away. And having been accused of having an overactive imagination more than once, she couldn't be entirely sure how much of this she might be conjuring out of her own mind.

Nothing of the ceremony was any too clear in her mind; everything seemed to be washed away in a flood of sadness and loss. She stood through it in a fog of pain, sure only now that she was in no way inflicting any of this on herself. When those assembled had begun dispersing, a locus of agony sharpened and defined.

It was the Queen.

Talia had not been this close to Selenay since her first day at the Collegium; she would not have dared to disturb her except that the Queen's emotional turmoil drew on her with an irresistible attraction. She approached shyly, as quietly as she could.

"Your Majesty?" she said hesitantly. "It's Talia."

"*I* sent him to his death," Selenay replied as if in answer to some internal question. "I knew what I was sending him into, and I sent him anyway. I murdered him, just as surely as if it had been my hand that pushed him to his death."

The pain and self-accusation of the Queen's words triggered something within Talia, something that impelled her to reply. "Why are you trying to convince yourself that he didn't know the kind of danger he was in?" she said, knowing that her own words were nothing less than the stark truth, but not knowing *how* she knew. "He was fully aware, and he went despite that knowledge. He wasn't *expecting* to die, but he knew it was a possibility. Majesty, we *all* know it can happen, and at any time. You had no choice either—wasn't it absolutely imperative that someone be sent?"

"Yes," the word came reluctantly.

"And wasn't he the best—perhaps the only—Herald for the task?"

"He was the only Herald with any hope of convincing the people of the area to part with the information I needed. He worked as my agent there for three years, and they knew and trusted him."

"And did he not succeed in sending you that information? Was there any substitute for it?"

"What he sent to me will save us a war," Selenay sighed. "Even among rulers blackmail sometimes works wonders, and I'll blackmail Relnethar with a cheerful heart if it will keep him off our borders and within his own. Lady knows I'd tried every other way to get it—"

"Then you had no choice at all; you acted for the good of *all* our people. It's the kind of decision that you and only you can make. Majesty, in Orientation class they told me in good plain terms that it is quite likely that a Herald will perish, perhaps horribly, before he ever has to think of retiring because of age. They tell everyone that— but it's never stopped anyone from becoming a Herald. It's something we *have* to do—just as making hard choices is something you have to do. And behind all of it, I think, is that we all have to choose to do what we *know* to be right; you as Queen, the rest of us as your Heralds. I *know* if Beltren could be standing here right at this moment, he'd tell you that the choice you made was the only one you could have made."

The Queen stared at Talia, her eyes bright with unshed tears, but Talia could feel the agony within her easing. "Child," she said slowly, "you very nearly perished yourself because of my actions—or lack of them. Can you stand there and tell me you would have been glad to die?"

"No," Talia said frankly. "I was awfully afraid—I didn't want to die, and I still don't, but if it happens, it happens. I made the choice to become a Herald, and if I knew I was going to die tomorrow, I still wouldn't choose otherwise."

"Oh, Talia—child—" the Queen sat abruptly on the side of the memorial, and Talia hesitantly touched her, then sat beside her and put one arm around her shoulders, feeling odd and a little awkward, and yet impelled to do so nevertheless. It was apparently the correct action, as Selenay suddenly relaxed long enough to shed a few, bitter tears, allowing herself the brief luxury of leaning on a strength outside her own.

"How have you become so wise, so young?" she said at last, composing herself. "Not yet even a year at the Collegium—yet, truly Queen's Own. Talamir would approve of you, I think. . . ." She rose gracefully, her face once again a serene mask. Talia sensed that while she still mourned, the burden of guilt had been lifted from her shoulders. "But you are not yet well, little one—and I see your keepers looking for you. And I must face the Ambassador of Karse, and dance in diplomatic circles about him until he knows with absolute certainty that I have the proof of his lord's double dealings. Thank you, Queen's Own."

She turned and walked swiftly back to the Palace, as Keren and Teren approached.

"When you didn't come back with the rest, we began to worry," Teren half-scolded. "Healer Devan wants you back in bed."

"You look like someone forced you through a sieve, lovey," Keren observed. "What's wrong?"

"The Queen—she was so guilty-feeling, so unhappy. I could feel it and I *had* to do something about it—"

"So you went to talk to her," Keren nodded with satisfaction at her twin. "All the right words just seemed to flow from you, right?"

"How did you guess?"

"Lovey, that's what makes *you* Queen's Own, and the rest of us ordinary Heralds. Grandfather used to claim he never knew what he was going to say to the King beforehand, yet it was always exactly the right thing. Trust those instincts."

"Grandfather?" Talia asked in a daze.

"Talamir was our grandfather," Teren explained. "I think he secretly hoped one of us would succeed him."

"Well I didn't," Keren replied firmly. "After seeing the kind of hell he went through, I wouldn't have the job under any circumstances. I don't envy you, Talia, not at all."

"I agree," Teren nodded. "Talia, you still look a bit wobbly. Will you be all right now?"

"I . . . think so," she said slowly, beginning to feel a bit better now that the overwhelming burden of the sorrows of the rest of the Heralds was dissipating.

"Let's get you back to your room then, and I'll have a little talk with Dean Elcarth. If nothing else, we should show you how to shield yourself so you don't take on more of other people's feelings than you can handle. If your Gift hasn't faded by now, it's not going to," Keren said as her twin nodded his agreement.

Keren stayed with her until Elcarth arrived, then left the two of them alone. Talia sat carefully on the edge of her chair, concentrating on what Elcarth had to say, afraid she might miss something vital. She was beginning to think she couldn't bear much more of this business of carrying other people's emotions and thoughts around inside of her. If there was a way to stop it from happening, she most devoutly wanted to learn it!

But this "shielding" was a simple trick to learn—for which Talia was very grateful.

"Think of a wall," Elcarth told her. "A wall all around you and between you and everyone else. See it and *feel* it—and believe that nothing and no one can reach you through it."

Talia concentrated with all her strength, and for the first time in days, she felt a blessed sense of relief from the pressure of minds around her. With its lessening her own confidence in the "shield" grew—and the shield grew stronger in response. At last Elcarth was satisfied that nothing could penetrate what she had built, and left her to her own devices.

"Don't ever hesitate to drop it, though," the Dean urged her. "Especially if you suspect danger—your Gift may give you the best warning you're likely to get."

Talia made a thoughtful gesture of acquiescence, thinking how, if she'd been able to detect the maliciousness of her tormentors, she'd have been warned enough to have gotten help with them long before things had come to so nearly fatal a conclusion.

A few days later the Healer pronounced her fit, and she returned to her normal round of classes. Outwardly her life seemed little different—yet there were some profound changes.

The first thing that had changed was her bond with Rolan; it was so much stronger now than it had been before the river incident that there was no comparison.

She discovered this not long after she had learned how to shield out the emotions of others.

She was sitting in a quiet corner of the Library; she had just finished her book and had closed it with a feeling of satisfaction, as it was one of the histories that concluded on a positive note. There wasn't enough time for her to start a new book before the next class, so she was simply sitting for a moment with her eyes closed, letting her mind wander where it would. Almost inevitably it wandered toward Rolan.

Suddenly she was seeing a corner of Companion's Field, but her view was curiously flat and distorted. There seemed to be a blind spot straight ahead of her, her peripheral vision was doubled, and she seemed to be several inches higher than she actually stood. There was that feeling of slight disorientation that she had come to associate with seeing through the eyes and memories of others—

Then a start of surprise, followed by an outpouring of love and welcome. It was then that she realized that she was sharing Rolan's thoughts.

From that moment on she had only to think briefly of him to know exactly where he was and what he was doing, and if she closed her eyes she could even see what he was seeing. Thoughts and images—though never words—flowed between them constantly. An emotion so profound it transcended every meaning Talia had ever heard attached to the word "love" tied them together now, and she understood how it was that Heralds and their Companions so seldom survived one another when death broke that bond that held them together.

It was shortly after this that her relationship with the Queen underwent a similarly abrupt change.

Selenay had sought the sanctuary of the barren gardens—a place where, with the last of winter still upon them, it was unlikely that she would be disturbed. Talia had found herself pulled inexorably to those same gardens; on seeing the Queen pacing the paths, she understood why.

"Majesty?" she called out softly. Selenay shaded her eyes against the weak afternoon sunlight and smiled when she saw who it was that had called her.

"Another lover of desolation? I thought *I* was the only person who found dead gardens attractive."

"But the potential is here for more. You only have to look ahead to what will be in the spring," Talia pointed out, falling into step beside the Queen. "It's not so much desolate and dead here as it is dormant. It's just a matter of seeing the possibilities."

"Seeing the possibilities—long-term instead of immediacy," Selenay became very thoughtful, then began to brighten visibly. "Yes! That's it *exactly!* Little one, you've done it again—and I have to get back to the Council. Thank you—"

She strode rapidly away, leaving Talia to wonder just what it was that she'd done.

But as time passed, such incidents became more and more commonplace. And as winter became spring, it was less often the case that Talia sought the Queen's company as it was the other way around. Selenay actively hunted her out at irregular intervals; they would talk together, sometimes for hours, sometimes only for a moment or two. Talia would find the words to express the things she knew, somehow, that the Queen needed to hear, and Selenay would take her leave, comforted or energized. Talia often thought of herself, with no little bewilderment, as two people; one, the ordiniary, everyday Talia, no more wise than the next half-grown adolescent, the other, some incredibly knowledgeable and ancient being who only manifested herself in Selenay's presence.

With this assumption of her duty as Queen's Own, Talia was reminded of yet another. The apparent reason that Rolan had Chosen her, after all, was because she was supposedly the one person who could civilize the Brat—yet in all this time she had seen Elspeth only once and that when she had first arrived. It was true that until now she had been too busy adjusting herself to the Collegium to have any time or emotional energy to spare for dealing with the child. Still, that wasn't the case anymore. It was definitely time to do something about the Heir-presumptive.

"Glory! What a long face!" Skif exclaimed, plopping himself down in the chair next to Talia in the Library, and earning himself a black look or two for disturbing the silence from the trainees sitting nearby. "What's the matter, or should I not ask?" he continued with less volume.

"It's the Brat. I'm supposed to be doing something about her, but I can't get anywhere near her!" Talia replied with gloom and self-disgust.

"Oh, so? And what's keeping you away?"

"Her nurse—I think. The foreigner, Hulda—I haven't once seen the old one. I can't prove anything, though. She seems very conscientious; the very model of respect and cooperation, yet somehow whenever I try to get anywhere near the child, *she's* there, too, with something Elspeth absolutely *has* to be doing right that very moment. And it's all very logical, all quite correct. It's just that it's happened too many times now."

" 'Once is chance, twice is coincidence,' " Skif quoted. " 'But three times is conspiracy.' Has it gotten to the conspiracy stage yet?"

"It got to that point a long time ago. But I can't see how I can prove it, or where everything fits in—"

He bounded to his feet and tapped her nose with an outstretched finger. "You just leave the proving it to good old Sneaky Skif. And as for figuring out how everything fits together, I should think Herald Jadus would be the best source for information. He's been stuck here at the Collegium since the Tedrel Wars were over; the servants tell him *everything,* and he's got the thought-sensing Gift to boot. If anyone would know the pieces of the puzzle that go back forever, he would. So ask him—you see him every night."

"I never thought of Jadus," Talia replied, beginning to smile. "But Skif—is this likely to get you into trouble?"

"Only if I get caught—in which case I'll have a good story ready. And you'd better be ready to back me up!"

"But—"

"Never you mind, but! Life's been too quiet around here. Nothing to get my blood stirred up. Besides, I don't intend to do this for nothing, you know. You owe me, lady-o."

"Skif," she replied unthinkingly, "If you can help me prove what I suspect, you can name your reward!"

"Thank you," he grinned, waggling his bushy eyebrows in what he obviously *thought* was a lascivious fashion, but which fell a lot closer to absurdity. "I'll do just that!"

Talia succeeded in sparing his feelings by smothering her laughter as he bounced jauntily out.

"Elspeth's nurse?" Jadus was so startled by Talia's question that he actually set My Lady down. "Talia, why in the name of the Nine would old Melidy want to keep you away from Elspeth?"

"It's not Melidy that's doing it, it's the other one," Talia replied, "Hulda. Melidy really doesn't seem to do very much, actually; she mostly just knits and nods. Hulda seems to be the one giving all the orders."

"That puts another complexion on things entirely," Jadus mused. "Youngling, how much do you know about the current situation—the background, I should say?"

"Not one thing—well, almost nothing. Selenay told me that her marriage with Elspeth's father wasn't a good one, and that she felt that a lot of Elspeth's Bratliness is due to her own neglect. And since nobody mentions him, I supposed her husband was either dead or vanished—or banished. That's about all."

"Hm. In that case, I'd better tell you starting from the Tedrel War. That was when Selenay's father was killed."

"That was at least fifteen years ago, wasn't it?"

"Just about. All right; Karse intended to overrun us without actually declaring war. They hired the entire nation of Tedrel Mercenaries to do their dirty work for them. The King was killed just as the last battle was won—and if I'd just been a little more agile he'd still be alive—" he sighed, and guilt washed briefly over his features. "Well, I wasn't. Selenay had only just completed her internship when the war broke out; she was duly crowned, completed the work of mopping up the last of the Tedrel, and settled down to rule. As was to be expected, anyone of rank with a younger son to dispose of sent him to the Court. One of those visiting sons was Prince Karathanelan."

"With a name like that, he could only have been from Rethwellan."

Jadus smiled, "They *are* rather fond of mouth-filling nominatives, aren't they? He was, indeed. He was also almost impossibly handsome, cultured, intelligent—Selenay was instantly infatuated, and there was nothing anyone could say that would make her change her mind about him. They were wedded less than a month after he'd first arrived. The trouble began soon after that."

"Why should there have been trouble?"

"Because he wanted something Selenay could never, by law, give him—the throne. Had he been Chosen, he could have reigned as equal consort, but no Companion would have anything to do with him. Selenay's Caryo even kicked him once, as I recall. He had brought a number of landless, titled friends with him, and the Lord knows we have unclaimed territory enough, so Selenay had granted them estates. He didn't see why she couldn't just as easily give him rank at least equal with hers."

"But why didn't he understand? I mean, everyone knows the law is the law for everybody."

"Except that outKingdom the monarch's word frequently *is* the law; he wouldn't or couldn't accept that such is not the case here. When he couldn't get what he wanted by gift, he began scheming to take it by force, under the mistaken assumption that it was his right to do so."

Talia shook her head in disbelief.

"At any rate, he and his friends, and even some of our own people, began plotting a way to remove Selenay and set him in her place. And to allay any suspicions, he reconciled with Selenay and had his own nurse travel here to help Melidy with Elspeth. I don't think that *his* intention was to kill Selenay—I really do believe he only intended to hold her until she agreed to abdicate in his favor or Elspeth's with him as Regent. I do know for a fact that his friends were far more ruthless. Their intention was assassination, and they planned it for when Selenay was alone, exercising Caryo. It might have worked, too—except for Alberich's Gift."

"Alberich has a Gift? I never guessed. . . ."

Jadus nodded; "It's hard to think of Alberich as a Herald, isn't it?"

"It is," Talia confessed. "He doesn't wear Whites. I scarcely ever *see* Kantor, with or without him. And that accent and the way he acts; he's so strange—where is he from, anyway? Nobody ever told me."

"Karse," Jadus said to her surprise, "Which is why you'll never hear a Herald use that old saying 'The only things that come out of Karse are bad weather and brigands.' He was a captain in their army—the youngest ever to hold that rank, or so

I'm told. Unfortunately for him—though not for us—his Gift, when it works, is very powerful. It caused him to slip a time or two too often, to seem to know far more than he should have, especially about the future. His own people—his own company of the army—were hunting him as a witch because of that. They had him cornered in a burning barn when Kantor galloped through the flames to save him. Well, that's another story and you should ask him to tell it to you some time; the pertinent thing to this story is that Alberich's Gift is Foresight. Without telling Selenay why, he insisted on accompanying her, along with a dozen of his best pupils. Every one of the ambushers was killed; among them was the Prince. The official story is that he was killed in a hunting accident along with his friends."

"I suppose that's marginally true. They *were* hunting Selenay."

Jadus grimaced. "Child, you have a macabre sense of humor."

"But didn't his own people have anything to say about such a flimsy tale?"

"They might have, except that circumstances had changed. As it happened, their King had since died and the Prince's brother was reigning, and there had been no love lost between the two of them. The new King knew what his power-hungry sibling was like and was just as pleased that the scandal was shoved beneath the rug so neatly. Well, after that Selenay was kept very busy in attempting to ferret out those conspirators who hadn't actually been among the ambushers—and to tell you the truth, I still don't think she's found all of them. I'll tell you now what I've suspected for some time—Talamir *was* murdered because he was about to propose to the Council that Elspeth be fostered out to some of his remote relations. They were isolated folk of very minor noble rank. They weren't going to put up with any nonsense from a child, and they were isolated enough that there was no chance Elspeth would be able to run away. But they are stubborn folk and Talamir was the only one likely to be able to persuade them to take the Brat on, and when he died, the plan was given up. But that all came later—after Selenay had been so busy that she had very little time to spare for Elspeth. Up until two years ago none of us had any inkling of trouble—we just turned around one day, and the sweet, tractable child had become the Royal Brat."

"What's all this got to do with Hulda?"

"That is something I can't tell you; I'd been under the impression that it was Melidy who was in charge of the nursery, but from what you've observed that doesn't seem to be the case. That's exceedingly disturbing since I would have bet any amount of money that Melidy was the equal of anyone, up to and including Alberich! I can't picture her just handing everything over to a foreigner."

"Something's changed drastically, then," Talia mused. "And it looks like it's up to me to find out what."

"I fear so, youngling," Jadus sighed, seeing the determination in her eyes. "I fear so."

Another change in Talia's life was in the way the other students treated her. Hitherto they had assumed Talia's reticence was due to a wish for privacy and had honored that wish. Now that they knew it was simply due to shyness, they went out of their way to include her in their gossip and pranks.

Sessions in the sewing room were no longer a time for Talia to hide behind a mound of mending. The change was signaled one afternoon when there were no boys sharing the task.

Nerrissa was the current target of teasing about her most recent amorous conquest. She was being quite good-humored about it, but the jibes were getting a little tiresome. She looked around for a possible victim to switch the attention to, and her eye lighted on Talia.

"Ridiculous! And old news as well," she replied to the most recent sally. "Besides, there's somebody here who's managed to captivate a lad who's a *lot* harder to catch than Baern is."

A chorus of "Who?" greeted the revelation.

"What?" Nerrissa's eyes glinted with mischief. "You mean none of you noticed *anything?* Bright Havens, you must be denser than I thought. I would have figured that *someone* else would have seen that our Skif's attentions to Talia are a great deal warmer than brotherly of late."

"Oh, *really?*" Sheri turned to look at Talia, who was blushing hotly. "I thought you were my friend, Talia! You might have told *me!*"

Talia blushed even redder and stammered out a disclaimer.

"Oh, my—" Sheri teased. "So vehement! Sounds to me a little too vehement."

After a while, Talia managed to stop blushing and to give as good as she got. From then on, her relationships with her fellow students were a great deal easier.

Meals were another time when she could forget the problems with getting closer to Elspeth. There had always been a certain amount of pranking about in the kitchen; Mero saw to it that their hands were always too full for them to get into mischief, but he put no such rein on their mouths. Mero himself was a favored target, and Talia, with her innocent face, was now the one generally picked to try and fool him.

"Haven't you forgotten something, Mero?"

"I? *I?* Talia, you are surely mistaken."

"I don't know, Mero," one of the others chimed in. "It seems to me that the salt cellar is missing—"

"By the Book! It is! What could I have done with the cursed thing?" He searched for it with feigned panic, watching out of the corner of his eye while they passed it from hand to hand, grinning hugely. At last Talia got it back again and placed it prominently on the table while his back was turned.

"Ha!" he shouted, pouncing on it. "Now I *know* I looked there before—" he stared directly at Talia, who shrugged guilelessly.

"Kobolds," he muttered, while they smothered giggles. "There must be kobolds in my kitchen. What's this place coming to?"

Five minutes later he got his revenge.

"Would you say, young Talia, that you are a fairly good hand in the kitchen?" he asked, as the hoist went up with the precious salt-cellar on it.

"I—guess so."

"And would you say that you know how to prepare just about any common dish of your Hold people?" he persisted.

"Definitely," she replied injudiciously.

"Ah, good! Then certainly you can show me what to do with *this*." He dropped an enormous gnarled and knobbly root in front of her.

Talia, who had never seen anything like it in her life, coughed and tried to temporize, while Mero's grin got wider and the rest of the kitchen helpers giggled.

Finally (since it was evident that he wasn't going to feed them unless she admitted her ignorance or told him how to prepare it) she confessed to being defeated.

Mero chuckled hugely and took the thing away, replacing it with their lunch. "What *is* it, anyway?" Griffon asked.

"A briar burl," Mero laughed. "I doubt Talia could have done anything with it that would please a human palate—but she might have managed a gourmet meal for a termite-ant!"

Meals themselves were high points of the day. She had a permanent seat now at the second table, sandwiched between Sherrill and Jeri, across from Skif, Griffon, and Keren. To the eternal amusement of the girls and their teacher, both Griffon and Skif insisted on cosseting her, Griffon with the air of a big brother, Skif's intentions obviously otherwise although he attempted to counterfeit Griffon's. Griffon wasn't fooled by Skif in the least.

"Watch yourself, you—" he growled under his breath. "You treat my Talia right, or I'll feed you to the river with your best clothes on!"

Sherrill and the others overheard this "subtle" threat, and their faces puckered with the effort not to laugh.

Skif retaliated by picking Griffon's pockets bare even of lint without the larger boy even being aware of the fact.

"More greens, brother?" he asked innocently, passing Griffon a plate containing his possessions.

Talia had to be saved from choking to death as she attempted to keep from giggling at the dumbfounded look on Griffon's face.

That night Talia was on the receiving end of unmerciful teasing when they all got their baths at the end of the day.

"Oh, Talia—" Jeri piled her hair on the top of her head and simpered at her in imitation of Skif. "Would you like a—mushroom? Take two! Take a hundred!"

"Oh, thank you, no, dear, *dear* Skif—" Sherrill batted her eyelashes coyly at "Skif." "I'd much rather have a—pickle."

"I'll just bet you would, wouldn't you?" "Skif" replied, with a leer.

About this time the real Talia was torn between hilarity and outraged embarrassment. "I don't know where you get your filthy minds—" she said, attacking both of them with a bar of soap and a sponge, "But they plainly need a good scrubbing!"

The episode degenerated at that point into a ducking and splashing match that soaked every towel in the room and brought down the wrath of the Housekeeper on all three of them.

"Hist!" someone hissed at Talia from behind

the bushes next to the entrance to the gardens. She jumped, remembering all too well the misery of the months previous—then relaxed as she realized the whisperer was Skif.

"What on earth are you doing in there?" she asked, getting down on hands and knees, and seeing him in a kind of tunnel between two planted rows of hedges.

"What I told you I'd do—spying on the Brat. There's something I want to show you. Squeeze on in here and follow me!"

She looked at him a bit doubtfully, then saw that he was completely serious, and did as he asked. They crawled through the prickly tunnel for some time before Skif stopped and Talia all but bumped into him. He signed at her to be quiet, and parted the twigs on one side, just enough for both of them to peer through.

Elspeth and her two nurses, Hulda and Melidy, were no more than a few feet away. They had no problem listening in on their conversation.

"Oh, no, dear," Hulda was saying gently. "It's quite out of the question. Your rank is *much* too high for you to be associating with Lord Delphor's children. You *are* the Heir to the Throne, after all."

Talia bit her lip angrily as Elspeth's face fell. Old Melidy seemed to wake up a little from her half-doze. Her wrinkled face was creased with a faint frown as she seemed to be struggling to remember something.

"Hulda, that . . ." she began slowly, " . . . that just doesn't seem *right* somehow. . . ."

"What doesn't seem right, dear?" Hulda asked with artificial sweetness.

"Elspeth isn't . . . she can't. . . ."

"Be expected to know these things, I know. Now don't you worry about a thing. Just drink your medicine like a dear love, and I'll take care of everything." Hulda poured a tiny glass of something red and sticky-looking and all but forced it into Melidy's hand. The old woman gave up the struggle for thought and obediently drank it down. Not long afterward she fell asleep again.

Skif motioned that they should leave, and they backed out of the hedgerow on all fours.

"That's what I wanted you to see," he said, as they exited the hedge in a distant part of the garden. "Hold still, you've got twigs in your hair." He began picking them out carefully.

"So've you. And leaves. She must be drugging Melidy, and keeping her drugged. Witch! But how did the old woman get into a state where she *allowed* herself to be drugged in the first place?"

"You've got me; *I* can't hazard a guess. Ask Jadus, maybe he knows. Want me to keep watching?"

"If you don't mind. I want to know if she's doing this on her own or at someone else's direction. And I want to know what else she's telling the child."

"Oh, I don't mind; this is fun! It's like being back on the streets again, except that now I'm not in danger of losing a hand or being hungry all the time," he grinned.

"Oh, Skif—" she stopped, unsure of what to say next. Then, greatly daring, she leaned forward on an impulse and kissed his cheek lightly, blushed, and scampered away.

Skif stared after her in surprise, one hand raised to touch the spot she'd kissed.

* * *

Jadus didn't know anything about the state of Melidy's health, but he directed her to one of the Healers who would.

"Melidy *was* ill about two years ago," she said thoughtfully. "Do you know what a 'brainstorm' is?"

"Isn't that where an old person suddenly can't move or talk—maybe even falls unconscious for a long time—and then gets better, slowly?"

The Healer nodded. "That's what happened to Melidy. She *seemed* to have recovered completely, at least to me. I might have been wrong, though. Lady knows we aren't infallible."

"Maybe you weren't wrong—or maybe she was affected in some way that you wouldn't have noticed," Talia replied, sounding much more adult than she appeared, and making the Healer's eyes widen in surprise. "Keldar's mother had a brainstorm after she brought her to live at our Hold. She seemed completely all right—except that you had to be very careful what you said to her because she'd believe *anything* you told her, no matter how absurd it was. That might have been what happened to Melidy."

And if it was, she thought grimly, *she'd have been easy prey for Hulda.*

"As for that medicine you saw Hulda giving her, I never prescribed anything like that for her, but it might be a folk remedy, or one of the other Healers might have ordered it for her. I can check if you'd like. . . ."

Talia belatedly realized that this might not be a wise idea. She didn't want Hulda alerted if the woman *was* up to something—and she didn't want her embarrassed if she wasn't.

"No, that's all right, thank you. It probably is just a folk remedy. In fact, now that I think of it, it looked a lot like a syrup Keldar used to give her mother for aching joints."

The Healer smiled, with obvious relief. "Melidy does have arthritis, and unfortunately there isn't much we can do for her other than try and ease the pain. The potion might very well be one of ours. I'm glad the other nurse seems to be taking care of her, then. Is there anything else I can do for you?"

"No—thank you," Talia replied. "You've answered everything I needed to ask."

But, she thought as she walked slowly back to her room, *you raised a lot more questions than you answered.*

Nine

"If only I could go back in time. . . ."

"If only you could *what?*" Skif asked, looking up from the book he'd been studying. Talia was perched in his open window, staring out at the moonlit trees, her own mind plainly not on study.

"I said, 'if only I could go back in time,' " she repeated. "I'd give half an arm to know if there was anyone besides Elspeth's father involved in bringing Hulda here—especially since she arrived after he was dead. But the only way I could find that out is to go back in time."

"Not—quite—"

Skif's expression was speculative, and Talia waited for him to finish the thought.

"There's the immigration records—everything about anyone who comes in from outKingdom is in them. If Hulda had any other sponsors, they'd be in there. And it seems to me there's something in the laws about immigrants having to have three sponsors to live here permanently. One would have been the Prince, and one Selenay—but the third might prove very interesting. . . ."

"Where are these records kept? Can anybody get at them?" Talia's voice was full of eagerness.

"They're kept right here at the palace, in the Provost-Marshal's office. Keeping those records is one of his duties. But as for getting at them—" Skif made a face "—we can't, not openly. Well, *you* could, but you'd have to invoke authority as Queen's Own, and Hulda would be sure to hear of it."

"Not a good idea," Talia agreed. "So we can't get at them openly—but?"

"But I could get at them. It's no big deal, just—"

"Just that The Book is there, too," Talia finished for him. "Well, you haven't had any misdemeanors down in The Book for nearly a year, have you?"

"Hell, no! You've been keeping me too busy!" he grinned, then the grin faded. "Still, if I got caught, they'd figure I was in there to alter The Book. Orthallen doesn't like me at all; I'm like a burr under his saddle. I don't grant him proper respect, I don't act like a sober Heraldic Trainee. He'd love the chance to really slap me down." He looked at Talia's troubled face, then his grin revived. "Oh, hell, what can he do to me, anyway? Confine me to the Collegium grounds? I haven't been off 'em since I met you, almost! I'll do it, by the gods!"

There was something wrong—there was something very wrong. Skif wasn't late—not yet—but Talia suddenly had the feeling that he was in a lot of trouble, and more than he could handle. And tonight was the night he was supposed to be getting into those immigration records. . . .

Although she had no clear idea of what she was going to do, Talia found herself running through the halls of the Collegium—then the halls of the

Palace itself. It was only when she neared Selenay's quarters that she paused her headlong flight, waited until she had her breath back, and then approached the door of the Queen's private chambers shyly. The guard there knew her well; he winked at her, and entered the door to announce her. She could hear the vague murmur of voices, then he opened the door again and waved her inside.

She drew in a trembling breath and prayed that *something* would guide her, and went in. The door closed quietly behind her.

Selenay was sitting at the worktable, flushed and disturbed-looking. Elcarth, Keren, and the Seneschal's Herald, Kyril, were standing like a screen between Talia and something behind them. Standing between Selenay and the Heralds was Lord Orthallen. Talia's heart sank. It *was* Skif, then. She had to save him. He'd been caught, and it must have been much worse than he thought. But how was she going to be able to get him off?

"Majesty—" she heard herself saying, "—I—I've got something to confess."

Selenay looked confused, and Talia continued, "I—I asked Skif to do something for me. It wasn't—quite—legal."

As Selenay waited, Talia continued in a rush, "I wanted him to get the Holderkin records for me."

"The Holderkin records?" Selenay repeated, puzzled. "But why?"

Talia had no notion where these ideas were coming from, but apparently they were good ones. She *hated* the notion of lying, but she daren't tell the truth, either. "I—I wanted to make sure I wasn't in them anymore." To her own surprise, she felt hot, angry tears starting to make her eyes smart. "They didn't want me—well, I don't want them, not any of them, not ever! Skif told me Sensholding could claim Privilege Tax when I earn my Whites, and I don't want them to have it!"

Now she was really crying with anger, flushed, and believing every word she'd told them herself. Selenay was smiling a smile bright with relief; Elcarth looked bemused, Keren vindicated, Kyril slightly amused, and Orthallen—Talia was startled by his expression. Orthallen looked for one brief instant like a man who has been cheated out of something he thought surely in his grasp. Then he resumed his normal expression—a cool, impassive mask, and try as she might, Talia couldn't get past it.

"You see, Orthallen, I told you there'd be a simple explanation," Elcarth was saying then, as the Heralds moved apart, and Talia could see who it was that they had been screening from her view. She wasn't surprised to see Skif, white and tense, sitting in a chair as if he'd been glued there.

"Then why wouldn't the boy tell us himself?" Orthallen asked coldly.

"Because I didn't want Talia in trouble, too!" Skif said in a surly tone of voice. "I *told* you I wasn't after The Book, so what business was it of yours what I did want? *You* aren't the Provost-Marshal!"

"Skif," Kyril said mildly, "He may not be the Provost-Marshal, but Lord Orthallen is entitled to a certain amount of respect from you."

"Yes, sir," Skif mumbled and looked steadfastly at his feet.

"Well, now that this matter seems to have cleared itself up, shall we let the miscreants go?" Selenay smiled slightly. "Talia, the next time you want something in the records, just ask Kyril or myself. And we'll make sure you aren't listed in the Census as Holderkin anymore, if that's what you want. But—well, I still don't quite understand why you didn't come to me in the first place."

Talia knew from the tightness of the skin of her face that she had gone from red to white. "I—it was selfish. UnHeraldlike. I didn't want anybody else to know. . . ."

Elcarth had crossed the space between them and placed an arm around her shoulders. "You're only human, little one—and your kin don't deserve any kindness from you after the way they've disowned you. Skif—" he held out his hand to the boy, who stood slowly, and came to stand beside Talia, taking one of her hands and staring at Orthallen defiantly. "—you and Tarlia go back to your rooms, why don't you? You've had a long night. Don't do this again, younglings, but—well, we understand. Now get along."

Skif all but dragged Talia from the room.

"Good gods—how the *hell* did you think of that? You were great! *I* started to believe you! And how did you know I was up to my ears in trouble?"

"I don't know—it just sort of came," Talia replied, "And I just knew you were in for it. What happened? How did you get caught?"

"Sheer bad luck," Skif said ruefully, slowing their headlong rush down the hall. "Selenay needed some of the Census reports and Orthallen came after them. He saw my light in the Provost-Marshal's office, and caught me red-handed. Gods, gods, was I stupid! It wouldn't have happened if

I'd been paying any attention at all to the sounds from the corridor."

"What was he going to do to you?"

"He was trying to get me suspended. He couldn't get me expelled unless Cymry repudiated me, but—well, he was trying to get me sent off to clean stables for the Army for the next four years—'until I learned what honest work means,' he said."

"Could—could he have done that?"

"Unfortunately, he could. I've got one too many marks in The Book. There's an obscure Collegium rule covering that, and he found out about it, somehow. If I didn't know better, I'd say he's been *looking* for a way to get me."

"You'd better stop helping me, then. . . ."

By now they were outside Talia's door.

"Be damned if I will! This is so frustrating—I'd just found Hulda's records, too! Well, we'll just have to give up on those, and stick with what we've been doing. But there's no way I'm going to let this stop me!"

He stopped, and gave her a quick hug, then pushed her toward her door. "Go on, get some sleep. You look like you could use it, and I feel like somebody's been using me for pells!"

Talia was studying alone in her room one night, when there was a light tapping on her door. She opened it—to find a black, demonic looking creature on the other side.

A hand clamped over her mouth before she could shriek, and the thing dragged her back inside, kicking the door closed behind it.

"Ssh! Don't yell—it's me, Skif!" the thing admonished her in a hoarse whisper.

He took his hand away from her mouth gingerly, ready to clamp it down again if she screamed.

She didn't; just stared at him with huge, round eyes. "Skif—what are you trying to *do* to me?" she said finally. "I nearly died of fright! Why are you rigged out like that?"

"Why do you think? You don't go climbing around in the restricted parts of the Palace dressed in Grays—and I'm a bit too young to look convincing in Whites. Get your breath back and calm yourself down because tonight you're coming with me."

"Me? But—"

"Don't argue, just get into these." He handed her a tight-fitting shirt and breeches of dusty black. "Good thing you're my size, or nearly. And don't ask me where I got them, or why, 'cause I can't tell you." He waited patiently while she laced herself into the garments, then handed her a box of greasy black soot. "Rub this anywhere there's skin showing, and don't miss anything—not even the back of your neck."

He went to her window, opened it to its widest extent, and looked down. "Good. We won't even have to go down to the ground from here."

He produced a rope and tied it around Talia's waist. "Now follow me—and do exactly what I do."

The scramble that followed was something Talia preferred not to remember in later years. Skif had them climbing from window to window across the entire length of the Collegium wing, and from there along the face of the Palace itself. Talia was profoundly grateful for the narrow ledge that ran most of the way, for she doubted she could have managed without it. At length he brought them to a halt just outside a darkened window. Talia clung with all her might to the wall, trying not to think of the drop behind her, as he peered cautiously in through the cracks in the shutter.

He seemed satisfied with what he found, for he took something out of a pouch at his belt and began working away at the chink between the two halves of the shutter. Before too long, they swung open. Skif climbed inside, and Talia followed him.

The room disclosed was bare of furniture and seemingly unused. Skif led her to the closet set into one wall, opened it, and felt along the back wall. Talia heard the scrape of wood on wood, and a pair of peepholes was revealed.

Light shone through them from the other side. Talia quickly put her eye to one, and as she did so, Skif handed her a common drinking glass. He pantomimed placing it to the wall and putting her ear against it. She did, and realized she could hear every word spoken in the other room, faintly, but clearly.

"—so at this rate, the child is unlikely ever to be Chosen, much less made Heir. You're dong quite well, quite well indeed," an unctuous baritone said with satisfaction. "Needless to say, we're quite well pleased with you."

"My lord is most gracious," Talia could see the second speaker, Hulda, but was unable to see the first, and his voice was too distorted by the glass for her to recognize it. "Shall I continue as I have gone?"

"Has the child-Herald made any further attempts at Elspeth?"

"No, my lord. She seems to have become discouraged."

"Still," the first speaker paused in thought, "we cannot take the chance. I suggest you continue your practice of telling 'bedtime tales'—you know the ones I mean."

"If my lord refers to those featuring Companions who carry off unwary children to a terrible fate, my lord can rest assured that I will do so."

"Excellent. Here is another supply of the drug for the nurse and your usual stipened."

Talia heard the chink of coins in one of the two pouches Hulda accepted.

"You will come out of this a wealthy woman, Hulda," the first speaker said as footsteps marked his retreat.

"Oh, I intend it so, my lord," Hulda said with venom to the closed door. Then she, too, turned and left the room by a second door.

Talia was too busy thinking about what she'd witnessed to worry about the return trip.

When they reached her room, Talia seized a towel and began ruthlessly scrubbing the soot away. "Is that the first time you've watched that?" she asked as she scrubbed.

"The third. The first time was by accident; I'd been following the witch and had to duck into that other room to hide from her; I found the cracks behind a patch in the closet. The second time I took a guess that the first was a regular meeting. I was right. You know something else—no, that's too far-fetched."

"What is?"

"Well, a couple of times Melidy started to refuse

that drug the witch has been feeding her, and—
well, she *did* something, I dunno what, but it made
her drink it anyway. If I didn't know better, I'd
have sworn she was using *real* magic, you know,
old magic, like in the legends, to hold power over
Melidy's mind."

"She's probably got some touch of a Gift."

"Yeah—yeah, I guess you're right."

"Here, get into these. They're too big for me, so
they might fit you." Talia handed Skif a set of
clothing.

"Why?" he asked, astonished.

"Because as soon as you're dressed, we're going
to Jadus."

Jadus was asleep when they reached his room.
Under ordinary circumstances Talia would never
have dared disturb him, but she felt the occasion
warranted her waking him. Skif opened his door
silently, and both of them slipped inside.

He roused before Talia and Skif could reach his
side, staring at them with a dagger suddenly in his
hand.

The elderly Herald had been sleeping uneasily
for several nights running and had taken to sleeping as he had in his younger days; with a knife
beneath his pillow. He woke with wary immediacy
and sat up with the knife in one hand before they
were halfway across his bedroom. He blinked in
surprise to see the two soot-streaked trainees frozen in midstep.

"Talia!" He was shocked at *her* presence—Skif,
with his penchant for pranks, he might have expected. "Why—"

"Please, sir, I'm sorry, but it's an emergency."

Jadus shook the last sleep from his head, sat up, and gathered a blanket around his shoulders. "Very well, then—I know you better than to think you'd be exaggerating. Blow up the fire, light some candles, and tell me about it."

He heard them out, Talia prompting Skif to tell his part. Before they'd told him more than a quarter of their tale, he knew that it definitely warranted the classification of "emergency." By the time they'd finished it, he was chilled.

"If I didn't know you both, I'd have sworn you were making up tales," he said finally. "And I almost wish you were."

"Sir?" Talia asked after a lengthy silence, her face drawn with exhaustion. "What should I do?"

"You, youngling? Nothing," he reached out to both of them, gathering one in each arm and hugging them, grateful for their intelligence and courage. "Talia, Skif, both of you have done far more than any of your elders have managed; I'm pleased and proud of both of you. But now you'll have to trust me to take care of the rest. There are those who need to be told who will listen to an adult, but not to the same words from the mouth of a child. I hope you'll let me speak for you?"

Skif sighed explosively. "*Let* you? Holy stars, I was afraid you were going to make me tell all this to Kyril or Selenay myself! And after getting caught going after those records, I'm afraid my credit isn't any too high with them right now. Oh, no, Herald, I'd much rather that *I* was not the bearer of the bad news. If you don't mind, I'd rather go find my bath and my bed."

"And you, Talia?"

"Please—if you would," she looked up at him with eyes full of exhaustion and entreaty. "I wouldn't know what to say. There's too many questions we can't answer. We don't know who 'my lord' is, for one thing, and if Lord Orthallen starts shouting at me, I—I—think I might cry."

"Then go, both of you. You can leave everything to me."

The two rose and padded out, and he sat in deep thought for a moment before ringing for his servant.

"Medren, I need you to have Selenay wakened; ask her to come to my room and tell her that it's quite urgent that she do so. Then do the same for the Seneschal, Herald Kyril, and Herald Elcarth. Build the fire up, and bring wine and food," he stared thoughtfully into the distance for a moment. "I have the feeling that it is going to be a very long night."

Talia heard no more about Hulda the next day—nor, in fact, did she really care to. She was content to leave the matter in the hands of the adults. The sweet smell of spring blossoms tempted her out into the garden that evening at dusk; since the banishment of the troublemakers there was no danger in roaming the grounds at any hour anymore. She was breathing in the heady scent of hicanth flowers, when she heard strangled sobs emanating from one of the garden grottoes that were so popular with couples after dark.

At first Talia thought that it must be a jilted lover or some other poor unfortunate of the same ilk that was weeping, but the sobs sounded childlike as they increased in strength. She began to feel the same compulsion to investigate them that had prompted her to the Queen's side the winter before.

She remembered what she'd been told about trusting her instincts, and acted on the impulse. She approached the grotto as noiselessly as she could, and peered inside. Lying face-down on the moss, weeping as if her heart were broken, was the Heir.

She entered and sat down beside the child. "You don't look much like a fish anymore," she said lightly, but putting as much sympathy as she could muster into her words. "You look more like a waterfall. What's wrong?"

"Th-th-they s-s-sent Hulda aw-w-way," the child wept.

"Who are 'they,' and why did they send her away?" Talia asked, not yet knowing the results of Jadus' conference.

"M-m-my mother, and that nasty Kyril, and I don't know why—she was my only, only friend, and nobody else likes me!"

"I'm sorry for you—it's awful to be lonely and alone. I know; when I was your age, they sent my best friend away to be married to a ghastly old man, and I never saw her again."

The tears stopped. "Did you cry?" the child asked with artless interest.

"I did when I was alone, but I didn't dare around other people. My elders told me that it was sinful to cry over something so unimportant. I think that that was very wrong of them because sometimes crying can make you feel better. Are you feeling a little better now?"

"Some," the child admitted. "What's your name?"

"Talia. What's yours?"

The girl's chin lifted arrogantly. "You should call me Highness."

"Not yet, I shouldn't. You're not *really* the Heir until you have a Companion and prove you can be a Herald first."

"I'm not? But—that's not what Hulda said!"

"It's true though, ask anybody. Perhaps she didn't know—or perhaps she lied to you."

"Why would she lie to me?" the child was bewildered.

"Well, I can think of at least one reason. Because she didn't want you to make friends with other children, so that she could be the only friend you had. So she made you think that you were more important than you are—and you've made other people so annoyed with you that they've left you all alone."

"How do I know that *you* aren't lying?" the girl asked belligerently.

"I'm a Herald—or I will be in a few years, and Heralds aren't allowed to lie."

The child digested this—and looked as if she found it very unpalatable indeed. "She—probably lied to me all the time then. She probably even lied to me about being my friend!" Her lip quivered, and it looked as if the weeping were about to break out anew. "Then—that means I don't have *any* friends!"

The threatened tears came, and Talia instinctively gathered the unresisting child to her. She stroked her soothingly while she cried herself to exhaustion again and produced a handkerchief to dry the sore eyes and nose when the weeping bout was over.

"You haven't any friends now, but that doesn't mean that you can't *make* friends," Talia told her. I'll be your friend, if you'd like, but you have to make me one promise."

"Tell me what I have to promise first," the child said with a hint of suspicion—which told Talia more about "nurse Hulda's" treatment of the girl than a thousand reports could have.

"The promise is very simple, but it's going to be awfully hard to keep. I'm not sure you'll be able to. . . ." Talia allowed doubt to creep into her voice.

"I can do it! I know I can! Just tell me!"

"It's in two parts. The first part is—no matter what I say to you, you won't get mad at me until you've gone away and thought about what I said. The second part is—you still won't get mad at me unless what I said wasn't true, and you can prove it."

"I promise! I promise!" she said recklessly.

"Since you're my friend now, won't you tell me your name?"

The child flushed with embarrassment. "Promise you won't laugh?"

"I promise—but I wouldn't laugh anyway."

"Hulda laughed. She said it was a stupid name," the child stared at her lap. "It's Elspeth."

"There was no reason for Hulda to laugh; you have a very nice name. It's nicer than Talia."

"Hulda said only peasants are named Elspeth."

Talia had a suspicion that she was going to grow very weary of the words "Hulda said" before too long. "That's not true; I know that for sure. There were three Queens of this Kingdom named Elspeth; Elspeth the Peacemaker, Elspeth the Wise, and Elspeth Clever-handed. You'll have a hard time living up to the name of Elspeth. Especially if you want to become the kind of person that could win a Companion and be the Heir."

Elspeth looked frightened and worried. "I—I don't know how—" she said in small voice. "And Companions—they—I'm afraid of them. Can you— help me? Please?" The last was spoken in a whisper.

"Well, first you could start by treating people nicer than you do now—and I mean *everybody*, highborn or low. If you do that, you'll start having more friends, too, and they'll be real friends who like being with you, not people who only act friendly because they think you can get them something."

"I treat people nicely!" Elspeth objected.

"Oh, really?" Talia screwed her face into an ugly scowl, and proceeded to do an imitation of the Brat at her worst. "If that's treating people nicely, I'd hate to have you mad at me! Do you really think that anyone would want to be a friend of someone like that?"

"N-no," Elspeth said in a shamed voice.

"If you want to change, you have to start by thinking about everything you say or do before you say or do it. Think about how you'd feel if someone acted like that to you," Talia reached out impulsively and hugged the forlorn child. "I can see that there's a very nice person named Elspeth sitting here, but there's an awful lot of people who can't see past the Brat. That's what they call you, you know."

"Can't my mother *make* me the Heir? Hulda said she could."

"The law is that the Heir must also be a Herald, and not even the Queen is above the law. If you're not careful, Jeri may get the title. She's got blood as good as yours, and she's already been Chosen."

The vulnerable child that looked out of Elspeth's eyes won Talia's heart completely. "You really will help me?"

"I already promised I would. I'm your friend, remember? That's what friends are for—to help each other."

Lord of Lights, what have I gotten myself in for? Talia frequently asked herself throughout the next few weeks. She found herself running from classes or chores to the Royal Nursery and back again on at least a thrice-daily basis. She had breakfast with Elspeth now, rather than with the Collegium. After supper (which was served at the Collegium at a much earlier hour than at Court) she would return. Then in the evening after supper she would spend the time until Elspeth returned to her rooms with Jadus; when Elspeth got back, they would walk in the gardens before the child's bedtime.

Hulda had vanished from her rooms before Selenay could have her taken into custody for questioning. Someone—presumably someone on the Council—had warned her in time for her to flee. Talia had little time to spare to wonder what had happened to the woman; she was too busy trying to unmake the Brat.

It was an uphill battle all the way.

                    *   *   *

Elspeth pulled temper tantrums over the smallest of things; her milk was too cold, her bath was too hot, her pillow was too soft, she didn't like the color of the clothing chosen for her. Talia put up with the first two of these displays of temper, hoping if she ignored them, Elspeth would stop. Unfortunately, this trick didn't work.

The third of Elspeth's tantrums brought Talia's first attempt at correcting her; it began when one of her maids pulled her hair while brushing it out. The child grabbed the brush and slapped the woman with it without thinking.

Talia took the brush away and handed it to the startled maid. "Hit her back," she ordered.

"But—miss, I can't—" the maid stuttered.

"I'll take the responsibility. Hit her back. As hard as she hit you."

To Elspeth's open amazement, the maid gave her a sturdy smack on the rear with the offending brush.

Elspeth opened her mouth to shriek, indulging in a full-scale fit, the kind that had always cowed others into doing things her way before.

Talia calmly picked up a glass of water and threw it in her face.

"Now," Talia said, as the child sputtered. "These are the *new* rules around here; anything you do to someone else, you'll get right back. If you can't learn to think before you act, you'll have to take what's coming to you. She didn't pull your hair on purpose, after all." She turned to the maid, "I'm sure you have other things to do than wait on an unruly little beast."

The maid recognized a dismissal when she heard one; her eyes gleamed with amusement. She could hardly wait to spread the word about the new ordering of things! "Yes, milady," she said and vanished.

"Now, since you can't be trusted not to abuse the privilege of having a servant do it, you'll just have to brush your own hair—and tend to everything else as well," Talia handed the brush back to Elspeth, who gaped in astonishment as she left.

So Elspeth struggled along without the aid of servants.

She looked like a rag-bag and knew it and hated it. The servants, on the Queen's orders, were not bothering to conceal their own enjoyment of the new state of things, nor were they backward in making it obvious that they thought Elspeth was only getting what was due her. The courtiers were worse; they smiled and acted as if nothing were wrong, but Elspeth could tell that they were inwardly laughing at her. Talia continued to spend time with her and would help her with hair or clothing—but only if she asked politely. It was an altogether unexpected and unsatisfactory state of affairs.

Elspeth's reaction was to prove she didn't care, by wrecking her nursery. She spent one very satisfying morning overturning furniture, tearing the bedclothes off the bed and heaping them in the middle of the room, breaking toys and flinging the bits about. She was sitting in the middle of the wreckage, slightly out of breath and quite satisfied, when Talia arrived.

Talia surveyed the ruins with a calm eye. "Well, she said, "I suppose you realize the nursery is going to stay this way until you clean it up."

Elspeth gaped at her; she'd expected Talia to be

angry. Then the implications began to dawn on her. "B-b-but where am I going to sleep?"

"Either in the middle of the floor or on the bare mattress, it's up to you. Either one is a better bed than Skif ever had in the street or I had on sheep-watch. For that matter, it's a better bed than I get now when I've got foal-watch."

Elspeth began to cry; Talia watched her impassively. When the tears didn't bring capitulation, Elspeth picked up a wooden block and threw it angrily at Talia's head.

That brought a response all right—but it wasn't the one Elspeth wanted. Talia dodged the missile with ease and advanced on the child with compressed lips. Before Elspeth realized what was happening, Talia had picked her up and administered three good, stinging swats to the girl's rear, then set her down again.

"Next time," Talia warned, before the real howls of outrage could begin and drown her out, "it'll be six swats."

Then she left the room (although, unknown to Elspeth, she stayed close by the door) and shut the door behind her. Elspeth cried herself nearly sick, missed dinner, and fell asleep in the tangle of blankets in the middle of the room.

Talia knew very well that one missed meal was hardly going to hurt the child, but made a point of appearing the next day with a very hearty breakfast on a tray, acting as if nothing was wrong. She helped the much-subdued youngster to bathe and dress, and got her hair untangled for the first time in three days. All was well until lunch—when Elspeth demanded to know when someone was going to clean up her room.

"It will get cleaned when you do it—not before," was Talia's adamant reply.

This elicited another tantrum, another hurled toy, and the promised six swats. And Talia left for afternoon classes, with Elspeth still crying in a corner.

After three days of this, Talia arrived at the nursery after dinner to find Elspeth struggling to untangle the heavy blankets. She had already gotten what furniture she could lift back in the upright position, and more-or-less back in place. Wordlessly Talia helped her with the rest, gathered the broken toys with her, and put them back on the shelves. That night Elspeth slept in her bed for the first time in a week, falling asleep with Talia holding her hand and singing to her.

The next battles were over the broken toys.

When the toys she'd smashed weren't "magically" replaced as they'd always been in the past, Elspeth wanted to know why.

"You obviously didn't care about them, so you won't get any more," Talia told her. "If you want toys to play with, you'll have to fix the broken ones yourself."

This occasioned a near-repeat of the previous week—though *this* time Elspeth had more sense than to throw anything at Talia. She cried herself sick again, though; and by the end of the fifth day Talia was heartily tired of this tactic. She figured it was about time to put a stop to it—so she picked the girl up, dumped her in the tub in her bathing-room, and doused her with cold water.

"You were making yourself sick," she said as

gently as she could while Elspeth sputtered. "Since you wouldn't stop, I figured I'd better stop you."

Elspeth took care never to cry herself sick again, though this time she held out for a full two weeks more. At the end of that time, Talia found her with a glue-brush in one hand and a broken wagon in the other. She had bits of paper sticking to her hair and face and arms and glue all over her, and was wearing a totally pathetic expression.

One slow, genuine tear crept down her cheek as she looked up at Talia. "I-I don't know how to fix it," she said quietly. "I tried—I really, really tried—but it just stays broken!"

Talia took the toy and the brush from her hands, and hugged and kissed her, oblivious to the glue. "Then I'll help you. All you ever had to do was ask."

It took the better part of a month to fix all the broken toys, and some were smashed beyond redemption. Talia did not offer to have these replaced; Elspeth had a tantrum or two over this, but compared to her earlier performances, they were half-hearted at worst. She was beginning to get the notion that Talia was a much better companion when Elspeth wasn't making fur fly. Then Talia judged that it was about time for the girl's schooling to start.

After the first day of screaming fits—only screaming, no attacks and no destruction, Elspeth had learned that much at least—Talia arranged to miss a week of her own morning classes. By the end of that week she felt as if she'd been breaking horses, but Elspeth had bowed beneath the yoke of learning, and was even (grudgingly) beginning to like it.

Gradually, Elspeth's good days began to out-number her bad ones; as they did so, more and more amenities came back into her life. Her servants returned (she treated them like glass—apparently afraid they'd vanish again if she so much as raised her voice); first the toys that had been totally destroyed were replaced, one by one, and without a word being said, then the ones that had been broken and inexpertly mended. All except for one doll—one that had been torn limb-from-limb, and which Talia had repaired. When Elspeth saw that the broken toys were being replaced, she took to keeping that one with her and sleeping with it at night. Talia smiled to herself, touched—and the doll remained.

Progress was being made.

Now there was a second problem to deal with. The child really had a horror of Companions; she had nightmares about them and couldn't be persuaded to go anywhere near the Field.

Talia began trying to undo the effects of Hulda's horror stories with Collegium gossip, which included as many tales about Companions as about the trainees. As soon as she thought it feasible, she started taking Elspeth on walks before bedtime, and those walks took them closer and closer to Companion's Field. Finally she took Elspeth right inside, having Rolan follow at a discreet distance. As days passed and the child became accustomed to his presence, Talia had him move in closer. Then came the triumphant day when she placed Elspeth on his back. The quick ride they shared cured the child of the last of her nightmares and hysterics and gave Talia a handy reward to offer for good behavior, for Elspeth had become as infatuated with Companions as she had been terrified before.

There were wonderful days after that—days when Elspeth was sweet and even-tempered, when being around her was a pleasure. And then there were the occasional miserable days, when she backslid into the Brat again.

On the bad days she had temper-tantrums, insulted the servants (though she never again laid a hand on one), called Talia names, and wrecked her nursery just for the sheer pleasure of destroying things. Talia would bear with this up to a point, then give her three warnings. If the third wasn't heeded, the Royal Brat got a Royal spanking and was left to her own devices for a time until she sought Talia out herself to apologize.

Gradually the good days came to outnumber the bad by a marked percentage, and it soon became possible to get the child to toe the line simply by reminding her of the fact that she was approaching "Bratly" behavior.

Talia was exhausted, but feeling well-rewarded. As a concession to the incredible amounts of time she was putting in on the girl, she was first excused from her chores for a time, then from foal-watch duty. As the Brat became more and more Elspeth, she began to take those tasks up again. As Elspeth became more interested in Companions and less afraid of them, she became enthralled with the notion of foal-watch (which, in summer, was a far from onerous duty, though it could be—and often was—pure misery in the winter).

Companion mares did not foal with the ease of horses; those who had Chosen, of course, had their Heralds or trainees to stay by them when the time came, but those who had not Chosen had no one. If there were complications, minutes could often mean the life of mare or foal. Keren did what she could, of course, but she couldn't be everywhere, and she needed a certain amount of sleep herself. So one of the duties of the trainees was to spend the nights when an unpartnered Companion mare was nearly ready to foal constantly by her side. Talia had one such stint just after Midsummer, and Elspeth begged so hard to share it with her that Talia relented and gave in.

She hadn't expected anything to come of it— nor, from what she could pick up from Rolan, was the mare herself expecting to drop for at least a week. But much to everyone's surprise, just before midnight the mare awakened Talia and her charge with urgent nudges, labor well under way.

It was Elspeth who ran to fetch Keren when it was evident to Talia's experienced eye that the foal was breech; Elspeth petted the mare's head and cooed to her (the creature a few months ago from which she would have fled in terror) while Keren and Talia got the foal turned. And it was Elspeth who helped the shaking little colt to his feet afterward and helped rub him down with coarse toweling. The mare imparted a message to Keren as the little one first began to suckle; Keren grinned, and carefully pulled a few hairs from her tail, and a sleepy but overjoyed Elspeth was presented with a ring and bracelet braided on the spot, as a "thank-you present from his mum." She put them on immediately and refused to take them off—and thereafter, when Talia was sometimes expecting a temperamental outburst, she would often see the child stroke the bracelet, gulp hard, and exert control over herself. That night signaled the real turning-point.

At last, well past Midsummer, Elspeth approached her mother, and asked permission (so politely that Selenay's mouth fell open) to watch Talia at her afternoon classes.

"Have you asked Talia if she minds an audience?" the Queen asked her transformed offspring.

"Yes, lady-mother. She said it was all right to come to the morning ones, too, but I've got different lessons from her then, so I didn't think that would be a very good idea. I'm supposed to be watching the fighters training in the afternoon though, and riding, so that's the same if I'm doing it with the Collegium students, isn't it? And—I'm tired of doing it alone. Please?"

The Queen gave her permission, and turned to Talia (who had accompanied Elspeth but had not spoken during the interview) as the child left the room.

"I can't believe my eyes and ears!" she exclaimed. "Is that the same child who terrorized her servants this winter? You've worked miracles!"

"*Elspeth's* worked miracles," Talia corrected. "I just had to give her reasons to change. I think we're all fortunate that this Hulda creature only had a really free hand with her for less than two years. If she'd had Elspeth at any earlier age, I don't think there would have been much anyone could have done to change her back."

"Then I thank all the gods that you discovered it was Hulda that was behind the change. All I knew for certain was that Elspeth gradually began to become a problem. I couldn't even take her on rides with me anymore; she had hysterics when Caryo came near—hysterics only Hulda could calm," Selenay said thoughtfully. "I can't believe how clever Hulda was about all this. The worst we thought she was doing was giving the child some inflated notions about her own importance. She claimed it was only a phase Elspeth was going through. And I was having some problems of my own in dealing with her. She was growing to look more and more like her father every day, and it was sometimes very hard for me to deal with her because of that. I could never be sure if I were making a rational judgment about her behavior or one based on dislike of the man she resembled. Talamir proposed fostering her; it's common enough to cause no comment. Poor old man, he simply didn't feel that he was capable of handling so young a child. Then, when we thought we had a solution, he was murdered."

Talia bit her lip. "So you know it for a fact now?"

"We found a vial of a rather strong heart medicine among the things she left behind. A little of it is beneficial—but too much, and the heart gives out in strain—exactly as Talamir's did. poor Talamir we always seemed to be stretching out to each other across a vast gulf of years—and never quite meeting. I *know* he did his very best for me, but he was too embarrassed by the situation to ever feel comfortable about being my confidant. And he was too much of a gentleman to give me a good set-down when I obviously needed it; not even verbally."

"Well, *I* certainly can't spank *you!*" Talia retorted, with a touch of exasperation at the self-pitying mood the Queen had fallen into.

"Oh, no?" Selenay laughed. "That sounded like a well-placed verbal spank to me!"

Talia reddened. "I-I apologize. I have no right to speak to you like that."

"Quite the contrary. You have *every* right to do so; the same right that Talamir had and didn't exercise." Selenay regarded the girl with her head cocked slightly to one side. "You know, the tales all claim that the wisdom of the Queen's Own knows no age barrier, and I'm beginning to believe the tales don't say everything. You're just as much my Herald as if you had twice your years, as well as being Elspeth's. And believe me, little one, I intend never to have to do without you!"

Ten

Several days later, the same topics came up again in conversation between Talia and the Queen.

"Bad enough that Hulda vanished," Selenay said, more than annoyed—angered, in fact—at herself for letting the woman escape almost literally out of her own hand. "I meant to have someone question her under the Truth Spell about 'my lord'; even though I don't think she would have been able to tell us much. But Kyril has discovered that the immigration records on her have vanished as well."

"Bright Havens! Then we may *never* learn who she was working with. According to Skif, the man she spoke with was always hooded and masked, and he doubts she even knew who he was," Talia was troubled; more troubled than she was willing to admit. "But is she likely to give us further problems?"

"I doubt it. What could she do, after all? Even Melidy is recovering—as much as she can."

"That's *very* good to hear," Talia sighed with relief. "Then whatever that drug was, it isn't going to have any lasting effects?"

"The Healers say not. And I can't tell you how

grateful I am to hear that you seem to have cured Elspeth's fear of Companions."

"It's rather remarkable how it vanished when Hulda did," Talia remarked dryly. "It didn't take more than a few visits to Rolan and the others to cure it. She adores them now."

"I'd noticed," Selenay replied with a wry twist of her mouth. "Especially after Elspeth suddenly decided she wanted to share my afternoon rides with Caryo again. That gives me a thought. I know you're busy, more so than ever before, but could you spare me an hour or so a week?"

Talia sighed. "I'll make the time, somehow. Why?"

"I'd like you to take Talamir's place at Council."

Talia choked. "*What*? Now? Why?"

"Why not? You'll have to take it sooner or later. I'd like you to get used to the machinations going on, and I'd like the Councilors to get used to seeing you there. You needn't say anything during the sessions at all, but you just might see something that I wouldn't, that would be useful to know."

"What could *I* possibly see?"

"Perhaps nothing—but perhaps a great deal. Besides, this will give you a certain amount of protection. Having you at my Council table will make it very clear that I will *not* ignore attempts to harm you just because you're not a 'real' Herald yet."

"May I make a condition?"

"Certainly."

"I'd like Elspeth with me; that way she won't feel left out, and it will show her more clearly than anything I could tell her that the job of reigning is *work*."

"I agree—and I would never have thought of that."

"That's not true," Talia protested.

"It is, and you know it. And since you're acting as Queen's Own, you might as well call me by my given name. I'm getting tired of being 'highnessed' and 'majestied.' To you, I am just Selenay."

"Yes, maj—Selenay," Talia replied, returning the Queen's smile.

"The next Council meeting is just after the noon meal, two days from now. Till then?"

Elspeth had arrived promptly for Talia's arms-lesson with Alberich, and thereafter never missed one. The child seemed to be fascinated by the different styles the Armsmaster was training them in. The rest of the trainees, warned in advance that Elspeth would be watching, went about their normal activities with only a hint of stiltedness. After a few moments, they began pausing now and again for a nod or a friendly word with the child, attempting to act as if she were just another trainee.

Before very long, they no longer had to act. It seemed natural to accept her as one of them.

Elspeth was a silent observer for a week or two when Alberich evidently decided he had an idea he wished to try. And in a fashion typical to Alberich, he did so without telling Talia about it beforehand.

When he'd finished with Talia, his eye lighted on Elspeth, seemingly by accident—though Talia was well aware that where lessons were concerned *nothing* Alberich did was by accident. "You—child!" he barked. "Come here!"

Talia saw Elspeth's chin begin to tighten and her nose to tilt up—a sure sign that she was about to revert to her old behavior. She managed to catch the girl's eye and made what Elspeth had taken to calling the "Royal Awful" face. Elspeth giggled and fingered her bracelet, all haughtiness evaporated, and she obeyed Alberich with commendable docility.

"Look, all of you," he said, giving a short practice blade to her. "At this age, she has learned no bad habits so there is nothing for her to unlearn. She has more flexibility than an acrobat, and she'll learn more quickly than any three of you put together. Name, child?"

"Elspeth, sir."

He demonstrated one of the primary exercises for her. "Can you do that?"

A tiny frown between her brows, Elspeth did her best to imitate his movements. He made some minor corrections, then ran her through the exercise several more times, the last at full speed.

"There, you see? *This* is what you are striving to imitate—the agile and receptive mind and body of the young child. And watch—"

He suddenly attacked her in such a way that the natural counter for her to make was the exercise he's just taught her. She performed so flawlessly that she drew impromptu applause from the other students.

"At this stage, once learned, never forgotten. Try to emulate her."

At Alberich's command, they returned to sparring with one another. He beckoned to Talia. "You have charge of this one?" he asked, as though he had no idea of Elspeth's identity.

"Yes, sir," she replied respectfully.

"I should like to include her in the lessons. This can be arranged?"

"Easily sir. Would you like to learn weapons-work, instead of just watching, Elspeth?"

"Oh, yes!" the child responded eagerly, her eyes shining. "Only—"

"Yes? Alberich prompted.

"You won't hit me *too* hard, please, sir? Not like you hit Griffon."

Alberich laughed, something Talia hadn't seen him do very often. "I gauge my punishments by the thickness of my students' skulls, child. Griffon has a *very* thick skull."

Griffon, who was close enough to hear every word, grinned and winked at the girl.

"I think," Alberich continued, "That you have not so thick a skull, so I shall only beat you a little. Now, we might as well begin with what I just taught you."

Talia realized as she watched them that Alberich had helped to deliver the death-blow to the Brat.

Now there was only Elspeth.

After that, though there were occasional brief lapses, the child was able to maintain her good behavior with very little effort. Throughout the hot days of that summer, she rapidly became the pet of the Collegium, although she was never in any danger of being spoiled as everyone remembered only too well what the Brat had been like.

Rather than simply watching things, she began volunteering to help. At archery practice she brought water and arrows to replace those broken, at weapons practice, chalk and dry towels. She did her best to help groom Companions and clean tack, and not just Rolan and his gear, but turning a hand to help anyone who happened to be there. When it was Talia's turn at chores during "their" afternoons, Elspeth even insisted on doing her share; Mero the Cook soon began looking forward to having her in the kitchen and always had a special treat for his helpers on the days that she and Talia shared the work. Elspeth even had a certain fascination for the mending chores, never having known before how it was that torn clothing came to be repaired. She was not very good at it though, not having the patience for tedious work, and preferred to do something active, like sorting the clothing into piles of "still good enough," "wear only to work out," and "hopeless"—her own terms, quickly adopted by the rest. "Hopeless" was a particular favorite—the mender in question enacting mourning scenes over the offending garment. It got to be a regular game, one all of them enjoyed to the hilt.

By the time the leaves were turning, no one could imagine the Collegium without Elspeth running about with the trainees.

One chilly afternoon, with the last dessicated leaves blowing against Talia's window, there was a quiet knock on her door. When Talia opened it, Sherrill was standing there—in Whites.

Talia was speechless for a moment—then hugged her friend as hard as she could, exclaiming breathlessly, "You did it! You did it!"

Sherrill hugged back, one happy tear escaping

from her eyes. "I guess I did," she said when Talia finally let her go. "You're the first to know, except for Elcarth."

"I am? Oh, Sherri—I don't know what to say—it's wonderful! I'm so glad for you! When are you leaving on your assignment?"

"Next week," she said, seeming to feel more than a little awkward suddenly, "and I had another reason for coming here—seeing as I'm sort of your mentor—well—there's something I have to tell you about before I leave."

"Go on," Talia replied, wondering why her friend was so ill-at-ease.

"Well—what do you think of—boys?"

"I never really thought about it, much," she replied.

"I mean, do you like them? You seem to—like Skif a lot."

"I'm not like Keren, if that's what you mean."

"No, it isn't," Sherrill squirmed in frustration. "You know—about babies and all that, right?"

"I should hope so, seeing as they'd planned on marrying me off before I came here!" Talia replied with some amusement. "And I think I've helped Keren with more foals than you ever have in just one year on foal-watch! I think they wait for me!"

"Well, do you know how *not* to have them? I mean, you must have noticed that you don't often see a pregnant Herald, and we're hardly a celibate bunch. . . ."

"Yes in answer to your second question," Talia said, thinking wryly of the nocturnal activities of her next-door neighbor Destria. "But *no* to your first!"

"We've got something the Healers make up for us," Sherrill said, obviously relieved that she wasn't going to have to explain the facts of life to her young friend. "It's a powder—you take some every day, except when you're having moon-days. It doesn't even taste bad, which is truly amazing considering the way most of their potions taste. You can also use it to adjust your cycles if you have to, if you know you're going to be in a situation where having your moon-days would be really awkward, for instance. You just stop taking it earlier, or keep on longer. I figured I'd better tell you about it, or it was possible no one would. I know you haven't needed it yet—but you might want it soon if the gleam I've been seeing in Skif's eyes means anything."

"You remembered to tell me this on the day you got your Whites?" Talia asked incredulously, ignoring the comment about Skif. "Oh, Sherri, whatever did I do to deserve a friend like you?"

The powder worked just as well as the little sponges Sherrill had shown her how to use in place of the rag-clouts for moon-days, and Talia was more than grateful to Sherrill for telling her about it. Being able to adjust her cycles was wonderful in and of itself—which was just as well, since she never really got a chance to test the efficacy of the other application.

She and Skif were so often thrown together that Talia had lost any self-consciousness around him, and had certainly long since unconsciously relegated him to the category of "safe" males, especially after the help he'd been with the Hulda affair. It helped that they were much of an age and size and that the normally rowdy Skif muted

his voice and actions around her, as if being aware
how easily she could be startled or frightened by a
male. They had started out being quite good
friends—but now he was being attracted to her in
another way, as his mealtime behavior had so ardently demonstrated. So what occurred next between them was hardly surprising.

After Talia had so nearly died in the icy water
of the river, Alberich had assigned Sherrill to give
her the same kind of swimming lessons a child of
the Lake would have. Sherrill's last act before going
out on her internship was to surprise Talia on the
bridge and toss her into the same spot she'd been
thrown before. The water was almost as cold,
though the ice was scarcely more than a thin skin
among the reeds. Sherri stood ready to haul her
out if she had to, but Talia "passed" this impromptu exam with flying colors and chattering
teeth.

Skif met her coming back to her room, laughing, shaking with cold, barefoot and dripping and
wrapped in a horseblanket.

"Holy stars!" he exclaimed in shock. "What happened to you?"

"Sherri pushed me in the river—no, wait," she
forestalled his rushing off to meet out the same
treatment to the innocent Sherrill. "It was on
Alberich's orders. She's been teaching me what
she knows, and she wanted a foolproof way of
testing whether I'd learned or not."

"Some test," Skif grumbled, then to Talia's surprise, picked her up and carried her to her room.

"They don't *ever* let up on you, do they?" he
complained, helping her out of her sodden clothing and building up the tiny fire in her room.

"Holy stars, you do *twice* the work of the rest of us, and you *never* get a break, and then they turn around and do things like this to you. . . ."

She turned unexpectedly and stumbled. He caught her, and she found herself staring into his brown eyes at a meager distance of an inch or two. He froze, then seized his opportunity and kissed her.

They broke apart in confusion a long moment later.

"Uh, Talia . . ." he mumbled.

"I like you, Skif," she said softly. "I like you a lot."

"You do?" he flushed. "I—you know I like you."

"And you know who my next-door neighbor is. Nobody'd notice if we—you know."

"You mean—" Skif could hardly believe his ears. Or his luck. "But you've got your good uniform on—you're going somewhere. Tonight maybe?"

"I've got a Council meeting, but after that. . . ."

Alas for poor Skif—the Council meeting was long and boring, and Talia was a good deal more tired from Sherri's "trial by water" than she realized. She arrived at her room a little before him and sat down on her bed to rest. By the time he got there, much to Skif's chagrin, she was fast asleep.

He bit his lip in annoyance; then his expression softened. He covered her carefully with a blanket and gave her a chaste kiss on one cheek; she was so weary she didn't even stir.

"No matter, lady-o," he whispered. "We can try again another time."

"Bright Havens, little one!" Jadus exclaimed,

seeing Talia's strained expression as she arrived for her nightly visit. "What ails you?"

"I—I'm not sure," she replied hesitantly. "But everyone's so *angry*—I thought I could keep it out, but it won't stay out—"

"You should have said something sooner," he scolded gently, using his own Gift to reinforce her shielding. "Elcarth could have helped you."

"Elcarth was busy, and everybody else was too angry to get near. Jadus, what's wrong with everyone? I thought Heralds didn't get angry—I've never felt anything like this before!"

"That's because you weren't in any shape to sense the mood of the Collegium last winter, dear heart."

"You're changing the subject," Talia said, a bit tartly. "And if this affects Selenay or Elspeth, I need to know what it's all about."

Jadus hesitated, then sighed and concluded that she was right. "It's not a pretty tale," he said. "There's a young Herald named Dirk who became infatuated with one of the Court beauties. That's not too uncommon, especially the first time a Herald is assigned to the Court or Collegium, but she apparently played on it, built it into something a great deal more serious on his part. And all the time she was simply toying with him—intended using him for the rather base end of getting at a friend of his. When she was found out, she said some very cruel things—deliberately came very close to destroying his fairly fragile ego. She totally shattered his self-esteem; she's got him convinced he's worth less than a mongrel dog. He's been sent back to his home for a while; hopefully in the company of his family and friends, he'll recover. I pray so; Dirk is a good lad, and a valuable Herald, and worth fifty of her. I knew his father at Bardic, and the lad did me the service of visiting me now and again to pay his respects. The anger you feel is largely due to the fact that we are legally and ethically unable to mete out to that—woman—the punishment she richly deserves. And child, we *do* get angry; we're only human—and it hurts to know we are helpless to avenge what has been done to one dear to us because *we* obey the spirit *and* the letter of the law."

Talia left Jadus deep in thought, wondering if *she'd* ever truly be worthy of that kind of caring.

Skif slipped Talia a note at breakfast. "My room, tonight?"

She smiled and nodded very slightly.

He arrived at his room, Talia and the proposed rendezvous temporarily forgotten. He was battered, bruised, and sore from his head to his heels, and all he was really thinking about was whether or not he could coax Drake or Edric into bringing him something from the kitchen so that he wouldn't have to drag his weary body to the commonroom.

He blinked in surprise to see food and hot tea waiting on his desk. He blinked again to see Talia sitting on his bed.

"Oh, Lord of Lights—Talia, I forgot!"

"I heard," she said simply. "But I thought you could use food and a friend—and we'll see if we can't get you in shape for other things with those two."

"He's a sadist, that Alberich," he moaned, lowering himself, wincing, into the chair, and reaching for the tea. " 'Time you had some responsibility,' he said. 'You're going to be my assistant,' he said. 'It'll give you less time for picking of pockets and evil habits.' He *didn't* say he'd be giving me extra lessons. He *didn't* say that he was going to make me the sparring partner for hulking brutes who've already *gotten* their Whites. He *didn't* tell me I was going to be teaching three giants who never saw anything more sophisticated than a club. Holy stars, Talia, you should *see* those three! They were farmers, or so they tell me. Farmers! Talia, if you asked directions from one of them, he'd probably pick up the plow, ox and all, to point the way!"

Talia murmured sympathetically, and massaged his shoulders.

"I hurt in places I didn't know I had," he complained, eating his dinner with what, for him, was unnatural slowness.

"I might be able to help with that," Talia smiled, continuing to massage his aches.

It was a short two steps to his bed; she got most of the clothing off him—and not so incidentally off herself. She had gotten hold of some kellwood-oil and warmed it to skin temperature, using it to help get the knots out of his bruised and battered muscles. Under her gentle ministrations he was even beginning to feel somewhat revived; then he made the mistake of closing his eyes.

Talia realized it was hopeless when she heard his gentle snores.

She sighed, eased herself out of his bed, tucked him in like a child, and returned to her own room.

This Midwinter, she stayed at the Collegium

quite gladly, enjoying the unusual freedom to read until all hours of the night if she chose, and greatly enjoying Jadus' company. She discovered that this year Mero and Gaytha were remaining over the holiday, along with Keren and Ylsa, and the six of them often met in Jadus' room for long discussions over hot cider.

Keren and Ylsa took her out with them on long rides into the countryside outside the capital. They even managed to persuade Jadus to accompany them on more than one of these expeditions—the first time he'd been off Collegium grounds for years. The three of them had found a pond that had frozen with a black-ice surface as smooth as the finest mirror. While Ylsa and Jadus stayed by the fire they built on the shore, laughing at the other two and keeping a careful eye on the rabbit and roots they were roasting for a snow-picnic, Karen taught Talia how to skate. With runners made of polished steel fastened to her boots, Keren glided on the surface of the pond with the grace of a falcon in flight.

Talia fell down a lot—at least at first.

"You're just trying to get back at me," she accused. "I never got a sore rear from riding, so you're trying some other way to make it hard for me to sit down!"

Keren just chuckled, helped her up again, and resumed towing her around the pond.

Eventually she acquired the knack of balancing, then of moving. By the time they quit to return home, she was thoroughly enjoying herself, even if she looked, as she said, "more like a goose than a falcon!"

They repeated this trip nearly every other day,

until by Midwinter itself Talia was proficient enough to be able to skate—shakily—backwards.

Once again they shared the revelry in the Servant's Hall, this time with the other four as additions to the group. It was altogether a most satisfactory Midwinter holiday.

When classes resumed, she added one in law and jurisprudence and another in languages and lost the free hour in the library. Often it seemed as if there simply weren't enough hours in the day to do everything, but somehow she managed.

Her bond with Rolan, if anything, continued to deepen; now it seemed as if he was always present at the back of her mind. She knew by now that *he* was the source of some of the wisdom that she'd had spring unbidden into her mind when the Queen needed it, and that it had been Rolan who had guided her when she'd needed to bail Skif out of Orthallen's ill graces. Rolan, after all, had the benefit of living in the mind of a man of great ability—the former King's Own, Talamir—for all of Talamir's life as a Herald, and made all of that wisdom available to his new Herald. Yet some of it, at least, was all Talia's own; the instinctive judgment that only the Monarch's Own Herald possessed.

Before she realized how much time had passed, the trees were budding again. There was a new crop of trainees, and Talia was amazed at how *young* these children looked. Sometimes she was just as surprised, when looking in a mirror, at how young *she* still looked—for she felt as if she must appear at least a hundred years old by now.

Spring did bring one respite; Keren had taught

her all she knew. There would be no more equitation classes, as such. From time to time she would help Keren with the younger students who needed individual help, but it was not the steady, draining demand that the class had been.

Now that Keren was no longer Talia's teacher, their relationship ripened into an incredibly close friendship, closer even than the relationship Talia had had with her sister Vris. For all of the difference in their ages—Keren was slightly more than twice Talia's age—they discovered that the difference was negligible once they really began to talk with one another. The closeness they had begun over the Midwinter holiday began to deepen and strengthen. Talia found that Keren was the one person in the entire Collegium with whom she felt free to unburden herself—perhaps because Keren was strongly sympathetic to the weight of responsibility on the shoulders of the Queen's Own, having had that burden in her own family. Being able to say exactly what she pleased to *somebody* made life a great deal easier for Talia.

As for Keren—Talia was one of the few people she'd ever met, even in the Heraldic circle, who was willing to accept her, her relationship with Ylsa, and all that this implied, without judgment. Once Talia's loyalty was given, it was unswerving and unshakable. Most Heralds liked and admired Keren, but many were uneasy about getting too close to her, as if her preferences were some kind of stain that might rub off on them. Talia was one of the few who gave her heart freely and openly to one she considered to be her best friend. And with Ylsa so often away, life up until now had been rather lonely—a loneliness Talia did much to alleviate, simply by being there.

Talia learned something new about her friend, something that few guessed. The outward strength and capability of the riding instructor masked the internal fragility of a snowflake. Her emotional stability rested on a tripod of three bonds—the one with Teren, the one with Dantris, her Companion, and the one with Ylsa. It was partially because of that that the Circle had assigned the twins to teaching full-time at the Collegium when the advance of middle years made it time to think of taking them from field duty (although the primary reasons were that they were experts in their areas—Keren with equitation and Teren for his talents in dealing with children and true gift for teaching). There was very little chance that anything untoward would occur to either Dantris or her brother here. Ylsa had been given her own assignment as Special Messenger because of the unusual endurance of Felara, second only to Rolan's—though it was true that the duty of special messenger was not as hazardous as many of the others, which had again been a minor consideration. Still, Talia often thought with a vague dread that if anything ever happened to Ylsa, Keren might well follow.

The night was warm; it was too early for insects, the moon was full. It was an altogether idyllic setting. There was even a lovely soft bed of young ferns to spread their cloaks on. Talia had met Skif quite by accident when she was coming back from walking with Elspeth in Companion's Field. With unspoken accord they had retraced their steps, and found this ideal trysting place. . . .

"Comfortable?"

"Mm-hm. And the stars—"

"They're gorgeous. I could watch them forever."

"I thought," Talia teased, "that you had something else in mind!"

"Oh I did—"

But *he* had just spent his afternoon dodging Alberich, and *she* had been up since well before dawn.

Talia returned his hesitant, but gentle caresses. She was both excited and a little apprehensive about this, but from the way Skif was acting she evidently wasn't being *too* awkward. She began to relax for the first time since early that morning, and she could feel the tension in his shoulders begin to go out—

—and they fell asleep simultaneously.

They woke with dew soaking them and birds overhead, and the sun just beginning to rise.

"I hate to say this," Skif began with a sigh.

"I know. This isn't going to work, is it?"

"I guess not. It's either the gods, fate, or the imp of the perverse."

"Or all three. I guess we're stuck just being good friends. Well, you can't say we didn't try!"

To Skif's delight, their classmates seemed totally unaware of the fact that their trysts had been abortive. Talia was thought of as being very hard to get; Skif was amazed to discover that his reputation had been made as a consequence, and proceeded immediately to try to live up to it. Coincident with this, Alberich dropped him as assistant, and appointed Jeri, so he never again had the problem that had plagued his "romance" with Talia. Talia simply smiled and held her peace when teased about Skif, so their secret remained a secret.

The Death Bell tolled four times that year; Talia found herself in a new role—one that she hadn't expected.

She'd attended the funeral of the first of that year's victims. It was just turning autumn, the air still had the feel of summer during the day, although the nights were growing colder. She had gone to Companion's Field afterward and had mounted Rolan without saddling him. They had not ambled along as was their usual habit; it was rather as if something was drawing both of them to a particular corner of the Field.

Companion's Field was not, as the name implied, a simple, flat field. Rather, it was a rolling, partially wooded complex of several acres in size, containing the Stable for foul-weather shelter, the barn and granary holding the Companions' fodder, and the tack shed—in reality a substantial building with fireplaces at either end. The heart of the field was the Grove, the origin-place of the original Companions, and the location of the tower containing the Death Bell. There were several spring-fed creeks and pools and many secluded, shady copses, as well as more open areas.

Talia's "feelings" led her to one of those secluded corners, a tiny pool at the bottom of an equally tiny valley, all overhung with golden-leaved willows. There was a Herald there, his own Companion nuzzling anxiously at his shoulder, staring vacantly into the water of the pool.

Talia dismounted and sat next to him. "Would

you like to talk about it?" she asked, after a long silence.

He tossed a scrap of bark into the pool. "I found him—Gerick, I mean."

"Bad?"

"I can't even begin to tell you. Whatever killed him can't have been human, not even close. And the worst of it was—"

"Go on."

"It was *my* circuit he was riding. If I hadn't broken my leg, it would have been me. Maybe."

"You don't think so?"

"There's been some odd things going on out there on the Western Border, especially on my circuit. I tried to warn him, but he just laughed and told me I'd been out there too long. Maybe, if it'd been me out there—I don't know."

Talia remained silent, knowing there was more he hadn't said.

"I can't sleep anymore," the Herald said at last, and indeed he looked haggard. "Every time I close my eyes, I see his face, the way he was when I found him. The blood—the—pain— Dammit to all the Twelve Hells!" he drove his fist into the ground beside him. "Why did it have to be Gerick? *Why?* I've never seen anybody so much in love with life—why did he have to die like *that?*"

"I wish I had an answer for you, but I don't," Talia replied. "I think we'll only know the *why* of things when we meet our own fates. . . ." Her voice trailed off as she searched for words to bring him some kind of comfort. "But surely, if he loved life as much as you say, Gerick must have made the most of every minute he had?"

"You know—you're right. I used to dig at him

for it, sometimes he'd just laugh, and tell me that since he didn't know what was around the corner, he planned to make the most of whatever he had at the moment. I swear, it seemed sometimes as if he were trying to live three men's lives, all at once. Why, I remember a time when—"

He continued with a string of reminiscences, at times almost oblivious of Talia's presence except as an ear in which to pour his words. He only stopped when his throat grew dry, and he realized with a start that he'd been talking for at least a couple of hours.

"Lord of the Mountain—what have I been telling you?" he said, seeing for the first time that his companion was only an adolescent girl. "Look I'm sorry. What is your name?"

"Talia," she replied and smiled as his eyes widened a little in recognition. "There's nothing to apologize for, you know. All I've been doing is listening—but now you're remembering your friend as he lived instead of as he died. Isn't that a better memorial?"

"Yes," he said thoughtfully. "Yes." The strain was gone from his face, and she could no longer sense the kind of tearing, destructive unhappiness that had led her here. There was sorrow, yes—but not the kind that would obsess and possess him.

"I've got to go now, and you should get some sleep before you're ill." She swung up on Rolan's back as he raised eyes that mirrored his gratitude to meet hers.

"Thank you, Queen's Own," was all he said—but the tone of his voice said much more.

The second Herald to die that year fell victim to an avalanche, but the lover he'd left behind had to be convinced that he hadn't been taking foolish risks because they'd quarreled previously. That was an all-night session, and Talia appeared at her first class looking so dragged out that the now-Herald Nerrissa, who was teaching it, ordered her back to bed and canceled all her morning work.

The third meant another soul-searching session with Selenay, guilt-wracked over having sent, this time, a young and inexperienced Herald into something she would never have been able to cope with—an explosive feud between two families of the lesser nobility of the East. It had devolved into open warfare between them, and while trying to reconcile the two parties, the Herald had gotten in the way of a stray arrow. Had she had more experience, she would not have so exposed herself.

Of course, Selenay had had no way of knowing that the feud had gotten that heated at the time she sent Beryl—but with the clear vision imparted by hindsight, she felt that she should have guessed.

But for the fourth, just after Midwinter holiday, it was Talia herself that was in dire need of comfort—for the Herald who died was Jadus.

She'd awakened one morning before dawn knowing immediately that something was wrong—that it involved Jadus, and had only taken enough time to pull her cloak on over her bedgown before running to his room. She all but ran into a Healer leaving it, and his eyes told her the truth.

Jadus' passing had been quite peaceful, he told her; Jadus had had no inkling of it, simply hadn't awakened. His Companion was also gone—probably simultaneously.

None of this was any comfort at all.

She retreated to her room and sat on the edge of her bed, staring at the chair he'd spent so many nights occupying, guarding her in her illness. She thought of all the things that she wished now she'd told him—how much he had meant to her, how much she'd learned from him. It was too late for any of that now—and too late to thank him.

"Lovey—I heard—" Keren stood beside her; Talia hadn't even noticed the door opening. As they stared at one another, the Bell began to toll.

As if the bell-tone had released something, Talia began to cry soundlessly. Keren held her on the edge of the bed, and they wept together for their old friend and for all that he'd meant to both of them.

Keren was not the only one to think of Talia when the news spread, for when they looked up at a small sound, Dean Elcarth had taken the chair across from Talia's bed.

"I have to tell you two things, my dear," he said with a little difficulty. "Jadus was a long-time friend of mine; he was my counselor on my internship in fact. He left all of his affairs in my hands. He knew he hadn't much longer to live, and he told me when—he wanted you to have—" Mutely he held out the harp case that held My Lady.

Talia took it in trembling hands and stared at it, unable to speak around the lump of tears in her throat.

"The other thing is this; he was happier these past two years than at any time since he lost his leg. When it came to strict academic subjects, he wasn't a very good teacher; his heart just wasn't in it. The classes we had him teach were just to keep him busy, and he knew it. Until you came, he'd been retreating more and more into the past, living in a time when he'd been useful. You made him feel useful again. And when you were sick—I don't think you realize how much your needing him, both to guard your safety and to chase the nightmares away with his music, made him *alive* again. And being able to counsel and guide you—it meant the world to him."

"He—knew? He knew how much I needed him?"

"Of course he knew; he had the thought-sensing Gift. No matter how well you think you shield, youngling, when you care for someone the way you two cared for each other, things are bound to get through—will you, nill you. And when you started coming to him for advice or for help, and when *he* was the one you came to over the Hulda affair—I don't think he was ever prouder of anything he'd done. He often told me he no longer missed not having a family because now he had a family in you and in the friends you'd brought to him. He was a very lonely man until you came to his door, little one. He died a happy and contented man."

Elcarth dropped his head and rubbed briefly at his eyes, unable to say more.

"I have to go," he said finally, and stood up. Talia caught his hand.

"Thank you—" she whispered.

He squeezed her hand in acknowledgment and left.

It was several months before she could bring herself to touch My Lady—but once she had (though she missed Jadus dreadfully every time she played), she never once neglected to practice.

And when she did, she tried to remember him

as he'd been that night, alert and alive, in the chair next to her bed with his harp on his lap, and a loaded crossbow hidden on the floor beside him, with his old cane exchanged for one that held concealed the blade of a sword.

And the incredulous smile of joy that had appeared when she had begged him to play for her.

Or the way he'd looked when he told her and Skif that they could leave the problem of Hulda in his hands—strong again; confident again—*needed*.

And the laughter and joy they'd shared that Midwinter day when Keren had taught her to skate.

Sometimes, it even helped a little. But only sometimes.

Eleven

"Tripe! I'm late!" Talia swore to herself, finally noticing the time by the sundial in the garden beneath her window. She gathered up the scattered notes around her desk, coerced them into a more-or-less neat pile, and flew out the door of her room.

She'd managed to learn a few shortcuts in the three years she'd been at the Collegium; that and longer legs managed to get her to her classroom scant seconds ahead of Herald Ylsa and the Dean. She ran her fingers through her unruly curls, hoping to smooth them down enough that her race through the halls wouldn't be blazoned in her appearance.

Three years had made quite a difference in the way she looked. The awkward adolescent whose arms and legs had always seemed a bit too long for her body was gone. Though she'd never be tall, growth and Alberich's training had honed her into a slender, supple, and athletic young woman. The face she showed to the world was self-confident, but that outward appearance covered a certain shyness and uncertainty that still remained. The muddy color of her hair had finally turned to a rich red-brown. She wore it just touching her shoulders; much to her dismay, since she secretly yearned for straight, midnight-black hair like Sherrill's, it had remained stubbornly curly. Her eyes now matched her hair, and while she would never be called beautiful, she charmed everyone when she smiled—which she did now more often than not. There was no one in the Collegium or among the full Heralds of the Circle who were acquainted with her that did not care deeply for her. The older trainees had taken it upon themselves to make it pointedly clear to the Blues that anyone harassing her would find life very uncomfortable indeed. Her teachers tried to keep her challenged, but at the same time went out of their way to coordinate their efforts so as to make it possible for her to keep up with all her commitments. The younger students—for she always had a moment to spare to soothe an anger, encourage the discouraged, or lend an ear to the homesick—frankly adored her. Her own contemporaries had formed a kind of honor guard for her headed by Griffon, always at hand to take over a chore or duty when the inevitable conflicts arose.

She returned all these attentions with an artless gratitude and affection that made it seem a privilege to have helped her.

And yet she still felt a kind of isolation from everyone but her few close friends—Skif, Keren, Sherri, and Jeri. It was almost as if she was *of* the Collegium and Circle, yet not truly at one with them.

A great part of that feeling had to do with the fact that it seemed to her as if she were continually receiving the affection and attention she so ardently craved, and yet was doing little or nothing to earn it. Exposing Hulda had been mostly Skif's work; civilizing Elspeth had been largely a matter of forcing her to take the consequences for her actions and returning her to her previous behavior patterns. It hardly seemed to her that being Selenay's sounding board required much effort on *her* part. She felt—when she had time to think about it—as if she would never truly belong until she earned her place, entirely by her own efforts, and by doing something for the benefit of the Circle that no one else could do.

She little realized that by helping to ease the emotional turmoils of others she was already accomplishing just that. As far as she was concerned, that was the kind of thing anyone would and could do under the same circumstances. Only Elcarth, Herald Kyril (who made a study of Heraldic Gifts), and Ylsa realized how rare her abilities and her Gift were—and how badly they would miss her, were she not there.

But since she still kept most of her inmost doubts to herself, none of them realized she felt this way. They saw only the cheerful exterior that she presented to the world at large.

Only Keren and Rolan ever witnessed the bouts of self-doubt and temper; the fits of self-pity and depression. And neither of those two (like Jadus before them) was likely to betray her trust, since it was given so rarely. For if she had a fault, it was this; even after three years, it was still hard for her to truly trust in others.

Today marked a new phase of her studies, and a strange and somewhat frightening one. Now she was to learn the full use of that ability to sense the distresses of others that had appeared so abruptly under stress. Today was the beginning of her lessons in "Herald's magic."

There were three others in the class besides herself; the twins Drake and Edric from her own year-group (Talia was still unable to tell them apart), and a silent, flame-haired lad from the year-group following Talia's. Neave's abilities had caused mild havoc among the trainees for a brief period until he had been identified as the source of disturbance. He was a "projector"—and he'd inadvertently projected his own nightmares into the dreams of those around him that were at all receptive and unshielded. Since his life up until he'd been Chosen had been rough enough to make even the ex-street-urchin Skif blanch, his nightmares had been grown from fertile ground and given his fellow students several sleepless and terror-filled nights.

As the Dean and Herald entered the room, Talia found she had tensed up all over. These were new and strange waters she was about to dive into; she'd more or less come to terms with the simpler manifestations of her Gift, but there remained her old Hold training to deal with. To Holderfolk, such abilities were "unnatural" at best, and demon-born at worst.

Talia was just grateful that the class was being taught by two so familiar to her. If it had been a stranger facing her, she would have been ready to have a litter of kittens with nerves! She tried to relax—this was nothing to fear; *every* Herald had to learn the working of his or her Gift—and Elcarth caught her eye, and gave her a brief, encouraging smile.

Dean Elcarth surveyed the four of them, noting their understandable nervousness. Only Drake and Edric appeared to be more excited than ill-at-ease— but then, *their* Gift had been a part of them since birth. He smiled reassuringly at Neave and Talia, lifted an eyebrow at the twins, and began his usual speech.

"We put the four of you in a class together because you all demonstrate Gifts in the same 'family' of talents," the Dean began, as his bright, round eyes met each of theirs' in turn. "Your Gifts of what we call 'magic' are all in the areas of communication. I want you all to know that although we refer to these things in the world outside these walls as 'magic,' there is nothing *whatsoever* unnatural about them. You have Talents, even as a Bard, an artist, or an artisan. You should never be afraid of what you have been gifted with—rather you should learn how to use these gifts to the benefit of yourselves and others."

"Talia and Neave already know Herald Ylsa; she was instrumental in discovering that both of you had prematurely awakened Gifts, since she is one of the best at the using and detecting 'communications' type abilities that we have among the Circle. For this reason, she will be in charge of this class, and I am merely here to assist her. Don't be afraid to ask her questions; despite her formidable reputation, she doesn't bite—"

"Not hard, anyway," Ylsa interrupted with a smile.

"—and if she doesn't know the answers to your questions, she certainly knows exactly where to look and who to ask! I'll be helping her, since next to Herald Kyril, I'm probably the second choice for an expert at the Collegium. Ylsa, the floor is yours."

"Well," she said, folding her arms and leaning back against the edge of the desk. "Where shall I start? Have any of you questions about all this?"

"Herald," Neave's expression was troubled. "All this—magic—it isn't evil, is it?"

"Is a crossbow evil?" she countered.

"Depends on who's holding it, Herald," one of the twins grinned and answered, "and who it's pointed at."

"Exactly. Your Gifts can be used for evil purposes. They're just like any weapon—and make no mistake about it, they can be weapons if you're so minded. But you wouldn't be sitting here now if you were inclined toward evil. Trust the judgment of your Companion in that, Neave, if you don't trust your own. They don't Choose where evil is—and on the very rare occasion where someone has been corrupted past redemption—and the last was two hundred years ago—they will repudiate their Chosen. So since you and Kyldathar still seem on very good terms, I think you can set your mind at rest about being evil."

"Herald, the Companions seem to be able to make our Gift stronger, somehow," said the other twin. "Edric and I could 'talk' a little to each other before, but since we were Chosen it's been *much* clearer and easier."

"Good!" Ylsa nodded. "I wondered if any of you had made that connection. Yes, the Companions seem to strengthen our Gifts and develop the ones that are latent. You'll probably find that your Gift gains enormously in power when you're in physical contact with your Companion and when you're under the influence of very strong emotions. No one is sure whether there's a connection there, between our bonds with our Companions and very strong emotions. Our Gifts are unfortunately not the kinds of things that yield easily to measurement."

"Herald Ylsa, we've all seen or heard about the 'Truth Spell'—are we going to learn *spells?*" Talia asked. "My folk say all spells are demon-work."

"Yes, you will be learning spells of a sort, though probably not what the Holderfolk had in mind. What *we* call a spell for the most part is an exercise that forces you to concentrate. When you concentrate, you boost your capability; it's as simple as that. The word 'spell' is just a handy term; in point of fact, most of them are rather like meditation chants or prayers of a sort."

"Then, does everybody have this kind of—uh—gift?" Neave asked.

"Again, yes. The catch is that most people don't have enough of the ability for it to be really useful to them. It's just like Talia sings very well but will never be a Bard, and I throw a decent pot but could never be a really *good* potter. As far as that goes, there are some of us whose Gifts are hardly stronger than those of nonHeralds—and even among Heralds a *really* powerful Gift is rare, though we all have enough to enable us to bond with our Companions and use the Truth Spell. From what we can tell, it seems to be that the very strongest gifts tend to be associated with those who become Healers rather than Heralds, although the Gifts of communication are very similar to the Healing Gifts. That is why in an emergency you may be called on to assist Healers. Sometimes the very strongest of our variety of Gifts hide themselves; I've known a case or two when persistent *inability* has actually hidden very strong *ability*. Mostly though, it seems that contact with your Companion triggers your Gift and continued development of the bond also develops the Gift to the point where you have direct conscious control of it. Once you can control it, you can be trained in the use of it, and you can learn its limits. Oh, I think I should mention something about the Truth Spell; *that* really is a spell, in the sense of the Bardic tales. It requires a Gift to use, apparently the one that makes the Companion-Herald bond possible. If you have a strong Gift, you'll be able to use it to actually force someone to speak only the truth; if your Gift is weak, you'll only be able to detect whether or not a person is lying. The Truth Spell will be the last thing we'll teach you. Now, if you're all ready, I think we're about at the point where we should stop talking and start doing.

For once, learning did not come easily to Talia. To her extreme frustration, mastering the use of her Gift proved to be far more elusive than she had dreamed. The others quickly outstripped her in progress as she strove to get some kind of control on her abilities. Directing her Gift seemed to be a greatly different thing than simply blocking it or letting it direct her actions passively, as she had been doing. It seemed to require a kind of combination of relaxation and concentration that she despaired of ever mastering. Several weeks passed without her attaining much more control than she had had before the class started.

"You know—" Ylsa said one day, with a look as

if she were slowly realizing something that should have been obvious. "—I think we're going after the wrong Gift. I'm not at all sure now that your prime Gift is thought-sensing."

"Well what could it be?" Talia cried in frustration.

"Everything you've told me and what I've seen for myself points not to the mind, but the heart. Look, your own mind-call to Rolan was fear; the times with Selenay and other Heralds—sorrow, pain, loss. Even what you picked up from me was an emotion—love. Or maybe lust," she winked at Talia, who coughed politely and blushed, "since I'm not sure exactly what you were getting from me that time, and it had been a *long* trip. Seriously, though—you *can* hear thoughts if you're properly prepared or you're in deep trance, but what you receive first and strongest is *emotion*. When there's no emotion involved, and there hasn't been in these training sessions, it's that much harder for you to receive meaning. I didn't think about that because the Gift for emotion-sensing—we call it 'empathy'—is almost *never* seen alone, or in a Chosen. The only times I can ever remember seeing it is in company with the Gift of true Healing, and the Companions never Choose someone with the Healing Gifts, probably because they're needed too much as Healers. What have I been telling you to do all this time?"

"Relax and clear my mind of everything—" Talia said, beginning to grasp what Ylsa was saying, "—and especially to clear my mind of emotions, *even the ones coming in from outside.*"

"So naturally you fail. Our Gifts are tricky things, you know; they depend very strongly on how much we believe in our own abilities. When you failed, you disbelieved a little and made it that much harder the next time. It's time we abandoned this tack and tried something different."

"Like what?"

"You'll see—just keep your shields down. If all this isn't moonshine, I don't want you expecting anything in particular, and maybe having your imagination supply it for you," Ylsa turned to Neave and whispered in his ear. He nodded and left the room, while Talia waited with half-perplexed anticipation for something to happen.

Suddenly she was inundated by terror, and hard upon the terror came a picture—and then it was something more than a picture. It was a vision of a filthy, smoke-filled taproom—a vision that she was a part of, for the room around her and her fellows had vanished. All around her loomed the slack bodies of drunken, half-crazed people; mostly men, but with a few slatternly women sprawled among them. They were very much bigger than she; she seemed to have shrunk down to the size of a ten-year-old. She was trying to slip through them with as little stir as possible, serving their cheap wine, when one of them woke from his daze and seized her arm in a grip that hurt. "Come here, little boy, pretty boy," he crooned, ignoring her struggles to free herself. "I only want to give you something. . . ."

She wanted to scream, knowing very well what it was he wanted, but found her throat so choked with fear that she could barely squeak. It was like a nightmare from which there could be no awakening. She began losing herself completely in panic when something broke the spell she was in.

"Talia!" Ylsa was shaking her, slapping her face lightly. "Talia, block it out!"

"Goddess. . . ." Talia slumped in her seat and held her head in both hands. "What happened?"

"I told Neave to project the most emotional image he could think of at you," Ylsa said, a bit grimly, "We succeeded better than I had guessed we would. You not only received it, you were trapped by it. Well, that answers *that* question— your Gift is empathy, beyond all doubt. And now that we know for certain what your Gift is, we can do more about training you properly."

"Lady of Light," Talia said, burying her face in her hands. "Poor, poor Neave! If you'd seen what I saw . . . how can such filth be allowed to exist?"

"It's not—not here," Neave himself came through the door, looking quite ordinary; far calmer, far more natural than Talia would have believed possible for someone whose mind held such memories. "I'm from outKingdom, remember? Where I come from, an orphaned child of the poor is fair game for whatever anyone wants to do with him. So long as the priests and the Peacekeepers aren't *officially* aware of what's going on, and there's no one to speak for the child, just about anything is tolerated. Are you all right? I could tell something was wrong, but not what. I stopped sending, but you'd already broken off contact. Talia, you had an awfully strong hold on me; I found myself reliving that whole filthy episode—"

"Neave—I'm so sorry—" she strove to express her horror at what he'd gone through, and failed utterly.

He touched her arm hesitantly, his eyes understanding. "Talia, it was long ago and far away.

Thanks to people like Ylsa and the Dean, it doesn't even hurt that much anymore. I know now it wasn't anything *I* did that caused it." He licked his lips, his calm shell cracking just a little. "Time does heal things, you know, time and love and help. I just wish that I could somehow make sure that nothing like that ever happens to another child."

"Someday, we hope, that's exactly what the Heralds will accomplish," the Dean said gravely. "Someday—when there isn't a Kingdom on this world that doesn't welcome us. But for now—well, Neave, we save the ones we can, and try not to think too hard about the others, the ones we couldn't save. We can't be everywhere. . . ."

But Elcarth's eyes told them how little it helped, at times, to know that, and how hard it was to forget the ones still trapped in their little hells.

Eventually, Ylsa declared the class to be officially over, saying that there was nothing else she could actually teach them. Now their proficiency depended on their own limits and how well they honed their Gifts with practice.

The end of the class meant that it was time to learn the only "real" magic that they were ever likely to see. It was time to learn the Truth Spell.

"Legend says this was discovered by a contemporary of Herald Vanyel, just before the incursions of the Dark Servants," she told them. "Since Vanyel himself was the last of what were called the 'Heraldic Mages,' this is the last real bit of magic ever created in Valdemar and is about all the 'real magic' we have left except for a few things the priests and Healers use. Most of the rest was lost to the Dark Servants, abandoned because of negative associations, or just plain forgotten. In some ways, it's too bad—it would be nice to still be able to build a fortress like the Palace—Collegium complex and to pave roads the way the old ones did. At any rate, this spell starts with a cantrip; a little rhyme, just like some of the others you've learned—"

With the rhyme came an image they were to hold in their minds, one that made very little sense to Talia, the image of a wisp of fog with blue eyes. While holding this image, they were to recite the rhyme mentally nine times; no more, no less. On the ninth repetition they were to imagine the fog enveloping the person they were casting the spell on.

Ylsa demonstrated on Dean Elcarth; closing her own eyes briefly then staring fixedly at him for a few moments. Within a few heartbeats, Elcarth was surrounded by a faint but readily visible glowing blue nimbus of light.

"I've just put the first stage on him," Ylsa told them. "I'm not forcing the truth out of him, but just registering whether or not he's telling it. Lie for me, Elcarth."

"I'm passionately in love with you, Ylsa."

The glow vanished, while Ylsa and her students laughed.

"Now tell me the truth."

"I consider you to be one of the most valuable assets of the Circle, but I'm rather glad you're not *my* lifemate. You're altogether too difficult a woman and you have a nasty temper."

The glow reappeared, and Ylsa sighed dramatically. "Ah, Elcarth, and here all this time I'd been hoping you secretly cared."

"Elcarth, sir, can *you* see what we're seeing?" Neave asked curiously.

"Not so much as a glimmer," he replied. "But anyone except the person bespelled sees the glow, whether or not they've got a Gift. Why don't you invoke the second stage, Ylsa?"

"If you're ready for it." Again she stared at him; Talia could see no perceptible change in the glow surrounding him.

"How old are you, Elcarth? Try to tell me 'twenty.' "

His face twisted with strain and beads of sweat appeared on his forehead. "T-t-t," he stuttered, "T-fifty-seven." He sighed heavily. "I'd forgotten what it felt like to try and fight Truth Spell, Ylsa. Take it off, would you, before I get tricked into revealing something I shouldn't?"

"Now why would I do something like that to you?" she teased, then closed her eyes briefly again, and the glow was gone. "You banish the spell easily enough—just picture the cloud lifting away from the person, close its eyes, and dissipate."

"You all have Gifts strong enough to bring both stages of the spell to bear," she said a moment later, "So why don't you start practicing? Neave and Talia, with me—the twins with Elcarth."

The feeling of having the second stage of the Truth Spell cast on her was decidedly eerie, Talia found. No matter what she had *intended* to say, she found her tongue would not obey her; only the exact truth came out. In cases where she didn't know the answer to a question, she was even forced to say so rather than temporize.

At last Ylsa declared them all proficient enough to close the class out.

"You know the 'spells'—though if we find out you've been using the Truth Spell as a prank, you'll find yourself in *very* hot water, so don't even consider it! Practice it if you wish, but do so only under the supervision of a full Herald. You know where your strengths and weaknesses lie," she continued, "Just like sparring practice will make you a better fighter, practicing with your Gifts will develop them to their full extent. If you run into any problems that are related to your Gifts, there are three of us who are probably the experts; you can come to any of us, day or night if it's an emergency. Myself, when I'm at the Collegium, the Dean, or Herald Kyril, the Seneschal's Herald. There are books in the Library as well that may help; I recommend you go up there and follow your instincts. Certainly you'll learn more about the abstract theory of our Gifts from them than you will from me, if that's what you want. I never was one for theory. I leave that up to Kyril! *He* enjoys trying to ferret out the 'whys' and 'hows' of our Gifts. I'm content with just knowing the usages, and never mind how it works."

Theirs was the first of the three groups being taught to finish formal training. The other two were much smaller, the 'communication' Gifts being by far and away the most common, and contained, respectively, Griffon and a younger girl, Christa; and Davan with one of Christa's year-mates, a boy called Wulf. Talia was extremely curious about these other Gifts and asked Ylsa about them as the last class broke up.

"The other two general groups have to do with moving things with thought alone, and seeing at a distance." Ylsa said. "We tend to lump them un-

der the names of 'Fetching' and 'Sight.' Oddly
enough, the two Heralds best at both those skills
happen to work together as a team; Dirk and Kris.
Well, maybe it's not so odd. Gifts that are needed
tend to appear just before they're needed."

The second name woke a vague feeling of recol-
lection; after a moment of thought, Talia remembered that she'd met Kris before, her first night at
the Collegium. "Kris is the one that's too good-
looking to be true, isn't he? she asked Ylsa with a
half-smile.

"That's the one. The fact that Dirk and Kris are
partners is one reason why we hold these classes—
particularly the latter two—all at the same time
and for more than one year-group; it makes more
sense to wait for a time of several weeks when
Dirk and Kris don't have to be out somewhere,"
Ylsa replied. "Why are you asking?"

"Insatiable curiosity," Talia confessed. "I—kind
of wonder how their Gifts are related to my own."

"Seeing's probably the closest; emotions are powerful attractants for the mind's eye. In fact, you
have more than a touch of that particular Gift
yourself, as you've noticed. I've told you that no
one ever has *just* one Gift with no hint of the
others, haven't I? You've got enough thought-
sensing and Sight to possibly be useful in an
emergency—maybe just a hint of Healing as well.
Anyway, the difference between their Gifts and
yours is that you will generally have to See things
through the eyes of someone present unless there's
a *lot* of emotional residuum to hold you, and then it
will be very vague. They can See things as if they
were observing them directly, even if there's nobody there. There isn't much to watch in that

class, though; just the three of them sitting around in trance-states. Quite boring if you're not linked in with them. Dirk's class is something else altogether—*that's* something to see! I know he won't mind; want to peek in on them?"

"Could I?" Talia didn't even try to conceal her eagerness.

"I don't see any reason why not. Queen's Own should probably see some of the other Gifts in action—especially since it seems your year-mate Griffon has one of the rarer and potentially more dangerous of the 'Fetching' family."

"He does? What does he do?" Talia found it difficult to envision the good-natured Griffon as dangerous.

"He's a Firestarter."

Because of Griffon's Gift, Dirk was holding his classes outside, away from any building, and near the well—just in case. Talia could see he had a bucket of water on the cobblestones beside him. He and his two pupils were sitting cross-legged on the bare paving, all three seeming to be too engrossed in what they were doing to notice any discomfort from the stone. He nodded agreeably to Ylsa and Talia as they approached, indicating with an eyebrow a safe place to stand and watch, and then turned his attention immediately back to his two pupils.

Talia discovered to her surprise that she recognized Herald Dirk as the young Herald she'd encountered just outside the capital. She had been far too overcome with bashfulness and the fear that she'd been wrong-doing to take more than a cursory look at him then; she took the opportu-

nity afforded by his deep involvement with his
pupils to do so now.

Her initial impression of homeliness was totally
confirmed. His face looked like a clay model that
had been constructed by someone with little or no
talent at all. His nose was much too long for his
face; his ears looked as if they'd just been stuck on
by guess and then left there. His jaw was square
and didn't match his rather high cheekbones; his
teeth looked like they'd be more at home in his
Companion's mouth than in his. His forehead didn't
match any of the rest of his face; it was much too
broad, and his overly generous mouth was lop-
sided. His straw-colored hair looked more like the
thatched roof of a cottage—provided that the
thatcher hadn't had the least notion of what he'd
been about. The only thing that redeemed him
from being repulsive was the good-natured smile
that always hovered around the corners of his
mouth, a smile that demanded that the onlooker
smile in response.

That, and his eyes—he had the most beautiful
eyes Talia had ever seen; brimming with kindness
and compassion. The only eyes she could compare
them to were Rolan's—and they were the same
living sapphire blue as a Companion's.

If she hadn't been so fascinated by what was
transpiring, she might have paused to wonder at
the strength of response she felt to the implied
kindness of those eyes.

As it was, though, Griffon was in the process of
demonstrating his gift, and that drove any other
thought from her head.

He seemed to be working his way up through
progressively less combustible materials; it was evi-

dent from some of the residue of this exercise that he'd already attained the control required to ignite normally volatile substances at will. In front of him were the remains of burned paper, shredded cloth, the tarry end of a bit of rope, and a charred piece of kindling-wood. Now Dirk placed in front of him an odd black rock.

"This stuff *will* burn if you get it hot enough, I promise you," he was saying to Griffon. "Smiths use it sometimes to get a really hot fire; they prefer it over charcoal. Give it a try."

Griffon stared at the bit of black stone, his face intent. After a tense moment, he sighed explosively.

"It's no use—" he began.

"You're trying too hard again," Dirk admonished. "Relax. It's no different than what you did with the wood; the stuff's just a bit more stubborn. Give it longer."

Once again Griffon stared at the lump. Then something extraordinary happened. His eyes suddenly unfocused, and Talia's stomach flipped over; she became disoriented for a moment—the experience was something rather as if she'd been part of the mating of two dissimilar objects into a new whole.

The black lump ignited with a preternatural and explosive fury.

"*Whoa!*" Dirk shouted, dousing the fire with the handy bucket of water. It had burned with such heat that the stone beneath it sizzled and actually cracked when the water hit it. There was a smell of scorched rock and steam rising in a cloud from the place it had been.

Griffon's eyes refocused, and he stared at the blackened area, dumbfounded. "Did *I* do that?"

"You certainly did. Congratulations," Dirk said cheerfully. "Now you see why we have this class outside. More importantly, can you do it again, and with a little more control this time?"

"I—think so—" Griffon's eyes once again took on the abstracted appearance they'd had before—and the soaked remains of the black rock sizzled, then began merrily burning away, in sublime indifference to the puddle around them.

"Now damp it," Dirk commanded.

The flames died completely. In seconds the rock was cool enough for Dirk to pick up.

"Well done, youngling!" Dirk applauded. "You've got the trick of it now! With practice you'll be able to call fire right out of the air if you want—but don't try yet. That's enough for today. Any more, and you'll have a headache."

The headaches were something Ylsa had warned Talia's class about, the direct result of overextending a Gift. Sometimes this was unavoidable, but for the most part it was better not to court them. Drake had gotten one one day, showing off; his example had reinforced that prohibition. Ylsa had given them each a packet of herbs to make into a tea that deadened the worst of the pain should they miscalculate and develop one anyway, and had told them that Mero kept a further supply on hand in the kitchen when they ran out.

"Now, Christa—your turn." Dirk moved his attention to the lanky, coltish girl to his left. "There's a message tube the mate to this one—" he laid a Herald's message container of the kind that Special Messengers usually carried on their belts in front of her, "—on the top of the first bookcase in the Library. It's lying along the top of *Spun of*

Shadow. I know this is bigger than anything you've tried before, but the distance is a bit less than you've reached in the past. Think you can visualize it and bring it here?"

She nodded without speaking, and took the message tube in her hands. There was a growing feeling of tension once again, it was plainly perceptible to Talia. She felt as if she were in the middle of two people pulling on her mind—then came a kind of popping noise; now not one, but two message tubes lay in Christa's hands.

Dirk took the new one from her and opened it. He displayed the contents to her with a grin—a small slip of parchment with the words "Exercise one, and well begun" on it. Christa's grin of accomplishment echoed Dirk's.

"Not good poetry, but the sentiment's right. Well, you managed that one. Now let's see if you can get a little farther. . . ."

Ylsa nudged Talia, who nodded reluctantly, and both moved quietly away.

"Gifts like Griffon's have been known to wreak absolute havoc if the owner fails to learn how to control them." Ylsa said gravely once they were out of earshot. "There have been instances in the past when the trainee's teacher, unprepared perhaps for the kind of explosion we saw today, reacted with fear—fear that the pupil in turn reacted to. Sometimes that causes the pupil to block his Gift entirely, making it impossible for him to learn full control; and then, at some later date, during a moment of stress or crisis, it flares up again with a fury that has to be seen to be believed. We've been very fortunate in that this fury has always been turned against the enemies of the Kingdom in the past."

"Lavan Firestorm—" Talia said in comprehension. "I remember now; he almost single-handedly drove back the Dark Servants at the Battle of White Foal Pass. But at Burning Pines his Companion was killed, and the last Firestorm he called up consumed him as well as the enemy."

"There's nothing but bare rock at Burning Pines to this day. Those who were there were just lucky he retained enough hold on his sanity to warn them before he called down the Fires. And there's no guarantee that the Firestorm *couldn't* be turned against friends as well as enemies—rage can often be blind. That's why Dirk makes such a good teacher; he never shows the slightest sign of fear to his pupils. We're lucky to have him in the Circle," Ylsa replied. "At any rate, you've got weapons drill to go to, and I have to report that I'm free for reassignment. I'll see you at dinner, kitten."

Talia continued to practice every night, choosing times when the sometimes volatile emotions of the students of the Collegium were damped by the weariness of day's end. For several weeks she simply observed what she was drawn to—though a time or two she quickly chose some *other* subject to observe after her initial contact proved highly intimate and rather embarrassing. When she became more sure of herself, though, she was tempted by encountering the fear of one of the youngest student's nightmares to try intervening.

To her great delight, she was successful in turning the fear away. Without that stimulus, the dream quickly changed to something more innocuous.

Her success prompted her to try intervention in the emotions of others several times more—though always choosing only to try to redirect the more negative emotions of anger, fear—or once, in the case of a quarrel and a gross misunderstanding on the part of two of the court servants, hatred. Her successes, though not always complete, were enough to encourage her in the belief that such interventions were "right."

There was a side effect to the complete awakening and training of her Gift, and it had to do with Rolan. He was, after all, a stallion—and *the* premier stallion of the Companion herd. And Companions, like their human partners, were always "in season." Rolan's company was much sought after of a night.

And now that Talia's Gift was at full strength, it was impossible to shield him out of her mind.

The enforced sharing of Rolan's amorous encounters vastly increased her education in certain areas—even if it wasn't something she'd have chosen of her own accord.

It was both curiosity and her growing sensitivity that led her to the House of Healing and the Healer's Collegium. Most of the patients there were Heralds, badly injured in the field. Once their conditions had been stabilized they were always sent here, where the combined efforts and knowledge of the Kingdom's best in the Healer's craft could be brought to their aid. There was not the crying need for her in the House of Healing that there had been at other times and places— but the distress was there all the same, and it drew her as a moth is drawn to flame. She was at a loss as to how to gain entrance there until impulse caused her to seek out the one teacher she knew among the Healers—the one who had treated her in her illness; Devan.

Her choice couldn't have been better. Devan had been briefed by Ylsa on the nature of Talia's Gift, and as an empath himself, he thoroughly understood the irresistible drawing power that the place had for her. He welcomed her presence on his rounds of his patients, guessing that she might well be able to accomplish something to aid in their recoveries.

It wasn't easy, but as she had told Selenay, when something needed to be done, she made the time for it. She began getting up an hour or so earlier, breakfasting in the kitchen, and making Devan's early-morning rounds with him, then returning during the time in the afternoon that Elspeth spent riding with her mother.

Talia learned a great deal, and not just about the Healing Gifts. With so many Healers and Healers-in-training available, it was not necessary for her to participate in Devan's treatments, but her observations gave her a profound respect for his abilities. His specialty—all Healers had one form of Healing that they studied more intensively than the others—was the kind of hurts caused by wounding, and what he referred to as "trauma"; injuries acquired suddenly and violently, and often accompanied by shock.

Talia had never quite realized down deep until she began visiting the House of Healing just how hazardous the life of a Herald could be. Until now, she'd only been aware of the deaths; accompanying Devan she saw what *usually* happened to Heralds who ran afoul of ill luck on duty.

"It's the Border sectors that are usually the worst, you know," Devan told her when she remarked that no less than three of his patients seemed to be from Sectors in and around her old home. "Take your home Sector for instance; the normal tour of duty for a Herald is a year and a half. Guess how long it is for the ones that ride the Holderkin Sector?"

"A year?" Talia hazarded.

"Nine or ten months. They're fine until the winter raids coming over from Karse. Sooner or later they catch more than an arrow or an axe, and then it's back here to recover. That's one of the worst, though some of the Sectors up on the North Border are just as bad, what with the barbarians coming down every time the food supply runs short. That's why we have Alberich teaching you combat and strategy, youngling. Get assigned to a Sector like the Holderkin one, and you're often as much soldier as Herald. The Herald in charge may well be the only trained fighter around until an Army detachment arrives."

Later, she asked him why it was that there wasn't anyone from the Lake Evendim area, when she knew from what Keren and Sherrill had told her that they, too, had their share of freebooters.

"Along Lake Evendim it isn't raiders and barbarians. It's pirates and bands of outlaws because it's easy to hide in the shore-caves. Not too many injured end up here because that type of opponent isn't really out to fight, just to thieve and run. Your compatriots usually wind up getting patched up at one of the Healing Temples, and then they're on their way again. We don't have anyone here from Southern Sectors, either."

"Why?"

"Southern's abutted by Menmelith, and they're friendly—but the weather's strange and unpredictable, especially in the summer. Lots of broken bones from accidents—but there, again, they're usually cared for locally unless it's something really bad, like a broken neck or back."

"But there's two from the Northwest corner—and one of them is poor Vostel—" Talia shuddered a little. Vostel was burned over most of his body, and in constant agony when not sustained by drugs. Talia had taken to spending a lot of time with him because the constant pain was a drain on his emotions. He felt free to let down his frail bulwark of courage with her; to weep from the hurt, to curse the gods, to confess his fear that he would never be well again. She did her best to comfort, reassure, and give back some of the emotional energy that his injuries drained from him.

"Northwest is uncanny," Devan replied. "And I say it, who come from there and should be used to it. Very odd things come out of that wilderness, and don't think I'm exaggerating because I've seen some of them. Just as an example, ninety-nine people out of a hundred will tell you that griffins don't exist outside of a Bard's fevered imagination—the hundredth has been up there and seen them in the sky, and knows them for the deadly reality that they are. I've seen them—I've hunted them, once; they're hard to kill and impossible to catch, and dangerous, just like every weird thing that lives in that wilderness. They say there were wars once somewhere out there fought with magic—

magic like in the Bardic tales, not our Gifts—and the things living out there are what's left of the weapons and armies that fought them."

"What do you think?" Talia asked.

"It's as good a way to explain it as any, I suppose," Devan shrugged. "All *I* know is that most people don't believe the half of my tales. Except the Heralds of course; they know better, especially after a griffin's taken a mouthful out of some of them, or a firebird's scorched them for coming too close to her nest—like Vostel. That's probably why I stay here; it's the only place I'll be believed!"

Talia shook her head at him; "You stay because you have to. You're needed too badly here—you couldn't do anything else, and you know it."

"Too wise, youngling," he replied, "You're too wise by half. Maybe I should be glad; you're certainly making it easier to get my patients on their feet again. If I haven't said so before, I appreciate your efforts. We don't have enough mind-Healers to care for the minor traumas; the two we've got have to be saved for the dangerously unbalanced. Now don't look innocent, I know *exactly* what you've been doing! As far as I'm concerned, you can go right on doing it."

For here among the injured she found yet another, and more subtle application of her own Gift. There wasn't the kind of self-destructive sorrow to deal with that came upon those left behind with a Herald's death, but there were other, more insidiously negative emotions to be transmuted.

Self-doubt, so familiar to her, was one of those emotions. There wasn't a Herald in the wards that wasn't prey to it. Often they blamed themselves for their own injuries or the deaths or injuries of those they had been trying to help. And when they were alone so much of the time, with only pain and memory as companions, that self-doubt tended to grow.

It was hardly surprising that some of them developed phobias either, especially not if they'd been trapped or lying alone for long periods before rescue.

And there was a complex muddle of guilt and hatred to be sorted out and worked through for most of them. They hated those who had caused their hurts, either directly or indirectly, and they felt terrible guilt because a Herald was simply not *supposed* to hate anyone. A Herald was supposed to understand. A Herald was supposed to be the kind of person who cured hatreds, not the kind who was prey to them himself. That a Herald was also not supposed to be some kind of superhuman demigod didn't occur to them. That a little honest hatred might be healthy didn't occur to them either.

But the most insidious emotion, and the hardest to do anything about was despair; and despair was more than understandable when a body was plainly too badly hurt to be fully Healed again. It sometimes happened that an injury had been left too long untended to be truly Healed, especially if it had become infected. That was why Jadus had lost his leg in the wars with Karse fought by the Tedrel mercenaries. Healers could realign even the tiniest fragments of bone to allow a crushed limb to be restored—but only if that bone had not yet begun to set. And nerve-damage left too long could never be restored. How did you ease the pain of one who could look at his maimed and broken flesh and know he would never be the same again?

And there was the steady toll on heart and courage inflicted by what seemed to be endless pain—pain such as the burned Vostel was enduring.

All these things called to her with a voice too strong to be denied, begging her to set them aright. So as she became more deft in the usage of her Gift, she began administering to these injured as well as the bereft, and doing it so subtly that few realized that she'd helped them until after she'd gone. It was hard: hard to find the time, hard to witness the kinds of mental torment that could not be set aright with one simple touch or an out-pouring of grief—but once she began, it was impossible to stop; the needs in the House of Healing drew her as implacably as the anguish left in the wake of death did. She didn't realize—though by now Kyril and one or two others did—that she was only following in the footsteps of many another Monarch's Own. Like Talia, those who had possessed the strongest Gifts in that capacity wound up ministering not only to the Monarch, but the entire Circle as well. The mounting evidence for these few was that when Talia earned her Whites, she was likely to prove to be one of the Heralds tales are written about. Unfortunately for their peace of mind, the Heralds tales are written about seldom had long or peaceful lives.

Twelve

"Make sure you get the blindfold good and tight," Elspeth told Skif. "Otherwise the test isn't any good."

Skif forbore to comment that he already knew that, and simply asked, "Is Keren done yet?"

"I'll go see," Elspeth ran off.

"Positive you can't see anything? Too tight? Too loose?" he asked Talia, making a few final adjustments to her blindfold.

"Black as a mousehole at midnight," she assured him, "And it's fine—it isn't going to slip any, I don't think, and it isn't uncomfortable."

"Keren says she's ready when you are," Elspeth called from beyond the screen of trees in Companion's Field where Keren stood.

"You ready?"

"Any time."

Skif led Talia carefully around the trees to where Keren stood, hands on her hips and a half-smile curving her lips.

"I took you at your word, little centaur; it's good and complicated," she said as they approached her. "Nobody's ever tried this sort of thing before to my knowledge; it should be interesting."

"Nobody seems to have this kind of Companion-bond either except me," Talia replied, "And I want to see how much of it is really there and how much is imagination."

"Well, this should do the trick. If you're really seeing through Rolan's eyes, you won't take a single misstep. If you're only imagining it, there's no way you'll be able to negotiate *this* maze."

The red and gold leaves had been carefully cleaned from the ground for at least a hundred feet in all directions in front of where Keren was standing, and laid out on the grass was a carefully plotted maze, the boundaries of its corridors marked by a line of paint on the grass. The corridors were only about two feet wide at the most, and it would take careful watching to avoid stepping on the paint. The maze itself was, as Keren had indicated, very complicated, and since the corridors were not demarcated by anything but the paint on the grass, there would be no way the blindfolded Talia would be able to tell where they were by feel.

Rolan stood beside Keren, on a little rise of ground that gave him a good view of the entire maze. According to Talia's plan, *he* would be her eyes for this task. If the bond between them were as deep and strong as she thought, she would be able to traverse the maze with relative ease.

While Keren, Skif, and Elspeth watched in fascination, she set out to make the attempt.

Halfway through, she hesitated for a long moment.

"She's going to end up in a dead end," Skif whispered to Keren.

"No, she's not—wait and see. There's more than

one way you can get through this, and I think she just chose the shorter route."

Finally Talia stopped and turned blindly back to her audience.

"Well?" she asked.

"Take the blindfold off and see for yourself."

She had threaded the maze so successfully that there wasn't even a smear of paint on her boots. "It worked—" she said, a little awed, "it really worked!"

"I must admit that this is one of the most amazing things I've ever seen," Keren said, picking her way across the grass followed by Rolan and the other two. "I thought Dantris and I were tight-bonded, but I don't think we could have managed this. Why did you stop halfway through?"

"Rolan was arguing with me—I wanted to go the way I finally did, and he wanted me to take the 'T' path."

"Either would have gotten you out; the one you wanted was the shorter, though. Ready for the second test?"

"I think so. Rolan seems to be."

"All right then—off with you, despoiler of gardens!" Keren slapped Rolan lightly on the rump; he snorted at her, and trotted off. Skif followed beside him.

Keren had a single die, which she threw for a set of twenty passes, as Talia carefully noted down the number of pips. Skif, with Rolan, had a set of six cards, one for each face of the die. Rolan was to indicate which face was up for each pass Keren made—for this time, *he* would be using Talia's eyes. This didn't take long; both of them were soon back, and Skif's and Talia's lists compared.

"Incredible—not even *one* wrong! We're going to have to tell Kyril about this; I don't doubt he'll want to give you even more tests together," Keren said with amazement.

"He's welcome if he wants to," Talia replied. "I just wanted to be sure that I was right about the bond. Now that we're done, I'll tell you what else I was testing. I was shielded the entire time for both tests."

"You're joking, surely!" Skif's mouth fell open.

"I was never more serious. You realize what this means, don't you? Not only is our bond one of the strongest I know of, but if *I* can't shield him out, nobody can block him away from me, either."

"That could be mighty useful, someday," Keren put in. "It means that even if you were unconscious, you could be reached through Rolan. We'll definitely have to tell Kyril about this now."

"Go right ahead. It's hardly something that needs to be kept secret."

"Talia, do you think I'll have a friend like Rolan someday?" Elspeth asked wistfully.

Talia gathered the child to her and hugged her shoulders. "Catling," she whispered, "Never doubt it for a minute. In fact, your Companion-friend may very well be even *better* than Rolan, and that's a promise."

Rolan did not respond to this with his usual snort of human-like derision. Instead, he nuzzled the child gently, almost as if to confirm Talia's promise.

A few evenings later Talia decided to determine exactly what the physical limit of the range of her Gift was.

She did not bother to light a candle in her room, but simply relaxed on her bed in the growing dusk, isolating and calming any disturbing influences in herself until she was no longer aware of her body except as a kind of anchor from which to move outward. She extended her sense of empathy slowly, reaching first beyond her room, then beyond the Collegium, then beyond the Palace and grounds. There were vague pockets in the Palace of ambition and unease, but nothing and no one strong enough to hold her there.

She brushed lightly past them, venturing beyond, out into the city itself. Emotions appeared as vivid colors to her; they were like mists to move through for the most part, with none of the negative sort being strong enough to stay her passage. Once or twice she stopped long enough to intervene; in a tavern brawl, and in the nightmares of a young soldier. Then she passed on.

She ranged out farther now, following the Northern road, moving from contact to contact with those dwelling or camped beside it as if she were following beacons along the wayside. They were like little lanterns along the darkened road, providing mostly guidepoints for her—or perhaps like stepping-stones across a brook since she needed them to move onward. The contacts here were fewer than in any other direction as the Northern road led through some of the most sparsely populated districts in the Kingdom. As Talia's consciousness flowed along this route, she remembered that this was the route Ylsa had been sent out on earlier in the week.

Suddenly, as if merely being reminded of Ylsa's existence were impetus enough, she found herself being pulled Northward, caught by a force too strong and too urgent to resist.

There was growing unease and apprehension as she was pulled along—and growing fear as well. She found herself unable to break the contact or to slow herself and became even more alarmed because of this. She was in a near panic when she was suddenly pulled into what had drawn her.

She found herself *there*. Looking out of another's eyes. Ylsa's eyes.

Ambushed!

Too many—there were too many of them to fight off. Felara lashed out with wicked hooves and laid about her with her teeth, trying to make a path for escape, but their attackers were canny and managed to keep them surrounded. She clamped her legs tightly around Felara's chest to stay with her, knowing she was as good as dead if she was thrown.

She drew her longsword and cut at them, but for every one she laid low, two sprang up to replace him. The sword was not really meant for fighting a-horseback, and before she'd managed to strike more than half-a-dozen blows, it was carried out of her hands by a falling foe, and she was forced to draw her dagger instead. Then, in a well-coordinated move, they all drew back as a horn sounded.

Terrible pain lanced through her shoulder and momentarily filmed her eyes. She looked down stupidly to see a feathered shaft sprouting from her upper chest.

Felara screamed in agony as a second shaft pierced the Companion's flank. Damn the moon!

They were illuminated clearly by it—clearly enough to make good targets for the archers that *must* be hidden underneath the trees. Their attackers fell back a little more—and more shafts hummed out of the darkness—

Felara cried once again, and collapsed, trapping her beneath her Companion's bulk. And she couldn't think or move, for the loss and the agony of Felara's death were all too much a part of her.

The archers' work done, the swordsmen closed anew. She saw *the* blade catch the moonlight, and arc down, and knew it for the one that would kill her—

:*Kyril! Tell the Queen—in the shaft!*:

Dozens of images flashed and vanished. One stayed. Arrows—ringed with black. Five of them. Hollow black-ringed arrows—

Then unbearable pain, followed by a terrifying silence and darkness, more terrible than the pain—she was trapped in the darkness, unable to escape. There was nothing to hold to, nothing to anchor to—then abruptly, there *was* something in the darkness with her.

It was Rolan—

And she took hold of him in panic fear and *pulled*—

Talia shrieked with a mortal pain not her own—and found herself sitting bolt upright in her bed. For one moment she sat, blinking and confused, and not at all sure that it all hadn't been a far too realistic nightmare.

Then the Death Bell tolled.

"No—oh no, no, no—" She began to sob brokenly in reaction—when a thought stilled her own tears as surely as if they'd been shut off.

Keren.

Keren, who was bound to Ylsa as strongly as to her Companion or her brother—who depended on those bonds. Who, Talia knew, made a habit of communicating with her lover every night she was gone if Ylsa was within range. Who *must* have felt Ylsa's death—if she hadn't been mentally searching for her at the time of the ambush, she would know it by the Herald's bond. And who, prostrated by grief and the shock of Ylsa's death, which she had experienced no less than Talia, might very well lose her hold on responsibility and duty long enough to succeed in death-willing herself.

Talia was still dressed except for boots. She ran for the Herald's quarters without stopping to put them on. She'd never been in Keren's rooms before, but there was no mistaking the fiery beacon of pain and loss that led her onward. She followed it unerringly.

The door was already open when she arrived; Keren's twin slumped next to her, his eyes dazed, his expression vacant. Keren was sitting frozen in her chair; she'd evidently been trying to reach Ylsa when Ylsa was struck down. She was totally locked away within herself. Her face was an expressionless mask, and only the wild eyes showed that she was alive. The look in those eyes was that of a creature wounded and near death, and not very human anymore.

Talia touched Keren's hand hesitantly; there was no response. With a tiny cry of dismay, she took both Keren's cold hands in her own, and strove to reach her with her mind.

She was dragged into a whirling maelstrom of pain. There was nothing to hold on to. There was only unbearable loneliness and loss. Caught within that whirlpool was Keren's twin—and now, Talia as well.

Again she reached blindly in panic for a mental anchor—and again, there was Rolan, a steady pillar to hold to. She reached for him; was caught and held firm. Now, no longer frightened, no longer at the mercy of the pain-storm, she could think of the others.

Keren could not be reached, but perhaps her brother could be freed. She reached for the "Terenspark," caught it, and held it long enough to try to pull both of them out.

With a convulsive lurch, Talia broke contact.

She found herself on the other side of the room, half-supported by Teren, half-supporting him herself.

"What happened?" she gasped.

"She cried out—I heard her, and found her like *that*. When I tried to get her to wake, when I touched her, she pulled me in with her—" Teren shook his head, trying to clear it. "Talia, I can't reach her at all. We've got to do something! You can reach her, can't you?"

"I tried; I can't come near. It's—too strong, too closed in. I can't catch hold of her, and she's destroying herself with her own grief. Somehow—" Talia tried to shake off the effects of her contact with that mindless chaos and loss. "Somehow I've got to find something to make her turn it outward instead of in—"

Talia's chaotic thoughts steadied, found a focus,

and held. With one of the intuitive leaps perhaps only she was capable of, she thought of Sherrill—

Sherrill, daring to follow Keren into the river. Follow *Keren*, that was the key; and now Talia could remember how Sherrill had always seemed to hover at the edge of wherever it was that Keren or Ylsa or both were. And how there had always been a kind of smothered longing in her eyes. Remembered how Sherrill had always kept from intruding *too* closely on them, perhaps fearing that her own presence might spoil something—

Sherrill, who came from the same people as Keren and Teren; from among folk who did not hold that love between those of the same sex was anathema as was so often the case elsewhere.

Sherrill, who had as many lovers as she wished, yet stayed with none.

"Teren, think hard—is Sherrill back from her internship yet?" Talia asked him urgently.

"I don't—I think so—" He was still a little dazed.

"Get her, then. Now! She'll know who the Bell is for—tell her Keren needs her!"

He did not pause to question her, impelled by the urgency in her voice. He scrambled to his feet and sprinted out the door; Talia returned to Keren's side and strove to touch her without being pulled in a second time.

Finally the sound she'd been hoping for reached her ears; the sound of two pairs of feet running up the corridor.

Sherrill led Teren by a good margin, and she plainly had only one goal in her mind—Keren.

Talia relinquished her place as Sherrill seized Keren's hands in her own and knelt by her side; sobbing heartbrokenly, calling Keren's name.

The sound of her weeping penetrated Keren's blankness as nothing Talia had tried had done. Her voice, or perhaps the unconcealed love in that voice, and the pain that equaled Keren's own, broke the hold Keren's grief had held over her.

Keren's face stirred, came to life again—her eyes went to the woman kneeling beside her.

"Sherrill—?" Keren whispered hoarsely.

Something else came forward from the back of her mind, and Talia remembered one thing more—Ylsa, saying "sometimes persistent inability can mask ability"—and Sherrill's own disclaimer of any but the most rudimentary abilities at thought-reading.

Before the wave of their combined grief, and her need to find and give comfort, Sherrill's mental walls collapsed.

Teren and Talia removed themselves and shut the door, giving them privacy to vent their sorrows. But not alone anymore, and not facing their grief unsupported.

Talia leaned up against the corridor walls, wanting to dissolve helplessly into tears herself.

Talia? Teren touched her elbow lightly.

"Coddess—oh, Teren, I saw her die! I saw Ylsa die! It was horrible—" Tears were coursing down her face, and yet this wasn't the kind of weeping that brought any relief. Other Heralds were beginning to gather around her; she hadn't had any time to reshield and their raw emotions melded painfully with her own. It felt as if she were being smothered or torn into dozens of little pieces and scattered on the wind.

Herald Kyril, a tall man considerably older than Teren, and accompanied by the Queen, pushed his way to Talia's side and caught hold of one of her hands. With that contact, he managed to shield her mind from the others. It gave her some respite, though the relief was only partial. He could not shield her from her own memories.

"Majesty!" he exclaimed. "*This* is the other presence I sensed!"

Selenay exercised her royal prerogatives and ordered the corridor cleared.

"Kyril—" she said when only Talia remained. "It is possible that she may have the answer—her Gift is empathy, to be as one with the person she touches."

Talia nodded to confirm what Selenay said, her face wet, her throat too choked to speak.

"My lady—" the iron-haired Herald had something about him that commanded her instant attention, "—you may be the key to a terrible dilemma. I hear the thoughts of others, it is true, but *only* as words. Ylsa cast a message to me with her last breath, but it means *nothing* to me, *nothing!* But if you can recall her thoughts, you who shared her mind—you alone know the meaning behind those words on the wind. Can you tell us what she meant?"

Those final images sprang all too readily to mind, invoking the rest of the experience. "The arrows—" she gasped, feeling Ylsa's death-throes in every cell of her own body, "—the black-ringed arrows she carried are metal; hollow. What you want is inside them."

" 'In the shaft'—of course!" Selenay breathed. "She meant the arrow-shaft!"

Talia closed her hands over her aching temples; she wished passionately that she could somehow hide in the darkness behind her eyes.

"Kyril, are Kris and Dirk in residence?" Selenay demanded.

"Yes, Majesty."

"Then we have a chance to snatch what Ylsa won for us before anyone has an opportunity to find it. Talia, I must ask still more of you. Come with me—Kyril, find Kris and Dirk and bring them with you."

Selenay half-ran down the hall; Talia was forced to ignore her pounding head and urge her trembling legs into a sprint to keep up with her. They left the Collegium area entirely, and entered the portion of the Palace reserved for the Royal Family—a portion of the area dating right back to Valdemar and the Founding.

The Queen opened the door on a room scarcely larger than a closet; round, and with a round table in the center. It was lit by one lantern, heavily shaded, suspended from the ceiling above the exact center of the table. Beneath it, resting on a padded base, was a sphere of crystal. The table itself was surrounded by padded benches with backs to them. As the door closed behind them, the "dead" feeling to the room showed that it was so well-insulated against outside noise that a small riot could take place outside the door without the occupants of the room being aware of it. It was no longer possible to hear even the grim tolling of the Death Bell.

Talia sank onto one of the benches, holding her furiously aching temples and closing her eyes against the light. Her respite was short-lived. The door opened again; Talia raised aching lids to see that Kyril had brought two more Heralds with him, both dressed in clothing that showed every evidence of being thrown on with extreme haste.

With a pang, Talia recognized Dirk and had no difficulty in identifying the angelically-beautiful Kris. They took the bench to her left, Kris sitting closest to her. Kyril sat to her immediate right, and Selenay next to him.

"Talia," Kyril said, "I want you to retrace where you sent your mind tonight. I think perhaps there will be enough emotional residue for you to find it again. This is not going to be easy for you; it will require every last bit of your strength, and I think I can predict that what you will find there may be even more distressing than what you already know. I'll try and cushion the effects for you, but since your Gift is tied up with emotions and feelings, it's bound to be painful. Kris will be following you with his sight. Put your hand in his, and don't let go until we tell you to. Dirk will be linked with him, and the Queen will be shielding all four of us from the outside world and the thoughts of others and keeping distractions from us," As he spoke, Kyril took Talia's unresisting right hand into his own.

She had no energy to spare to reply; she simply leaned back into the padded support of the bench back and put herself back into the interrupted trance. The pain of her head interfered with that. There was a whisper, and a hand rested for a brief moment on the one resting in Kris'—"Selenay" her mind recognized absently—and the pain receded. She retraced her movements now with a kind of double inner vision, seeing the swirls of emotion she had followed, and Seeing the actual landmarks with Kris' Gift as well. Darkness did not hamper his sight in the least, for everything seemed to be illuminated from within, living things the most.

Time lost meaning. Then as she began to recognize things she had passed, she began to dread what she would find at the end of the journey.

Finding the site of the ambush again was probably the worst experience she had ever had in her life.

Ylsa's body had been searched—with complete and callous thoroughness. She was only grateful that it was not Keren who was linked in with her, to see the bestial things they'd done to her lifemate. She wanted to retch; started to feel her grasp on the place slip, then felt someone else's strength supporting her. She held to her task until she began to lose herself as her strength faded. She couldn't feel her own body anymore, even remotely. A luminous mist began to obscure her inner vision. She knew she should have been frightened, for she had gone beyond the limits of her own abilities and energies and was in grave danger of being lost, but she could not even summon up enough force to be afraid.

Then, for the third time, she felt Rolan with her, adding his energy to her own, and she held on for far longer than she would have thought anyone would have been able to bear. Then she heard Kris' voice say, "Got it," and felt him loose her hand.

"Your part's over, Talia," Kyril murmured.

She fled back to herself in a rush, and with a tiny sob of release she buried her head in her arms on the table and let the true tears of mourning flow at last. She wept in silence, only the shaking of her shoulders betraying her. The attention of the others was directed elsewhere now, and she felt free to let her grief loose.

Something clattered down onto the table with a faint metallic clash. The sound was repeated four more times.

Dirk's voice, harsh with fatigue, said, "That's the lot."

There was a stirring to her right, a sound of metal grating on metal, and the whisper of paper.

There was utter silence; then the Queen sighed. Her bench grated a little on the floor as she stood. "This is the proof I needed," she said grimly, "I must summon the Council. There will be necks in the noose after this night's work; high-born necks."

There was a whisper of cooler air from the door, and she was gone.

Talia felt Kyril rise beside her. "My place is at the Council board to represent the Circle," he said, then hesitated.

"Go, Kyril," Kris replied in answer to his hesitation. "We'll see to her."

He sighed with relief, obviously having been torn between his responsibilities to Talia and to the Circle. "Bless you, brothers. Talia—" his hand rested briefly on her head. "You are more than worthy to be Queen's Own. This would not have been remotely possible without your help. Oh, damn, words mean less than nothing now! You'll learn soon enough what this night's agony has won for all of us in the way of long-overdue justice. I think—Ylsa would be proud of you."

The door sighed; he was gone.

"Talia?" Someone had taken Kyril's place on her right; the voice was Dirk's. She stemmed the flood of tears with an effort, and regained at least a fragile semblance of control over herself. Surreptitiously drying her eyes on her sleeve, she raised her aching head.

The weariness on both their faces matched her own, and there were tears in Kris' eyes and the marks of weeping on Dirk's cheeks as well. Both of them tried to reach out of their own grief to comfort her, but were not really sure what to say.

"I—think I'd like—to go back to my room," she said carefully, between surges of pain. Her head throbbed in time with her pulse, and her vision faded every time the pain worsened. She tried to stand, but as she did so, the chamber spun around her like a top, the lamplight dimmed, and there was a roaring in her ears. Kris shoved the table out of the way so that she wouldn't crack her skull open on it while Dirk knocked over the bench in his haste to reach her before she fell; then everything seemed to fade, even her own body, and her thoughts vanished in the wave of anguish that followed.

It was Ylsa—and Felara with her. At least, Talia thought it was Felara; the Companion didn't look the same from moment to moment, a fascinating and luminous, eternally shifting form. And *where* they were—it was sort of a ghost of her own room, all gray and shadowy; insubstantial. You could see the Moon and the stars through the walls.

"Ylsa?" she said, doubtfully—for the Herald looked scarcely older than herself.

"Kitten," Ylsa replied, her tone a benediction. "Oh, kitten! You won't remember this clearly—but you *will* remember it. Tell Keren not to grieve too long; tell her I said so! And if she doesn't behave herself and take what Sherri's offering, I'll come haunt her! The darkness isn't the end to everything, kitten, the Havens are beyond it, and I'm overdue. But before I go—I have a few things to tell you, and to give you—"

She woke the next morning with burning eyes and a still-pounding skull, yet with an oddly comforted soul. There had been a dream—or was it a dream? Ylsa, no longer the mutilated, ravaged thing Talia had seen, but miraculously restored and somehow younger-looking, had spoken to her. She'd seemed awfully substantial for a ghost, if indeed that was what she was.

She'd spoken with Talia for a long, long time; some things she'd said were so clear that Talia could almost hear them now—what to tell Keren, for instance, when Keren's grief had ebbed somewhat; to make it clear to Sherri that she was not to consider herself an interloper. Then she'd taken Talia's hand in her own, and done—what?

She couldn't remember exactly, but somehow the anguish of last night had been replaced by a gentle sorrow that was much easier to bear. The memories, too—those that were her own were still crystal clear, but those which had been Ylsa's were blurred, set at one remove, and no longer so agonizingly a part of her. She couldn't remember now what it had felt like to die.

Someone had removed her outer tunic, tucking her into bed wearing her loose shirt and breeches. As she sat up, nausea joined the ache in her skull and her temples throbbed. The symptoms were very easy to recognize; after all, she'd badly overtaxed herself. Now she was paying the price. Ylsa had said something about that, too, in the dream—

She dragged herself out of bed and went to the desk, only to discover that someone had anticipated her need, readying a mug of Ylsa's herbal remedy and putting a kettle of water over the tiny fire on her pocket-sized hearth. She needed only to pour the hot water over the crushed botanicals and wait for them to steep. She counted to one hundred, slowly, then drank the brew off without bothering to sweeten or strain it.

When the pounding in her head had subsided a bit, and her stomach had settled, she sought the bathing room. A long, hot bath was also part of the prescription, and she soaked for at least an hour. By then, her headache had receded to manageable proportions, and she dressed in clean clothing and descended to the kitchen.

Mero was working like a fiend possessed; his round face displaying a grief as deep as any Herald's. He greeted her appearance with an exclamation of surprise; she soon found herself tucked into a corner of the kitchen with another mug of the herb tea in one hand and a slice of honeycake to kill the taste in another.

"Has anything happened since last night?" she asked, knowing that Mero heard everything as soon as it transpired.

"Not a great deal," he replied. "But—they brought her home in the dawn—"

His face crumpled for a moment, and Talia remembered belatedly that Mero and Ylsa had been longtime friends, that he had "adopted" her much as he had taken Elspeth as a special pet, in Ylsa's long-ago student days.

"And Keren?" she asked, hesitating to intrude on his grief.

"She—is coping. Is better than I would have expected. That was a wise thing—a kind thing, that you did; to bring to her side one who could most truly feel and share in her loss and sorrow," he replied, giving her a look of sad approval. "The Book of One says 'That love is most true that thinks first of the pain of others before its own.' She—the lady—she must be proud of you, I think—" he stumbled to a halt, not knowing what else to say.

"I hope she is, Mero," Talia replied with sincerity. "What of the Queen and the Council—and Teren?"

"Teren helps Sherrill to tend his sister; he seems well enough. I think it is enough for him to know that she is safe again. Oh, and Sherrill has been ordered to bide at the Collegium until this newly-woken Gift of hers be properly trained. Kyril himself is to tend to that. As for the rest—the Council are still closeted together. There was some coming and going of the palace Guard in the hour before dawn, however. Rumor says that there are some highborn ones missing from their beds. But—you do not eat—" he frowned at her, and she hastily began to nibble at the cake. "*She* told me, long ago, that those who spend much of themselves in magic must soon replace what they spent or suffer as a consequence." He stood over her until she'd finished, then pressed another slice into her hand.

"It's so quiet," she said, suddenly missing the sound of feet and voices that usually filled the Collegium. "Where is everybody?"

"In the Great Hall, waiting on the word from the Council. Perhaps you should be there as well."

"No—I don't think I need to be," she replied, closing weary eyes. "Now that my head is working again, I know what the decisions will be."

Whether she'd sorted out the confused memories alone, or with the aid of someone—or something—else, she knew now what it was that Ylsa had died to obtain. It was nothing less than the proofs, written in their own hands, of treason against Selenay and murder of many of the Heralds by five of the Court's highly placed nobles. These were the incontrovertible proofs that the Queen had long desired to obtain—and two of the nobles named in those letters were previously unsuspected, and both were Council members. There would be no denying their own letters; before nightfall the heart and soul of the conspiracy begun by the Queen's husband would be destroyed, root and branch. These documents, hidden in the hollow arrows and transported to the dim chamber of the Palace by Dirk and Kris, would be the instruments of vengeance for Ylsa herself, and Talamir, and many another Herald whose names Talia didn't even know. How Ylsa had obtained these things, Talia had no idea—nor, with the effect of the drug she'd been drinking finally taking hold, did she much care.

She began to doze a little, her head nodding, when the Death Bell suddenly ceased its tolling. She woke at the sudden silence; then other bells began ringing—the bells that only rang to announce vital decisions made by the Council. They were tolling a death-knell.

Mero nodded, as if to himself. "The Council has decided, the Queen has confirmed it. They have chosen the death-sentence." he said. "They will probably grant the condemned ones the right to die by their own hands, but if they have not the courage, the executioner will have them in the morning. I wish—" his face registered both grief and fury. "It is not the way of the One, may He forgive me—but I could wish they had a dozen lives each, that they might truly pay for what they did! And I wish that it could be I who metes out that vengeance to them—"

Talia briefly closed her eyes on his raw grief, then took up the task of easing it.

The petals falling from the apple trees were of a match for Rolan's coat—and the pristine state of Skif's traveling leathers.

"Do I look that different?" he asked Talia anxiously. "I mean, I don't *feel* any different."

"I'm afraid you do look different," she told him with a perfectly straight face. "Like someone else altogether."

"How?"

"Well, to tell you the absolute truth," she muted her voice as if she were giving him the worst of bad news, "you look—"

"What? What?"

"Responsible. Serious. *Adult*."

"Talia!"

"No, really, you don't look any different," she giggled. "All it looks like is that you fell into a vat of bleach and your Grays got accidentally upgraded."

"Oh, Talia," he joined her laughter for a while, then grew serious. "I'll miss you."

"I'll miss you, too."

They walked together in silence through the falling blossoms. It was Skif who finally broke the silence between them.

"At least I won't be as worried about you now—not like I'd have been if I'd gone last fall."

"Worried? About me? Why? What is there to be worried about *here*?"

"For one thing, you're safer now; there isn't anybody left to be out after your blood. For another, well, I don't know why, but before, you never seemed to belong here. Now you do."

"Now I feel like I've earned my place here, that's all."

"You never needed to earn it."

"I thought I did." They drew within sight of the tack shed, where Skif's Companion Cymry waited, and with her, his internship instructor, Dirk. "Promise me something?"

"What?"

"You won't forget how to laugh."

He grinned. "If you'll promise me that you'll learn."

"Clown."

"Pedant."

"Scoundrel."

"Shrew." Then, unexpectedly, "You're the best friend I'll ever have."

Her throat suddenly closed with tears. Unable to speak, she buried her face in his shoulder, holding him as tightly as she could. A few moments later, she noticed he was doing the same.

"Just look at us," she managed to get out. "A pair of great blubbering babies!"

"All in a good cause," he wiped his eyes on his sleeve. "Talia, I really do have something I'd like to ask you before I leave. Something I'd like you to do."

"Anything," she managed to grin, "So long as it's not going to get me in too much trouble!"

"Well—I never had any family—at least not that

I know of. Would—you be my family? My sister? Since it doesn't seem like we were meant to be anything else?

"Oh, Skif! I—" she swallowed. "Nothing would make me happier, not even getting my Whites. I don't have any family anymore either, but you're worth twelve Holds all by yourself."

"Then, just like we used to on the street—" He solemnly nicked his wrist and handed her his knife; she followed suit, and they held their wrists together   . . .

"Blood to blood, till death binding," he whispered.

"And after," she replied.

"And after."

He tore his handkerchief in half, and bound up both their wrists. "It's time, I guess. If I dally around much more, Dirk's going to be annoyed. Well—take care."

"Be very careful out there, promise? If you manage to get yourself hurt—I'll—I'll turn Alberich loose on you!"

"Lord of Lights, you *are* vicious, aren't you!" He turned toward her, and caught her in a fierce hug that nearly squeezed all the breath from her lungs, then planted a hard, quick kiss on her lips, and ran off toward his waiting mentor. As he ran, he looked back over this shoulder, waving farewell.

She waved after him until he was completely out of sight.

She was unaware that she was being watched.

"And off goes her last friend," Selenay sighed, guilt in her eyes.

"I think not," Kyril replied from just behind her. They had just turned their own Companions loose and had been walking together slowly back to the Palace; the gentle warmth and the perfumed rain of blossoms had made both of them reluctant to return to duty. Kyril had spotted Talia first; they'd turned aside into a copse to avoid disturbing what was obviously meant to be a private farewell.

"Why?" Selenay asked. "Lady knows she's little enough time for making friends."

"She doesn't have to *make* them; they make themselves her friends. As little as I see the trainees, I've noticed *that*. And it isn't just the younglings—there's Keren, Sherrill—even Alberich."

"Enough to hold her here without regret? We've stolen her childhood, Kyril—we've made her a woman in a child's body, and forced responsibilities on her an adult would blanch at."

"We steal *all* their childhoods, Lady; it comes with being Chosen," he sighed. "There isn't a one of us who's had the opportunity to truly be a child. Responsibility comes on us all early. As to Talia—she never really had a childhood to steal; her own people saw to that."

"It isn't fair—"

"Life isn't fair. Even so, given the chance to choose, she'd take being Chosen over any other fate. I know I would. Don't you think she's happier with us than she would be anywhere else?"

"If I could only be sure of that."

"Then watch her—you'll see."

Talia stared as long as anything of Skif and his mentor could be seen, then turned back toward the Collegium. As she turned, Selenay could clearly see her face; with no one watching her, she had erected no barriers. As she turned away, her pensive expression lightened until, as she faced the Collegium most of the sorrow of parting had left her eyes. And Selenay's heart lifted again, as she read all Kyril had promised she would find in those eyes.

Talia sighed, turning back toward the Collegium. As she did so, she felt Rolan reaching tentatively for her. For one long moment after Skif had vanished off on his own, she had felt bereft and terribly lonely. But now—

How could she *ever* be lonely when there was Rolan?

And Skif wasn't the only friend she had; Jeri was off somewhere, but Sherrill was still here— and Keren, Devan, little Elspeth, Selenay—even dear, overly-gallant Griffon.

They were all of them, more than friends; they were kin—the important kind, soul-kindred. Her family. Her *real* family. *This* was where she'd belonged all along; as she'd told Skif, it had just taken her this long to see it.

And with a lighter heart, she turned back down the path that led to the Collegium.

The Collegium—and home.